BONES ARE FOREVER

As a forensic anthropologist to the province of Quebec, Canada, Kathy Reichs has often said that she works *with* the dead, but *for* the living.

Forensics are an integral part of her world, with cases constantly coming in to her lab. And yet her chosen profession is, she says, like any other job. However, though you may get used to what's happening around you, and to the sounds and smells and sights of death, this doesn't mean you become immune to it.

Each of her books is based loosely on the cases she's worked on, or an experience she's had. She believes that her stories remain fresh because they originate from her being enmeshed and engaged in forensic work on a regular basis.

Kathy Reichs is one of only eighty-two forensic anthropologists ever certified by the American Board of Forensic Anthropology. She served on the Board of Directors and as Vice President of both the American Academy of Forensic Sciences and the American Board of Forensic Anthropology, and is currently a member of the National Police Services Advisory Council in Canada. She is a Professor in the Department at the University of North Carolina – Charlotte. She is a native of Chicago, where she received her PhD at Northwestern. She now divides her time between Charlotte, NC and Montreal, Quebec.

www.kathyreichs.com
www.facebook.com/kathyreichsbooks
twitter.com/kathyreichs

Also available by Kathy Reichs

The Virals Series
with Brendan Reichs

Kathy
REICHS

BONES ARE FOREVER

arrow books

Published by Arrow Books in 2013

4 6 8 10 9 7 5 3

Copyright © Temperance Brennan, L.P., 2012

Kathy Reichs has asserted her right under the Copyright, Designs and
Patents Act, 1988, to be identified as the author of this work.

Published by arrangement with the original publisher, Scribner,
an imprint of Simon & Schuster, Inc.

First published in Great Britain in 2012 by William Heinemann

Arrow Books
The Random House Group Limited
20 Vauxhall Bridge Road, London, SW1V 2SA

www.randomhouse.co.uk

Addresses for companies within The Random House Group Limited can
be found at: www.randomhouse.co.uk/offices.htm

The Random House Group Limited Reg. No. 954009

A CIP catalogue record for this book is available from the British Library

Typeset in Palatino by SX Composing DTP, Rayleigh, Essex, SS6 7XF

Penguin Random House is committed to a sustainable future for
our business, our readers and our planet. This book is made from
Forest Stewardship Council® certified paper.

Printed and bound in Great Britain by Clays Ltd, Elcograf S.p.A.

For my very, very old friend
Bob "Airborne" Abel

Acknowledgments

I would like to thank Gilles Ethier, Chief Deputy coroner of Quebec, for information pertaining to laws covering the disposal of deceased infants in the province. Dr. Robert Dorion, Dr. Michael Baden, and Dr. Bill Rodriguez helped with aspects of forensic science outside my specialty.

At the RCMP, Sgt. Valerie Lehaie and Cpl. Leander Turner shared information concerning Project KARE and the Alberta Missing Persons and Unidentified Human Remains project. John Yee provided valuable contacts. Judy Jasper answered a myriad of questions.

At the Giant Mine Remediation Project, Tara Kramers, Environmental Scientist, and Ben Nordahn, Mine Systems Officer, led me deep underground on a kick-ass tour of the Giant Gold Mine. Tara responded to my many follow-up queries.

Cathie Bolstad of De Beers Canada replied to my inquiry about exploration and staking. Gladys

King took my call at the Mining Records Office in Yellowknife.

Mike Warns and Ronnie Harrison helped with scores of picky little details.

Kevin Hanson and Amy Cormier of Simon and Schuster Canada made my trip to Yellowknife possible. Judith and Ian Drinnan, Annaliese Poole, Larry Adamson, Jamie Bastedo, and Colin Henderson were warm and generous hosts at the NorthWords Literary Festival.

I appreciate the continued support of Chancellor Philip L. Dubois of the University of North Carolina–Charlotte.

Heartfelt thanks to my agent, Jennifer Rudolph Walsh, and to my editors, Nan Graham and Susan Sandon. I also want to acknowledge all those who work so very hard on my behalf, including Lauren Lavelle, Paul Whitlatch, Rex Bonomelli, Daniel Burgess, Simon Littlewood, Tim Vanderpump, Emma Finnigan, Rob Waddington, Glenn O'Neill, Kathleen Nishimoto, Caitlin Moore, Tracy Fisher, Michelle Feehan, Cathryn Summerhayes, Raffaella De Angelis, and the whole Canadian crew.

I am grateful to my family for putting up with my moods and absences. Paul Reichs read and commented on the manuscript when he really wanted to get on with retirement.

Fire into Ice: Charles Fipke and the Great Diamond Hunt, Vernon Frolick, 2002, Raincoast Books, and

Treasure Under the Tundra: Canada's Arctic Diamonds, L. D. Cross, 2011, Heritage House, were useful resources.

Most of all, big thanks go out to my readers. I appreciate you reading about Tempe, coming to my talks and signings, visiting my website (KathyReichs. com), liking me on Facebook, and following me on Twitter (@kathyreichs). Love you, guys!

If I forgot someone, I am really, really sorry. If I made mistakes, they are my fault.

1

The baby's eyes startled me. So round and white and pulsing with movement.

Like the tiny mouth and nasal openings.

Ignoring the maggot masses, I inserted gloved fingers beneath the small torso and gently lifted one shoulder. The baby rose, chin and limbs tucked tight to its chest.

Flies scattered in a whine of protest.

My mind took in details. Delicate eyebrows, almost invisible on a face barely recognizable as human. Bloated belly. Translucent skin peeling from perfect little fingers. Green-brown liquid pooled below the head and buttocks.

The baby was inside a bathroom vanity, wedged between the vanity's back wall and a rusty drainpipe looping down from above. It lay in a fetal curl, head twisted, chin jutting skyward.

It was a girl. Shiny green missiles ricocheted from her body and everything around it.

For a moment I could only stare.

The wiggly-white eyes stared back, as though puzzled by their owner's hopeless predicament.

My thoughts roamed to the baby's last moments. Had she died in the darkness of the womb, victim of some heartless double-helix twist? Struggling for life, pressed to her mother's sobbing chest? Or cold and alone, deliberately abandoned and unable to make herself heard?

How long does it take for a newborn to give up life?

A torrent of images rushed my brain. Gasping mouth. Flailing limbs. Trembling hands.

Anger and sorrow knotted my gut.

Focus, Brennan!

Easing the miniature corpse back into place, I drew a deep breath. My knee popped as I straightened and yanked a spiral from my pack.

Facts. Focus on facts.

The vanity top held a bar of soap, a grimy plastic cup, a badly chipped ceramic toothbrush holder, and a dead roach. The medicine cabinet yielded an aspirin bottle containing two pills, cotton swabs, nasal spray, decongestant tablets, razor blades, and a package of corn-remover adhesive pads. Not a single prescription medication.

Warm air moving through the open window fluttered the toilet paper hanging beside the commode. My eyes shifted that way. A box of tissue sat on the tank. A slimy brown oval rimmed the bowl.

I swept my gaze left.

Lank fabric draped the peeling window frame, a floral print long gone gray. The view through the dirt-crusted screen consisted of a Petro-Canada station and the backside of a dépanneur.

Since I entered the apartment, my mind had been offering up the word "yellow." The mud-spattered stucco on the building's exterior? The dreary mustard paint on the inside stairwell? The dingy maize carpet?

Whatever. The old gray cells kept harping. *Yellow.*

I fanned my face with my notebook. Already my hair was damp.

It was nine a.m., Monday, June 4. I'd been awakened at seven by a call from Pierre LaManche, chief of the medico-legal section at the Laboratoire de sciences judiciaires et de médecine légale in Montreal. LaManche had been roused by Jean-Claude Hubert, chief coroner of the province of Quebec. Hubert's wake-up had come from an SQ cop named Louis Bédard.

According to LaManche, Caporal Bédard had reported the following:

At approximately two-forty a.m. Sunday, June 3, a twenty-seven-year-old female named Amy Roberts presented at the Hôpital Honoré-Mercier in Saint-Hyacinthe complaining of excessive vaginal bleeding. The ER attending, Dr. Arash Kutchemeshgi, noted that Roberts seemed disoriented. Observing the presence of placental remnants and enlargement of the uterus, he suspected she had recently given birth. When asked about pregnancy, labor, or an infant, Roberts was evasive. She carried no ID. Kutchemeshgi resolved to phone the local Sûreté du Québec post.

At approximately three-twenty A.M., a five-car pileup on Autoroute 20 sent seven ambulances to the Hôpital Honoré-Mercier ER department. By the time the blood cleared, Kutchemeshgi was too exhausted to remember the patient who might have delivered a baby. In any case, by then the patient was gone.

At approximately two-fifteen p.m., refreshed by four hours of sleep, Kutchemeshgi remembered Amy Roberts and phoned the SQ.

At approximately five-ten p.m., Caporal Bédard visited the address Kutchemeshgi had obtained from Roberts's intake form. Getting no response to his knock, he left.

At approximately six-twenty p.m., Kutchemeshgi discussed Amy Roberts with ER nurse Rose Buchannan, who, like the doctor, was working a twenty-four-hour shift and had been present when Roberts arrived. Buchannan recalled that Roberts simply vanished without notifying staff; she also thought she remembered Roberts from a previous visit.

At approximately eight p.m., Kutchemeshgi did a records search and learned that Amy Roberts had come to the Hôpital Honoré-Mercier ER eleven months earlier complaining of vaginal bleeding. The examining physician had noted in her chart the possibility of a recent delivery but wrote nothing further.

Fearing a newborn was at risk, and feeling guilty about failing to follow through promptly on his intention to phone the authorities, Kutchemeshgi again contacted the SQ.

At approximately eleven p.m., Caporal Bédard returned to Roberts's apartment. The windows were dark, and as before, no one came to the door. This time Bédard took a walk around the exterior of the building. Upon checking a Dumpster in back, he spotted a jumble of bloody towels.

Bédard requested a warrant and called the coroner. When the warrant was issued Monday morning, Hubert called LaManche. Anticipating the possibility of decomposed remains, LaManche called me.

So.

On a beautiful June day, I stood in the bathroom of a seedy third-floor walk-up that hadn't seen a paintbrush since 1953.

Behind me was a bedroom. A gouged and battered dresser occupied the south wall, one broken leg supported by an inverted frying pan. Its drawers were open and empty. A box spring and mattress sat on the floor, dingy linens surrounding them. A small closet held only hangers and old magazines.

Beyond the bedroom, through folding double doors—the left one hanging at an angle from its track—was a living room furnished in Salvation Army chic. Moth-eaten sofa. Cigarette-scarred coffee table. Ancient TV on a wobbly metal stand. Chrome and Formica table and chairs.

The room's sole hint of architectural charm came from a shallow bay window facing the street. Below its sill, a built-in tripartite wooden bench ran to the floor.

A shotgun kitchen, entered from the living room, shared a wall with the bedroom. On peeking in earlier, I'd seen round-cornered appliances resembling those from my childhood. The counters were topped with cracked ceramic tile, the grout blackened by years of neglect. The sink was deep and rectangular, the farmhouse style now back in vogue.

A plastic bowl on the linoleum beside the refrigerator held a small amount of water. I wondered vaguely about a pet.

The whole flat measured maybe eight hundred square feet. A cloying odor crammed every inch, fetid and sour, like rotting grapefruit. Most of the stench came from spoiled garbage in a kitchen waste pail. Some came from the bathroom.

A cop was manning the apartment's only door, open and crisscrossed with orange tape stamped with the SQ logo and the words *Accès interdit—Sûreté du Québec. Info-Crime.* The cop's name tag said Tirone.

Tirone was in his early thirties, a strong guy gone to fat with straw-colored hair, iron-gray eyes, and apparently, a sensitive nose. Vicks VapoRub glistened on his upper lip.

LaManche stood beside the bay window talking to Gilles Pomier, an LSJML autopsy technician. Both looked grim and spoke in hushed tones.

I had no need to hear the conversation. As a forensic anthropologist, I've worked more death scenes than I care to count. My specialty is decomposed, burned, mummified, dismembered, and skeletal human remains.

I knew others were speeding our way. Service de l'identité judiciaire, Division des scènes de crime, Quebec's version of CSI. Soon the place would be crawling with specialists intent on recording and collecting every fingerprint, skin cell, blood spatter, and eyelash present in the squalid little flat.

My eyes drifted back to the vanity. Again my gut clenched.

I knew what lay ahead for this baby who might have been. The assault on her person had only begun. She would become a case number, physical evidence to be scrutinized and assessed. Her delicate body would be weighed and measured. Her chest and skull would be entered, her brain and organs extracted and sliced and scoped. Her bones would be tapped for DNA. Her blood and vitreous fluids would be sampled for toxicology screening.

The dead are powerless, but those whose passing is suspected to be the result of wrongdoing by others suffer further indignities. Their deaths go on display as evidence transferred from lab to lab, from desk to desk. Crime scene technicians, forensic experts, police, attorneys, judges, jurors. I know such personal violation is necessary in the pursuit of justice. Still, I hate it. Even as I participate.

At least this victim would be spared the cruelties the criminal justice machine reserves for adult victims— the parading of their lives for public consumption. How much did she drink? What did she wear? Whom did she date? Wouldn't happen here. This baby girl never had a life to put under the microscope. For her, there would be no first tooth, no junior prom, no questionable bustier.

I flipped a page in my spiral with one angry finger.

Rest easy, little one. I'll watch over you.

I was jotting a note when an unexpected voice caught my attention. I turned. Through the cockeyed bedroom door, I saw a familiar figure.

Lean and long-legged. Strong jaw. Sandy hair. You get the picture.

For me, it's a picture with a whole lot of history.

Lieutenant-détective Andrew Ryan, Section de crimes contre la personne, Sûreté du Québec.

Ryan is a homicide cop. Over the years, we've spent a lot of time together. In and out of the lab.

The out part was over. Didn't mean the guy wasn't still smoking hot.

Ryan had joined LaManche and Pomier.

Jamming my pen into the wire binding, I closed my spiral and walked to the living room.

Pomier greeted me. LaManche raised his hound-dog eyes but said nothing.

"Dr. Brennan." Ryan was all business. Our MO, even in the good times. *Especially* in the good times.

"Detective." I stripped off my gloves.

"So. Temperance." LaManche is the only person on the planet who uses the formal version of my name. In his starched, proper French, it comes out rhyming with "France." "How long has this little person been dead?"

LaManche has been a forensic pathologist for over forty years and has no need to query my opinion on postmortem interval. It's a tactic he employs to make colleagues feel they are his equals. Few are.

"The first wave of flies probably arrived and oviposited within one to three hours of death. Hatching could have begun as early as twelve hours after the eggs were laid."

"It's pretty warm in that bathroom," Pomier said.

"Twenty-nine Celsius. At night it would have been cooler."

"So the maggots in the eyes, nose, and mouth suggest a minimum PMI of thirteen to fifteen hours."

"Yes," I said. "Though some fly species are inactive after dark. An entomologist should determine what types are present and their stage of development."

Through the open window, I heard a siren wail in the distance.

"Rigor mortis is maximal," I added, mostly for

Ryan's benefit. The other two knew that. "So that's consistent."

Rigor mortis refers to stiffening due to chemical changes in the musculature of a corpse. The condition is transient, beginning at approximately three hours, peaking at approximately twelve hours, and dissipating at approximately seventy-two hours after death.

LaManche nodded glumly, arms folded over his chest. "Placing possible time of death somewhere between six and nine o'clock last night."

"The mother arrived at the hospital around two-forty yesterday morning," Ryan said.

For a long moment no one spoke. The implication was too sad. The baby might have lived over fifteen hours after her birth.

Discarded in the cabinet? Without so much as a blanket or towel? Once more I pushed the anger aside.

"I'm finished," I said to Pomier. "You can bag the body."

He nodded but didn't move away.

"Where's the mother?" I asked Ryan.

"Appears she may have split. Bédard is running down the landlord and canvassing the neighbors."

Outside, the siren grew louder.

"The closet and dresser are empty," I said. "There are few personal items in the bathroom. No toothbrush, toothpaste, deodorant."

"You're assuming the heartless bitch bothered with the niceties of hygiene."

I glanced at Pomier, surprised by the bitterness in his tone. Then I remembered. Pomier and his wife had been trying to start a family. Four months earlier she'd miscarried for the second time.

The siren screamed its arrival up the street and cut off. Doors slammed. Voices called out in French. Others answered. Boots clanged on the iron stairs leading to the first floor from the sidewalk.

Shortly, two men slipped under the crime scene tape. Uniform jumpsuits. I recognized both: Alex Gioretti and Jacques Demers.

Trailing Gioretti and Demers was an SQ corporal I assumed to be Bédard. His eyes were small and dark behind wire-rimmed glasses. His face was blotchy with excitement. Or exertion. I guessed his age to be mid-forties.

LaManche, Pomier, and I watched Ryan cross to the newcomers. Words were exchanged, then Gioretti and Demers began opening their kits and camera cases.

Face tense, LaManche shot a cuff and checked his watch.

"Busy day?" I asked.

"Five autopsies. Dr. Ayers is away."

"If you prefer to get back to the lab, I'm happy to stay."

"Perhaps that is best."

In case more bodies are found. It didn't need saying.

Experience told me it would be a long morning. When LaManche was gone, I glanced around for a place to settle.

Two days earlier I'd read an article on the diversity of fauna inhabiting couches. Head lice. Bedbugs. Fleas. Mites. The ratty sofa and its vermin held no appeal. I opted for the window bench.

Twenty minutes later, I'd finished jotting my observations. When I looked up, Demers was brushing black powder onto the kitchen stove. An intermittent flash told me Gioretti was shooting photos in the bathroom. Ryan and Bédard were nowhere to be seen.

I glanced out the window. Pomier was leaning against a tree, smoking. Ryan's Jeep had joined my Mazda and the crime scene truck at the curb. So had two sedans. One had a CTV logo on its driver's-side door. The other said *Le Courrier de Saint-Hyacinthe*.

The media were sniffing blood.

As I swiveled back, the plank under my bum wobbled slightly. Leaning close, I spotted a crack paralleling the window wall.

Did the middle section of the bench function as a storage cabinet? I pushed off and squatted to check underneath.

The front of the horizontal plank overhung the frame of the structure. Using my pen, I pushed up from below. The plank lifted and flopped back against the windowsill.

The smell of dust and mold floated from the dark interior.

I peered into the shadows.

And saw what I'd been dreading.

2

The second baby was wrapped in a towel. Blood or decompositional fluids had spread brown blossoms across the yellow terry cloth.

The shrouded little corpse lay in a back corner of the window seat, surrounded by a cracked and sunbleached catcher's mitt, a broken tennis racket, a plastic truck, a deflated basketball, and several pairs of worn-out sneakers. Dust and dead insects completed the assemblage.

The crown of a tiny head was visible at one end of the bundle, the squiggly sutures newborn-wide. The membrane-thin bone was dusted with soft downy hair.

I closed my eyes. Saw another infantile face. Dark flesh circling startling blue eyes. Pudgy cheeks shrunk tight to delicate bones.

"Oh, no," someone said.

I raised my lids and looked out toward the street.

A hearse had joined the vehicles lining the curb. The reporters stood talking outside their cars.

A puff of breeze through the screen felt warm on my face. Or perhaps it was the adrenaline-pumped blood flaming my cheeks.

"*Avez-vous quelque chose?*" Do you have something? I turned.

Demers was looking in my direction, brush poised in midair. I realized the "oh, no" had come from my own lips.

I nodded, not trusting my voice.

Demers called to Gioretti, then crossed to me. After staring at the baby a very long time, he yanked a mobile from his belt and began punching keys. "I'll see if we can get a dog."

Shortly, Gioretti joined us. His gaze took in the window seat. "*Tabarnouche.*"

Positioning a case identifier, Gioretti began shooting pictures from different angles and distances.

I stepped off a few paces to phone LaManche. He issued the instructions I expected. Disturb the remains as little as possible. Keep looking.

Twenty minutes later, Gioretti had finished with video and stills. Demers had dusted the window box and its contents.

As I snapped on latex gloves, Demers spread a body bag on the floor beside the displaced shoes and sports paraphernalia. His jaw muscles bulged as he opened the zipper.

Reaching into the window seat, I gently lifted our second little victim. Based on weight and the absence of smell, I suspected the remains were mummified.

With two hands, I transferred the bundle to the body bag. Like the vanity baby lying by the sofa, it looked pitifully small in its adult-sized sack.

While Demers held a flashlight, I tweezed half a dozen bones from the interior of the window seat. Each was smaller than a thumbnail. Three phalanges. Two metacarpals. A vertebral body.

After sealing the isolated bones in a plastic vial, I wrote the case number, the date, and my initials on the cover with a Sharpie. Then I tucked the container below one edge of the stained yellow bundle.

Demers and I watched in silence as Gioretti shot his final photos. Out on the street, a car door slammed, followed by another. Footfalls sounded on the stairs.

Gioretti looked a question at me. I nodded.

Gioretti had just zipped the body bag and folded and strapped its ends when Pomier reappeared. With him were a woman and a border collie. The woman's name was Madeleine Caron. The collie went by Pepper.

Trained to respond to the smell of rotting human flesh, cadaver dogs find hidden bodies like infrared systems pinpoint heat. A truly skilled sniffer can nail the former resting place of a corpse even long after its removal. But these hounds of death are as variable as their handlers. Some are good, some are lousy, some are outright scams.

I was pleased to see this pair. Both were top-notch.

I crossed to Caron, gloved hands held away from my body. Pepper watched my approach with large caramel eyes.

"Nice place," Caron said.

"A palace. Pomier brief you?"

Caron nodded.

"We've got two so far. One from the bath, one from the window seat." I jabbed a thumb over my shoulder. "I'm about to release them for transport. Once the body bags are out of here, run Pepper around, see if anything piques her interest."

"You've got it."

"There's garbage in the kitchen."

"Unless the stuff's human, it won't ring her chimes."

First Caron took Pepper to the places where the babies had been stashed. Some dogs are taught to alert by barking, some by sitting or dropping to the ground. Pepper was a sitter. At both spots, she parked on her haunches and whined. Each time Caron scratched the dog's ears and said, "Good girl." Then she reached down and unclipped the leash.

After sniffing her way through the kitchen and living room, Pepper padded into the bedroom. Caron and I followed at a polite distance.

Nothing at the dresser. A slight hesitation at the bed. Then the dog froze. Took a step. Paused, one forepaw six inches off the floor.

"Good girl," Caron said softly.

17

Muzzle sweeping from side to side, Pepper crept across the room. At the open closet door, her snout went up and her nostrils worked the air.

Five seconds of testing, then Pepper sat, craned her head toward us, and whined.

"Good girl," Caron said. "Down."

Eyes glued to her handler, the dog dropped to her belly.

"Shit," Caron said.

"What?"

Caron and I turned. Neither of us had heard Ryan step up behind us.

"She's hit on something," Caron said.

"How often is she right?"

"Often."

"She alert anywhere else?"

Caron and I shook our heads.

"She ever miss?"

"Not so far." Caron's tone was grim. "I'll spin her around in here once more, then take her outside."

"Please ask the transport driver to wait," I said. "And tell Pomier. He's accompanying the remains to the morgue."

"You've got it."

As Caron led Pepper out, Ryan and I crossed to the closet.

The enclosure was no more than three feet by five. I pulled a chain to light the bare bulb overhead.

An iron rod held hangers, the solid kind that must

have been decades old. They'd been bunched to one side, I assumed by Demers.

A wooden shelf ran the length of the closet above the rod. A collection of magazines had been transferred to the bedroom floor. Like the shelf, the door, the rod, and the knob, they were coated with Demers's fingerprint powder.

Ryan and I spotted the vent simultaneously. It was on the ceiling, roughly centered in the closet. As our eyes met, Gioretti appeared in the doorway.

"You photograph in here?" I asked.

Gioretti nodded.

"We're going to need a ladder and the snakehead camera."

While we waited, Ryan filled me in on the landlord. "Stephan Paxton." He switched to English. "The guy'll never be addressing a Harvard graduation."

"Meaning?"

"He's got the brainpower of a moth. Beats me how he owns three buildings." Ryan shook his head. "The tenant here is Alma Rogers. Paxton says she pays cash, usually three or four months in advance. Has for at least three years."

"Rogers used an alias at the hospital?"

"Or here. But it's the same gal. Paxton's physical description matches that of the ER doc."

"Yet she gave her actual address."

"Apparently."

I found that odd but let it go. "Is there a lease?"

"Rogers moved in with a guy named Smith. Paxton thinks maybe Smith signed something at the outset, but he's not so good at keeping records. Says the cash in advance was lease enough for him."

"Does Rogers work?"

"Paxton hadn't a clue."

"Smith?"

Ryan shrugged.

"What about the neighbors?"

"Bédard's still making the rounds."

At that moment the equipment arrived. As Demers positioned the ladder, Gioretti connected an apparatus that looked like a plumber's snake to a portable DVR unit. He pushed a button, and the monitor beeped to life.

While Ryan held the ladder, Demers climbed the rungs and tested the grate with one finger. It wiggled, and plaster dust cascaded down.

Demers pulled a screwdriver from his belt. A couple of twists, and the screws came loose. More plaster dropped as he removed and handed down the grate. He drew a mask up over his mouth, then reached a hand into the dark rectangle in the ceiling. Palm flat, he gingerly explored. "There's a beam."

I held my breath as his arm went this way and that.

"Insulation." Finally, Demers shook his head. "I'll need the camera."

Gioretti handed up the snakelike tool. The tip held a fiber-optic image sensor with a lens under four millimeters across. The tiny camera would take pictures inside the wall and allow us to view images in real time.

Demers thumbed a switch, and a bright beam shot into the darkness. After adjusting its curvature, he inserted the snake into the recess. A blurry gray image appeared on the monitor down below.

"We're reading you." Gioretti turned a dial, and the gray blur crystallized into a wooden beam. Below the beam was what looked like old-fashioned vermiculite insulation.

"Must be a ceiling joist," Ryan said.

We watched the camera inch right along the joist, on-screen.

"Try the other way," Ryan said. "You should hit a wall stud and a rafter."

Demers reversed direction.

Ryan was right. Two and a half feet beyond the vent's left end, beams joined the joist from below and above.

Tucked in the upper V was another towel-wrapped bundle.

"Sonofabitch," Gioretti said.

Ninety minutes later, the closet ceiling was gone, and the third baby lay zipped inside its thirty-six-by-ninety-inch pouch.

Fortunately, the small attic produced no other infants.

Pepper had not alerted outside the building.

The three body bags lay side by side in the hearse, each with a pitifully small bulge in the middle.

Up the block, the journalists were practically wetting themselves. They maintained their distance. I wondered what Ryan had threatened to keep them in check.

I stood at the hearse's back bumper. I'd removed my jumpsuit, and the sun felt warm on my shoulders and head.

Though it was past two and I'd eaten nothing since dawn, I had no appetite. I kept staring at the bags, wondering about the woman who had done this thing. Did she feel remorse over murdering her newborns? Or did she proceed with her life, not reflecting at all on the enormity of her crimes?

Images kept intruding from my past. Unbidden. Unwanted.

My baby brother, Kevin, dead of leukemia at age three. I wasn't allowed to see Kevin's body. To my eight-year-old mind, his death had somehow seemed unreal. One day he was with us, then he wasn't.

In my child's way, I'd understood that Kevin was sick, that his life would end too soon. Still, when it happened, I was left bewildered. I'd needed to say good-bye.

Up the street, Ryan was talking to Bédard. Again.

Earlier the corporal had reported that so far, the canvas had turned up only one person who recalled ever seeing Alma Rogers. The aged widow Robertina Hurteau lived in the building opposite and kept watch on the block through her living room blinds.

The old woman described her across-the-way neighbor as *ordinaire*. She couldn't remember the last time she'd seen Rogers enter or leave the apartment. She'd occasionally seen her with a man but never a baby. The man was *barbu*.

What about a dog? I wondered. Or was it a cat? Had anyone asked? The missing pet bothered me. Where was it? Had Roberts/Rogers taken it with her? Had she abandoned or killed it as she had her own offspring?

Three dead babies and I was worried about a missing pet. Go figure.

You're out there somewhere, I thought. Amy Roberts, Alma Rogers. Traveling unnoticed. In a car? On a bus or train? Alone? With the father of your poor dead children? One of them? How many fathers were there?

I hoped Ryan was getting new information.

Demers and Gioretti were packing their gear. As I watched idly, a green Kia pulled to the curb behind their truck. The driver's door swung open, and a man hauled himself out. He wore jeans and a tank that revealed way too much flesh. His hair was lank, his face flushed and splotchy above an unkept beard.

Arm-draping the car door, the man scanned the vehicles lining the street. Then he turned and slid back behind the wheel.

My weary brain coughed up a translation.

Barbu.
Bearded.
I turned to call out.
Ryan was already sprinting up the sidewalk.

3

Ryan hit the Kia as the driver slammed the door. Reaching through the open window, Ryan snatched the key from the ignition.

Halfway up the block, I heard "What the fuck?"

Bédard arrived as Ryan badged the guy.

"What the fuck?"

The driver was Anglophone. With a limited vocabulary.

"Move!" Ryan yanked the handle.

"What the—"

"Now!"

Sandaled feet swung out, followed by a beluga body.

As Bédard drew his Glock, Ryan spun Beluga, pushed him to the Kia, kicked his legs wide, and frisked him.

"What? You're not going to buy me a few drinks first?"

Ryan didn't laugh at Beluga's wit.

A rear jeans pocket produced a canvas wallet. Satisfied that his suspect was unarmed, Ryan stepped back and began checking its contents. Bédard stood with his feet spread, gun double-grip pointed at Beluga.

"Turn around, but keep the hands up."

Beluga did as ordered.

"Ralph Trees?" Ryan looked up from a plastic card I assumed to be a license to its bearer's face.

Beluga stood in sullen silence, hands above his head. Hair crawled from his armpits down the sides of his rib cage.

"You Ralph Trees?"

Still, Beluga said nothing.

Ryan reached back and unclipped cuffs from his belt.

"What the shit?" Beluga splayed beefy fingers. "OK. OK. But it's Rocky, not Ralph."

"What are you doing here?"

"What are *you* doing here?"

"You're a really funny guy, Rocky."

"How about you tell Dirty Harry over there to ease up on the firepower."

Ryan nodded to Bédard. The corporal lowered but did not holster his weapon.

Ryan turned back to Trees and waggled the license. Trees mumbled an answer I couldn't hear.

I walked toward the trio. They paid no attention to me.

Up close, I could see that Trees's eyes were spiderwebbed with tiny red veins. I guessed his height at six-four, his weight at 350 or more. Tattooed between his lower lip and the top of his beard was an inverted smile composed of teeth. Classy.

"I come to see my lady. Last I checked, that ain't a crime."

"Murder is."

"What the fuck are you talking about?"

"Who's your girlfriend?"

"She's not my girlfriend."

"You're starting to piss me off, Rocky."

"Look, I bang her when I'm horny. Don't mean I send her chocolates on Valentine's Day."

Ryan just looked at him.

"Alva Rodriguez." The bloodshot eyes flicked from Ryan to Bédard and back. "That it? Someone offed Alva?"

"When's the last time you saw or talked to Ms. Rodriguez?"

"Shit, I don't know. A couple, three weeks ago."

"Try a little harder."

"This is harassment."

"File a complaint."

Trees's gaze shifted to me. "Who's the chick?"

"You just focus here."

"This is bullshit."

"When's the last time you had contact with Ms. Rodriguez?"

Trees made a show of giving the question some thought. His jittery eyes and sweaty hairline suggested the bravado was an act. "Two weeks Thursday. No, Wednesday. I was just back from a ride out to Calgary."

"Why Calgary?"

"I do some long-haul driving for my brother-in-law."

"Where is Ms. Rodriguez now?"

"Man, can I lower my arms?"

"No."

"How the hell should I know? She don't check in with me. Like I said, I come by, I get laid, I go about my business."

"You pay for these little rendezvous?"

"Me? You gotta be kiddin'." The oily smirk made me crave a very hot shower. "I bring the bitch a bottle, she's grateful. Ya know what I mean?"

"You also bring her a little toot?"

"I don't roll with that stuff. Just sauce."

"You know what, Rocky? I think maybe you're lying to me. I look at you, I see a guy who enjoys his flake. Maybe a guy who deals. What do you say I toss that funny little car of yours?"

"You can't do that."

"What do you think, Corporal Bédard?" Ryan's eyes remained on Trees. "You think we can do that?"

"We can do that."

Ryan passed the license to Bédard. "How about you

check ole Romeo out, see if he's got any interesting history."

Bédard holstered his gun and strode to his cruiser. While he ran Trees's name through the system, Ryan and I waited in silence. Like many under stress, Trees felt the need to fill it. "Look, I'm telling you what I know. It's jack shit. Alva and I didn't spend our time talking."

"Where does Ms. Rodriguez work?" Ryan asked.

"You're not listening to me."

"She have a steady income? A way to pay the rent?"

Trees shrugged—as well as he could with his hands in the air.

"You maybe turn her out, Rocky? Hook her on snow so she's there when you need a quick jolt? Is that the business you're talking about? You pimp more women than Rodriguez?"

"No way. I watched out for her. Alva isn't what you'd call a genius."

Ryan started firing questions, shifting topics to keep Trees off balance. "You know of her using a name other than Rodriguez?"

Trees shook his head.

"Where did she live before coming here?"

"She's Mexican, right? Or one of those."

"Why do you think that?"

"The name. And she had a sort of accent. Not French. I figured it was Mexican. Didn't matter to me."

"That's touching, you being so open-minded and all."

Trees rolled his eyes skyward. His forearms were now V-ing down, hanging deadweight from his upraised elbows.

"You the baby daddy?"

"What?"

"You help her kill them?"

"Kill what?"

"You crank up some tunes to drown out their crying?"

"Are you out of your fucking mind?"

"Or did she do the babies herself because you gave the word?"

Trees's eyes bounced from Ryan to me to his car, repeated the circuit. I wondered if he was about to bolt.

"Three, Rocky. Three newborns. Presently on their way to the morgue."

"You're freakin' nuts. Alva wasn't pregnant. Isn't pregnant. Where the hell is she?" Trees forgot all about hands-up. Both palms slapped his chest. "What do you want from me?"

"We believe Ms. Rodriguez gave birth early Sunday morning." Ryan tipped his head toward the three-flat in which we'd spent our day. "We found the baby under the bathroom sink. Two others hidden in the apartment."

"Jesus freakin' Christ." The color drained from Trees's cheeks, leaving his nose a bright beacon in a field of pitted gray. "I don't know nothing about Alva being pregnant."

"How can that be, Rocky? You being her devoted guardian and all."

"Alva is, you know, heavy. Wears baggy clothes. Looks like a goddamn tent on legs."

"Don't worry. DNA will answer all those messy paternity questions. If you're the daddy, you can buy flowers to lay on their graves."

"This is fucking horseshit."

"Where would she go, Rocky?"

"Look, I keep telling you, I don't know where she come from. I don't know where she'd go. I just know her to—"

"Yeah. You're a real romantic. Where did you two meet?"

"At a bar."

"When?"

"Two, maybe three years ago."

"Where have you been since Saturday?"

Trees brightened, as though sensing a sliver of hope. "I did a run over to Kamloops. You can ask my brother-in-law."

"Bet on it."

"Can I get something out of my car?"

Ryan nodded once. "Don't pull any cowboy moves."

Trees reached into the backseat of the Kia, yanked some papers from under an empty KFC bag, and gave them to Ryan. "That top one's a flyer for my brother-in-law's company. The green one's my work order. Check the date. I was in Kamloops."

Ryan read from the flyer. "'Got it here? Want it there? We move fast.' Pure poetry."

Trees missed the sarcasm. "Yeah. Phil's good with writing and shit."

"Phil looks like a skunk."

"Hey, he can't help it. He was born that way."

Ryan skimmed the work order, then handed both papers to me. Curious about his comment, I glanced at the flyer.

A happy driver I assumed to be Phil sat smiling and waving behind the wheel of a truck. His hair was black and combed straight back from his face. A white crescent streaked from his forehead toward the crown of his head.

Bédard rejoined us. Shook his head.

Ryan spread his feet and stared at Trees as though weighing options. Then, "Here's what you're going to do. You'll go with Corporal Bédard. You'll write down contact information for yourself and your brother-in-law and anyone else who can vouch for your sorry ass. You can write, can't you, Rocky?"

"You're the funny guy."

"Downright hilarious when I'm searching a glove compartment."

"OK. OK." Two placating palms came up.

"You will record everything you remember about Alva Rodriguez. Right down to the last time she flushed the toilet. You got it?"

Trees nodded.

Ryan raised his brows at me.

"Does Alva have a dog or cat?" I asked.

"A dog."

"What kind?"

"Just a dog." The oaf looked confused by the question.

"Big? Small? Long-eared? Brown? White?"

"A little gray yappy thing. Shits all over the place."

"What's the dog's name?"

"Fuck if I know."

"If Alva left, would she take the dog with her?"

"Fuck if I know."

Ryan shot me a quizzical look but said nothing. Then to Trees, "Go, Rocky. And dig real deep."

While Trees followed Bédard to his unit, Ryan walked me to my car.

"What do you think?" I asked.

"The guy couldn't find his own ass with GPS. Brain's probably fried."

"You think he's using?"

Ryan pulled his "you've got to be kidding" face.

"I thought he sounded genuinely shocked at the mention of the babies."

"Maybe," Ryan said. "But I'm going to be on that prick like fleas on a hound."

"Anything new on Roberts?"

"Demers doubts he got any useful prints. Those he lifted will take time to process. If Roberts isn't in the system, that's a dead end anyway. The landlord paid the utilities. There's no phone. No computer. No paper trail of any kind. If Mama's in the wind, it could take a while to find her."

"And the baby can't help us."

Turned out I was dead wrong.

4

The next morning I spent twenty minutes snaking up and down the narrow streets of Hochelaga-Maisonneuve, a working-class neighborhood a bump east of *centre-ville*. I passed iron staircase-fronted two-flats, convenience stores, a school, a small park. But no curbside usable at eight a.m. on a Tuesday in June.

Don't get me started. One needs a degree in civil engineering to understand when and where it is legal to park in Montreal, and the luck of a lotto winner to find footage that qualifies.

On my fifth pass down Parthenais, a Mini Cooper pulled out half a block up. I shot forward and, with much shifting and swearing, wedged my Mazda into the vacated space.

The clock on the dash said 8:39. Great. Morning meeting would begin in about six minutes.

After gathering my laptop and purse from the

backseat, I got out and assessed my handiwork. Six inches in front, eight behind. Not bad.

Pleased with my achievement, I headed toward the thirteen-story glass-and-steel structure recently renamed Édifice Wilfrid-Derome in honor of Quebec's famous pioneer criminalist. Famous by Quebec standards. In forensic circles.

Hurrying along the sidewalk, I could see the T-shaped black hulk looming over the quartier. Somehow, the brooding structure looked wrong against the cheery blue sky.

Old-timers still refer to Wilfrid-Derome as the QPP or SQ building. Quebec Provincial Police for Anglophones, Sûreté du Québec for Francophones. Makes sense. For decades the provincial force has laid claim to most of the square footage.

But the cops aren't alone in the édifice. The Laboratoire de sciences judiciaires et de médecine légale, Quebec's combined medico-legal and crime lab, occupies the top two floors. The Bureau du coroner is on eleven. The morgue and autopsy suites are in the basement. Hail, the gang's all here. Makes my job easier in many ways, harder in some. Ryan's office is just eight floors below mine.

I swiped my security pass in the lobby, in the elevator, at the entrance to the twelfth floor, and at the glass doors separating the medico-legal wing from the rest of the T. At eight-forty-five the corridor was relatively quiet.

As I passed windows opening onto microbiology, histology, and pathology labs, I could see white-coated men and women working at microtomes, desks, and sinks. Several waved or mouthed greetings through the glass. I returned their *bonjour* and hustled to my office, not in the mood to chat. I hate being late.

I'd barely dumped my laptop and stowed my purse when my desk phone rang. LaManche was eager to begin the meeting.

When I entered the conference room, only the chief and one other pathologist, Jean Pelletier, were seated at the table. Both did that half-standing thing older men do when women enter a room.

LaManche asked about events following his departure from the apartment in Saint-Hyacinthe. As I briefed him, Pelletier listened in silence. He is a small, compact man with thin gray hair and bags under his eyes the size of catfish. Though subordinate to LaManche, Pelletier had been at the lab a full decade when the chief hired on.

"I will begin the baby's autopsy as soon as we adjourn," LaManche said to me in his perfect Sorbonne French. "If the other infants have been reduced to bone, as you suspect, those cases will be assigned to you."

I nodded. I already knew they would be.

Hearing Pelletier sigh, I looked in his direction.

"So sad." Pelletier drummed the tabletop with his fingers, the first two permanently yellowed from half a century of smoking Gauloises cigarettes. "So very, very sad."

At that moment Marcel Morin and Emily Santangelo joined us. More pathologists. *Bonjour* and *Comment ça va* all around. After distributing copies of the day's lineup, LaManche began discussing and assigning cases.

A thirty-nine-year-old woman had been found dead, tangled up in a plastic dry-cleaning bag in Longueuil. Alcohol intoxication was suspected.

A man's body had washed ashore under the Pont des Îles on Île Sainte-Hélène.

A forty-three-year-old woman had been bludgeoned by her husband following an argument over the TV remote. The couple's fourteen-year-old daughter had called the Dorval police.

An eighty-four-year-old farmer had been found dead of a gunshot wound in a home he shared with his eighty-two-year-old brother in Saint-Augustin.

"Where's the brother?" Santangelo asked.

"Call me crazy, but I expect the SQ is pondering that very question." Pelletier's dentures clacked as he spoke.

The Saint-Hyacinthe infants had been assigned LSJML numbers 49276, 49277, and 49278.

"Detective Ryan is attempting to locate the mother?" LaManche said it more as statement than question.

"Yes," I said. "But there's little to go on, so it could take time."

"Monsieur Ryan is a man of many talents." Though Pelletier's expression was deadpan, I wasn't fooled. The old codger knew that Ryan and I had been an item, and loved to tease. I didn't take his bait.

Santangelo got the floater and the plastic-bag vic. The bludgeoning went to Pelletier, the gunshot death to Morin. As each case was dispensed, LaManche marked his master sheet with the appropriate initials. Pe. Sa. Mo.

La went onto dossier LSJML-49276, the newborn from the bathroom sink. Br went onto LSJML-49277 and LSJML-49278, the babies from the window seat and the attic.

When we dispersed, I returned to my office, pulled two case forms from my plastic shelving, and snapped them onto clipboards inside folders. Each of us uses a different color. Pink is Marc Bergeron, the odontologist. Green is Jean Pelletier. LaManche uses red. A bright yellow jacket means anthropology.

As I was digging for a pen, I noticed the flashing red light on my phone.

And felt the tiniest of flutters. *Ryan?*

Jesus, Brennan. It's over.

I dropped into my chair, picked up the receiver, and entered my mailbox and code numbers.

A journalist from *Le Courrier de Saint-Hyacinthe.*

A journalist from *Allô Police.*

After deleting the messages, I went to the women's locker room, changed into surgical scrubs, and proceeded out of the medico-legal section to a side corridor running past the secretarial office to the library. Located there was an elevator requiring special clearance.

When the doors opened, I stepped in and pressed a button that would take me to the morgue. There were only two other options: Bureau du coroner. LSJML.

Downstairs, a left and then a right brought me to a Santorini-blue door marked *Entrée interdite*. Entrance prohibited. I swiped my card and started down a long narrow hall shooting the length of the building.

On the left I passed an X-ray room and four autopsy suites, three with single tables, one with a pair. On the right, lining the wall, were drying racks for soggy clothing, evidence, and personal effects recovered with bodies, computer stations, and wheeled tubs and carts for transporting specimens to the labs upstairs.

Through small windows in the doors, I could see that Santangelo and Morin were beginning their externals in rooms one and two. With each pathologist was a police photographer and an autopsy technician, or diener.

Gilles Pomier and a tech named Roy Robitaille were arranging instruments in the large autopsy suite. They would be assisting Pelletier and LaManche, respectively.

I continued on to number four, a room specially ventilated for decomps, floaters, mummified corpses, and other aromatics. My kind of cases.

As did every autopsy suite, room four had double

doors leading to a morgue bay. The bay was lined with refrigerated compartments designed to hold one gurney each.

Tossing my clipboard on a counter, I pulled a plastic apron from one drawer, gloves and a mask from another, donned them, and pushed through the double doors.

Head count.

Seven white cards. Seven temporary residents.

I located those cards with my initials, LSJML-49277 and LSJML-49278. Both had been affixed to the same door.

Dead babies need so little room, I thought.

Both cards bore the same sad notation. *Ossements d'enfant.* Baby bones. *Inconnu.* Unknown.

Flashback. Rocking Kevin in my arms, afraid to squeeze lest I snap the brittle little bones, lest I add more bruises to the milky white flesh.

Standing amid the cold stainless steel, I could still feel the feathery weight of my brother's body against my chest, hear the soft cadence of his breathing, recall the perfume of little-boy sweat and baby shampoo.

Shake it off, Brennan. Do your job.

I pulled the handle and the door swung open. Cold air whooshed, bringing with it the odor of refrigerated death.

Two folded body bags lay side by side on the top shelf of one gurney. I toed the brake and yanked the gurney out.

When I backed through the double doors, Lisa was arranging equipment on a side counter. Together we maneuvered the gurney parallel to the stainless-steel table floor-bolted in the middle of the room.

"SIJ is shorthanded today." Wanting practice, Lisa usually speaks English to me. "One photographer will float between us and Dr. LaManche."

"That's fine. We'll do our own pics."

Fortysomething, Lisa has been a diener since receiving certification at age nineteen. Clever and knowledgeable, with hands as adept as any surgeon's, she is, far and away, the best autopsy tech at the LSJML.

Lisa is also the favorite of every cop in Quebec. I suspect that, besides her skill and sunny disposition, her blond hair and large bra size figure in.

"They look so little." Lisa was staring at the bags, sadness on her face.

"Let's get a series of pics before we remove them."

While Lisa filled out a case identifier and checked the Nikon, I entered information onto the first of my case forms.

Name: *Inconnu*. Date of birth: blank. Laboratoire de sciences judiciaires et de médecine légale number: 49277. Morgue number: 589. Police incident number: 43729. Pathologist: Pierre LaManche. Coroner: Jean-Claude Hubert. Investigator: Andrew Ryan. Section des crimes contre la personne, Sûreté du Québec.

As I added the date and began a form for the attic baby, Lisa took pictures of the two black pouches. Then she snapped on gloves, pulled a plastic sheet from a below-counter drawer, spread it across the autopsy table, and looked a question at me.

"Unzip them," I said.

The rolled towels were as I remembered, one green, one yellow, both dappled brown by the liquids of death. Using two hands, Lisa transferred each to the table. I made notes as she shot more photos.

"We'll start with the baby from the window seat." I indicated the yellow bundle.

Using her fingertips, Lisa gently teased free and laid back the outer layer of toweling. Then she rolled the bundle sideways, slowly revealing its contents.

A human baby is a very small biomass. Following death, the scarcity of body fat may lead to mummification instead of putrefaction. Such had been the case in the window seat.

The little corpse was tightly compressed, the head down, the arms and legs flexed and crossed over each other. Desiccated skin, muscle, and ligament wrapped the thorax, abdomen, and limbs, and stretched across the delicate bones of the face. The empty orbits held masses that looked like shriveled grapes.

Lisa was reaching for the Nikon when Pomier stuck his head through the door and spoke to me. "Dr. LaManche has a question."

"Now?" Slightly annoyed.

Pomier nodded.

Though anxious to begin my analysis, I knew the chief would never interrupt with anything trivial.

"Shoot from every angle, close-up and overview," I said to Lisa. "Then get a full set of X-rays."

"All the bones will be superimposed. There is nothing I can do about that."

"Taking measurements from the X-rays may prove impossible. But do your best. If I'm not back when you finish, unroll and photograph the second baby. Any questions, you know where to find me."

Lisa nodded.

"Let's go," I said to Pomier.

Every morgue is characterized by its own blend of odors, sometimes subtle, sometimes overpowering, but always present. These smells have been a part of my life for so long, I sometimes imagine them in my sleep.

Bodies recovered from water are among the most pungent. In the corridor, the stench of Santangelo's drowning victim was overtaking the ever-present aromas of disinfectant and deodorizer.

The bludgeoning victim lay on the far table in room three. The woman's face was swollen and distorted, her left side purpled due to livor mortis, the postmortem settling of blood in a corpse's downside.

Robitaille was picking through the woman's hair, searching her scalp section by section. Pelletier was examining her toes.

LaManche and the SIJ photographer were at the

near table. She was very tall and very pale. A tag on her shirt said S. Tanenbaum. I didn't know her.

Not so the third party. Andrew Ryan.

As we crossed to him, LaManche tucked the baby's right hand back to her side, lifted and studied her left. He made no comment, jotted no note.

I knew where the chief's thoughts were pointed. No defense wounds. Of course not. The infant was far too helpless to take action to save her own life, and the manner of death probably had not involved a blow. There would not have been even reflexive reaction.

One thing struck me right off. Everyone in the room was working quietly, talking in hushed tones when a question was posed or an instruction was given. No jokes. No quips. None of the irreverent humor used to ease tension at crime scenes and autopsies.

The baby looked far too vulnerable lying naked on the cold stainless steel.

"Temperance. Thank you." Over his mask, LaManche's eyes looked weary and sad. "The child measures thirty-seven centimeters long."

Haase's rule: during the last five months of gestation, fetal length in centimeters divided by five equals the number of months of pregnancy. I did a quick calculation.

"She's small for a full-term baby," I said.

"*Oui*. Crown-rump length. Biparietal diameter. Every measure. The detective and I are wondering with what accuracy you can determine her age."

I knew what LaManche wanted. A fetus is considered viable after seven months of gestation. If born earlier, survival is possible but unlikely without medical intervention.

"In case you find no abnormality but the mother claims the baby was premature and stillborn," I said.

"That's usually their story. The kid was dead, I panicked and stashed the body." Ryan's jaw muscles bunched, relaxed. "Without a witness or evidence to the contrary, such cases are bastards to prosecute."

I thought a moment. "I haven't looked at the attic baby yet, but the one from the window seat is desiccated and contorted. The tissue is so adhered, it will be tough removing the bones without damaging them. And standard X-rays will be of limited use due to bone and tissue superimposition. I'm thinking the best approach with the mummified remains might be MSCT."

Four blank looks.

"Multislice computed tomography. I suggest we use it for this baby, too. That way I can measure and observe the skeleton while it's articulated by soft tissue. A big advantage of MSCT is that it gives an isotopic image and doesn't distort the anatomical reality. I can measure the long bones on 2-D reconstructions and get anatomical length directly without need for a correction factor. After we view the scans, you can proceed with your regular autopsy."

As I spoke, my eyes roved the tiny girl on the table. She'd been brushed clean but not yet water-sprayed.

"It cannot hurt." LaManche looked at Pomier. "The staff at St. Mary's has been helpful in the past. Phone the radiology department. See if it is possible to use their scanner."

In his haste to do as directed, Pomier pivoted too quickly. His shoe knocked a caster on a portable light snugged to one end of the table. The floor stand wobbled. Ryan grabbed and steadied the extension arm holding the halogen bulb.

As the light jumped, my eyes caught something my brain didn't process.

What?

"Shift it again," I said, leaning close to the baby.

Ryan did.

Yes. There. Where the right shoulder met the curve of the baby's neck. Not so much a spot as an absence of luminosity, a dullness compared to the surrounding skin.

A few gray cells offered up a suggestion.

Hardly daring to hope, I crossed to the counter, grabbed a hand lens, and viewed the irregularity under magnification.

"Look at this," I said.

5

"*Câlisse,*" LaManche whispered.

"You're thinking print." Ryan's tone was so flat, I wondered if he was dubious or simply trying to be objective.

"ALS?" Pomier asked.

"Please," I said.

"I'll get the powder," Tanenbaum said.

Both techs left, reappeared shortly. Pomier was carrying goggles and a black box with a handle on top and a flexible wand projecting from one end. Tanenbaum had a fingerprint kit.

"May we go dark for a few minutes?" I called down to Pelletier.

"No problem. Madame is going for X-rays."

As I pointed out the area in question, Tanenbaum dusted bright orange powder onto the baby's neck.

Pomier hooked up the CrimeScope CS-16-500, an alternate light source capable of providing wavelengths ranging from infrared to ultraviolet. When done, he distributed orange-tinted plastic goggles. LaManche, Ryan, Tanenbaum, and I donned them.

"Ready?" Pomier asked.

LaManche nodded.

Pomier killed the overheads, slipped on his goggles, adjusted dials on the CrimeScope, then positioned the wand over the baby.

Slowly, the light crept up the pale little feet. It probed the hills and valleys of the perfect toes, the knees, the groin, the belly. Lit the hollow from which the shriveled umbilical cord hung.

Here and there, filaments lit up like hot white wires. Hairs? Fibers? Maybe useful, maybe not. I tweezed and transferred each into a plastic vial.

Finally, the beam swept the gentle curve where the baby's right shoulder met its neck. Pomier twisted a knob to return to the lower end of the green spectrum, then slowly moved up the wavelengths.

And there it was. An oval composed of concentric loops and whirls.

We all leaned closer.

"Bonjour," Pomier said in the darkness.

"I'll be damned."

Ryan's voice at my ear made me aware of decidedly non-morgue smells. Bay Rum cologne, starched cotton, a hint of male perspiration.

Feeling awkward, I straightened. "Because the skin is so soft and finely textured, it's easier to get a latent from an infant than from an adult," I said crisply.

I heard rattling and knew Tanenbaum was placing an orange filter over the lens of her digital camera. We all waited out a long series of clicks. The next sequence of noises told me she was using an adhesive lifter to transfer the print.

"*Je l'ai*," she said after several minutes. "I've got it."

Though we worked another half hour in the dark, our efforts revealed nothing else of interest. Still, we were all pumped as hell.

Pomier restored the lights, then went to inquire about the use of the CT scanner at St. Mary's Hospital.

Tanenbaum hurried off to run our prize through CPIC, the Canadian Police Information Center. Like the U.S.'s AFIS, the Automated Fingerprint Identification System, CPIC functions as a database for fingerprints and other information critical to police investigations.

LaManche resumed his external examination of the baby. Ryan headed upstairs to check for responses to queries he'd circulated about Amy Roberts/Alma Rogers/Alva Rodriguez and Ralph Trees.

When I returned to autopsy room four, Lisa had finished photographing both LSJML-49277 and LSJML-49278. She'd also popped X-rays of the former onto light boxes ringing the room.

I moved through the films, pessimistic. I was right. The window-seat baby was so tightly constricted that overlap of the bones made assessment difficult and measurement impossible. Frustrated, I crossed to the table where LSJML-49278 now lay on its unrolled towel beside the window-seat baby.

The attic baby had been reduced to a skeleton and fragments of dry ligament. Lisa had arranged some of the bones to form a miniature person. Most lay to one side on the grimy green terry cloth.

I wasn't surprised she'd failed to identify more. In a newborn, the cranial bones are unfinished and unfused. The vertebral arches are separate from the little disk bodies. Each pelvic half is composed of three disconnected bits. The long bones are amorphous shafts lacking the anatomical detail and joint surfaces that make femora, tibiae, fibulae, humeri, radii, and ulnae distinct. Ditto the teeny bones of the hands and feet.

Bottom line: most people wouldn't recognize a fetal skeleton if it hit them on the head. Even with training in juvenile osteology, classification of specific elements can be tough.

I checked the clock. Already it was going on eleven.

"This will be slow," I said to Lisa. "If you have things to do, I'm good working alone."

She seemed undecided, then, "Call if you need me."

I began by arranging the cranium in a pattern that looked like an exploded rose blossom. The frontal, the parietals, the sphenoid, the temporal and occipital segments. While sorting, I processed detail.

The occipital bone contributes to the back and the base of the skull. In a fetus, it consists of four pieces. The *pars squama* is the upper, rounded portion. The paired *pars lateralis* and the single *pars basilaris* lie down under, surrounding the foreman magnum, the hole through which the spinal cord enters the brain.

I used sliding calipers to measure the chunky little *pars basilaris*. Its width exceeded its length, placing the baby's gestational age at over seven months.

I positioned the needles on each end of the left *pars lateralis* and read the dial. Its length exceeded that of the *pars basilaris*. That nudged the gestational age to eight months.

I selected the flat, serrate-edged portion of the temporal, the part that had formed the right side of the baby's skull. A delicate circle of bone, the tympanic ring, was fused to an opening I knew to be the auditory canal.

Ring fusion bumped the gestational age to nine months.

Next I identified the facial bones. The maxillae and zygomatics, the ethmoid, the nasals, the palatines, the swirly little conchae from inside the nose. The mandible.

Until approximately one year postnatal, the human lower jaw remains unfused at the midline. As I examined the right and left halves, tiny teeth rolled around deep in the sockets. No surprise there. Tooth buds appear at nine to eleven weeks in utero. Though I could see the partially formed crowns, X-rays would be needed to evaluate dental development.

Moving on, I laid out the postcranial skeleton, measured the arm and leg bones, and compared the figures to a standardized chart. Each length supported the gestational age suggested by cranial development.

Satisfied that I'd learned what I could about age, I began teasing desiccated tissue from each tiny bone.

At noon Pomier popped in to report that St. Mary's would make a scanner available after nine that night. A radiologist named Leclerc would meet us in the hospital lobby. Dr. Leclerc was urging discretion. Live patients. Dead babies. I was on the same page.

Lisa stopped by every half hour. Each time I told her I was fine working solo.

Which was true. I didn't trust the emotions swirling inside me. Flashbacks to Kevin. Anguish for these infants. Fury at the woman who had killed them. I preferred to be alone.

By one I'd finished cleaning the bones. My stomach was growling, and a headache was gathering in my frontal lobe. I knew I should stop for lunch. Couldn't. I felt driven to learn everything possible before returning the babies to the cold, dark cooler.

After placing a stool by the dissecting scope, I began the painstaking process of observing every bone under magnification. Millimeter by millimeter, I inspected each shaft, metaphysis, epiphysis, groove, foramen, suture, and fossa, looking for indications of disease, malformation, or trauma.

Just past three Ryan called to report that Ralph "Rocky" Trees had no sheet as an adult, but he did have a juvenile jacket. Though the record was closed, Ryan was requesting access.

Rocky's story checked out. He drove pickup jobs for his brother-in-law, Philippe "Phil" Fast. The brother-in-law owned a small operation with a couple of trucks and a warehouse. Trees was away from Saint-Hyacinthe last Tuesday morning through late Sunday afternoon. Phil scoffed at the notion that Rocky might have a girlfriend.

That was it. No greeting. No "how are you doing." No good-bye.

By four-forty my gut was acid, my head was a bongo, and my back was on fire. But I'd completed my analysis. Sadly, my form held scant information.

Sex: Unknown.

There are studies that claim jaw or pelvic shape or differentials in postcranial bone growth indicate the gender of a fetus or neonate. I'm not convinced.

Race: Unknown.

Though a broad, low nasal bridge and wide cheekbones hinted at non-European input, there was no way to verify ancestry.

Congenital abnormalities: None.

Pathologies: None.

Trauma: None.

Age: Full-term fetus.

So little to say. Such a short life.

Already in the cellar, my spirits sank further.

Rather than call Lisa or Tanenbaum, I shot a final set of photos myself. Then I gathered the bones into a small plastic tub and wrote *LSJML-49278* on the lid and one side.

With robotic motions, I set the tub on the gurney and pushed it through the double doors to the morgue. "Good-bye, little one," I said softly as the bay clicked shut.

I was wrapping LSJML-49277 in padded plastic sheeting when the desk phone rang. In no mood to talk or even be cordial, I ignored it.

I placed the window-seat baby inside a square plastic tub, packed it with more wadded sheeting, and marked the case number on the outside. Then I filled out and signed an evidence transfer form. Since the mummified baby would leave the morgue with me, chain of custody had to be maintained.

Finished with the remains, I turned to the towels.

Like the filaments I'd plucked from LaManche's bathroom-vanity baby, the towels would be sent to the hair and fiber guys, perhaps to the folks in biology or DNA. Again, maybe useful, maybe not.

I sealed the attic towel in an evidence bag, jotted relevant information on the label, and set the bag to one side on the counter.

When I lifted the window-seat towel, something dropped with the sound of a tiny bean bag. Curious, I picked the thing up.

Between my gloved fingers was a small velvet sack with a drawstring closure. I teased it open. Inside was what looked like coarse-grain gravel. I poured some onto my palm. In the mix were a few green pebbles measuring a couple centimeters at most.

"Yowza. This'll crack the case wide open." My sarcasm was lost on the empty room.

After taking a few photos, I sealed the inclusion in a vial and placed it in a second evidence bag with the yellow towel. Then I called Lisa.

No answer.

I looked at the clock. Six-ten. Of course she was gone. Everyone was gone.

Feeling a heaviness the atomic weight of uranium, I took the tub containing the window-seat baby to a morgue bay adjoining autopsy room three and placed it on a gurney beside the bathroom-vanity baby, now wrapped and sealed in its own container. Then I wound my way to the elevator.

The basement was deserted. So was the twelfth floor. The building hummed with that eerie after-hours quiet unique to abandoned workplaces.

At the desk in my lab, I left Lisa a message asking that she transfer the bagged towels to the trace evidence section. As I cradled the receiver, my eyes drifted to the expanse of glass above my desk.

A dozen floors down, I could see the tops of apartment buildings, church spires, small patches of green I knew to be gardens. In the distance, the

Maison de Radio-Canada rose like a giant brick cylinder on boulevard René-Lévesque. Beyond it, the St. Lawrence River yawned gray and forbidding, even in June.

Past the black girders of the pont Champlain, the skyscrapers of *centre-ville* cut sharp silhouettes against the early summer dusk. I recognized Place Ville-Marie, Complexe Desjardins, the Centre-Mont-Royal, the Marriott Château Champlain.

The streets I'd searched for parking spaces that morning were clogged with traffic. Parents returning to the burbs for dinner and homework with the kids, lovers hurrying to nocturnal trysts, night-shifters dragging themselves to punch clocks on which time would seem to stand still.

How often Ryan and I had driven together from Wilfrid-Derome, discussing victims, suspects, aspects of a case. I can't share my work with those close to me who are not on the job—Pete, Katy, Harry, my best friend, Anne. I can't tell them what I've seen lying in a Dumpster or buried in a shallow grave. Can't describe the congealed blood, the bloated body, the seething maggots. I missed having someone to talk to, someone who understood. Ryan had kept me balanced. Kept me caring.

I wondered at Ryan's current coolness. Yes, we'd always danced around emotion, kept our innermost feelings to ourselves. Even in the good times.

Yes, the slaughter of innocents outraged him.

Women. Children. The elderly. I knew that. But this current moodiness seemed different. More than me. More than dead babies.

Whatever. He'd tell me when he was ready. Or not.

While changing into street clothes, I decided on dinner at home before heading to St. Mary's.

And remembered.

"Damn."

I detest grocery shopping. Irrational, but there it is. I'll make any excuse to avoid the supermarket. Then I pay the price. Like tonight. I hadn't bought food since arriving in Montreal two days earlier.

As I tossed my soiled scrubs into a biohazard bin, another thought heightened my melancholy.

When I'd departed Charlotte, Birdie had been recovering from a urinary tract infection. Knowing he hated air travel, and feeling the trip might compromise his wee bladder, I'd left him in Dixie. The cat offered no protest.

Frozen dinner. Alone.

As I walked up the corridor, my spirits went subterranean. I was considering take-out options when, through the window, I noticed a figure in my lab.

I froze. Then recognition.

Ryan. Jabbing digits on a cell phone.

At six-thirty? What the hell?

Ryan turned when I pushed through the door. Before I could speak, he cut me off. "We got her."

"Amy Roberts et cet?"

Ryan nodded.

"And?"

"You won't believe it."

6

"Her real name is Annaliese Ruben. She was popped twice for prostitution, once in 2005, again in 2008. Both arrests were in Edmonton. First time she got probation. Second time she was a no-show for the court date."

Ryan handed me three printouts.

The first was a response to the fingerprint search. Skipping the part about points of correspondence, I skimmed the physical descriptors. Annaliese Ruben had black hair, brown eyes, stood five feet tall, and weighed 195 pounds.

The second printout was a report on Ruben's criminal history. The third provided her most recent mug shot, obtained using the fingerprint system number. Ruben's thumbnail showed a woman with a moon face and dark tangled hair that badly needed grooming.

I handed back the sheets. "Might have an overactive thyroid."

"Yeah?"

"The bulging eyeballs. Or it could be the lighting. Mug shots don't bring out the best in folks."

"Edmonton PD says the address Ruben provided after the second collar turned out to be an abandoned warehouse. They've had no contact with her since '08, know nothing about her current whereabouts."

Ryan pocketed his iPhone and hip-planted his hands. There was stiffness in his movements, tension in his shoulders and jaw. Familiar signs. This case had gotten to him.

But there was more. A hardness in Ryan's eyes that I hadn't seen before.

I wanted to ask if there was something wrong, to say I was here if he wanted to talk. I didn't. Just waited.

"Are you familiar with Project KARE?" Ryan spelled out the acronym.

"Isn't it an RCMP task force created to investigate deaths and disappearances of women in and around Edmonton? I understand there have been quite a few."

"That's an understatement. But yeah, essentially, you're right. Their mandate is to collar the scumbags responsible for HRMP murders."

"High-risk missing persons."

"Yes." Ryan was keeping his voice carefully modulated.

"Meaning those involved in prostitution and drugs." I sensed where this was going.

"Yes."

"Annaliese Ruben is on the Project KARE list," I guessed.

"Since 2009."

"Who reported her missing?"

"Another prossie."

That surprised me. "Sex-trade workers usually steer clear of the cops."

"No shit. But the hookers in Edmonton are totally freaked."

"Wasn't someone arrested for those killings?"

"Thomas Svekla. A real piece of work. Charged with two murders, convicted of one." Ryan shook his head in disgust. "He'd stuffed his victim into a hockey bag and hauled her from High Level to Fort Saskatchewan."

"At least they got him."

"Word is there's more than one perp responsible."

"So a predator may still be out there."

"Yeah. Predator or predators."

Ryan's eyes looked dark and troubled. And too intensely blue to be real.

"But if Annaliese Ruben gave birth in Saint-Hyacinthe last Sunday, obviously she's alive," I said.

"And murdering babies."

"We don't know that."

"Who but the mother could kill three different newborns at three times? And why'd she go rabbit?"

"What's your next move?"

"Run the mug shot past Ralph Trees. See if Annaliese Ruben is Amy Roberts/Alma Rogers/Alva Rodriguez."

"Then?"

"Then find her ass and haul it to the bag."

I went with pad thai from the Bangkok at Le Faubourg on rue Sainte-Catherine. The line was short and I was running late.

St. Mary's Hospital started life in 1924 as a forty-five-bed affair in Shaughnessy House, now the Canadian Centre for Architecture. A decade later, operations moved from there to avenue Lacombe in the Côte-des-Neiges neighborhood, just over the mountain from *centre-ville*. Today the old girl is a multipavilion institution offering 316 patient beds and a staff active in teaching and research.

Le stationnement was a replay of twelve hours earlier. At eight-fifty a car finally pulled out on rue Jean-Brillant. I fired into the spot, grabbed my things, and bolted.

The area was surprisingly active for nine p.m. on a Tuesday. Cars filled the streets, and pedestrians chugged along the walks—shoppers clutching plastic grocery bags; hospital visitors, empty-handed, probably heading home; backpacked students from Université de Montréal or Collège Notre-Dame.

St. Mary's is not one of Quebec's architectural gems. The main building is a multilevel concrete and redbrick box with a castlelike tower jutting up at its center. I beelined to the entrance and pushed through the glass doors.

The lobby was mostly deserted. An old man sat with legs outstretched, chin on chest, snoring softly. A woman pushed a stroller in endless circles, looking exhausted. Two orderlies discussed a physician's printed order, or a menu, or a recipe for lentil soup.

LaManche stood on the lobby's far side by a bank of elevators. Pomier was beside him, string-handled bags hanging from his curled fingers. With them was a tall man in wire-rimmed glasses whom I assumed was Dr. Leclerc.

When I joined the trio, Leclerc spread his feet and crossed his arms in a posture more characteristic of a bouncer than a physician.

"How many more?" Leclerc's French hinted at stone gargoyles and *arrondissements*. I guessed he wasn't from around these parts.

"We are all here," LaManche said.

"This must be handled with the greatest of delicacy."

"Of course."

Leclerc shook his head, kept shaking it while repeatedly punching the button for an elevator. When the car came, I got in first and moved to the back. As we ascended, I scoped out our host.

Leclerc's thin brown hair was parted with military precision. His lab coat was eye-blistering white, his khakis creased sharp enough to draw blood. I guessed flexibility was not the guy's strong suit.

When the doors opened, Leclerc led us down a shiny tile corridor to an X-ray room reminiscent of the one at the LSJML. One difference: no changing rooms at Wilfrid-Derome. Our patients arrived and departed naked.

Through a window, I could see a woman seated beside a machine that looked like a large square donut with a narrow cot projecting from the hole. The woman's hair was black, her skin the color of walnuts. From her scrubs, I assumed she was a radiology nurse or technician.

"Mrs. Tong will assist you. I have explained"— Leclerc's lips twisted to one side as he sought the right word—"the situation."

When Leclerc rapped on the glass, Mrs. Tong looked up. As she rose, set down her magazine, and crossed to the door separating us from the scanning room, Leclerc continued talking.

"I have authorized Mrs. Tong to do full-body MSCTs on both subjects. Each axial scan will be performed with sixteen-by-three-quarter-millimeter collimation. The apparatus is a Sensation 16 unit. I have instructed Mrs. Tong to use two filters, one for bone and one for soft-tissue analysis."

Leclerc's delivery was so stiff, he sounded like a recording. "Mrs. Tong has agreed to remain beyond her normal shift. Please do not delay her any longer than necessary. Please follow her directives."

"Oh, goodness me. I'm happy to help." Mrs. Tong smiled warmly. "Got no kids to hurry home to. No church tonight. Fact is—"

"Thank you."

The woman's smile faded under her boss's flinty glance.

Leclerc turned to LaManche. "Who will handle the subjects?"

LaManche's gaze rolled to me. I nodded.

"I think this guy slept with a broom up his ass," Pomier said under his breath as I took the bags from him.

Three pairs of eyes followed Mrs. Tong and me into the scanning room. She started talking as soon as the door clicked shut.

"I call her Felix the Cat." She flapped a hand at the scanner. "You know, for CAT scan. That's what they used to be called. It's silly, I know. But a lot of patients are nervous as jackrabbits when they get shoved into a big whirring box. Naming the thing after a cartoon character helps ease the jitters."

"Mrs. Tong—"

"What are we, dining with the queen here? Call me Opaline. You know how Felix works?" As she spoke, she adjusted dials and flipped switches.

"I understand—"

"No magic. The old boy uses a computer and a rotating X-ray device to create cross-sectional images of organs and body parts. I'm talking slices with detail that'll blow your socks off."

It was clear that Opaline Tong loved to talk. Or was nervous as hell around dead babies. Her eyes avoided mine as I opened the first tub.

"The T in 'CT' stands for 'tomography.' You know what that means?"

"Imaging by sections using penetrating waves." I placed the tiny mummy designated LSJML-49277 on the patient couch, face-up, and secured it by buckling the straps.

"OK, then. You're a smart one."

Opaline pushed a button to move the couch up, then forward and backward inside the hole. When the baby was properly positioned, she stepped sideways and slapped the donut.

"The scanner itself is this circular rotating frame. It's got an X-ray tube on one side and a detector on the other that looks kind of like a banana. The rotating frame will spin the X-ray tube and detector around our poor little fella here, creating a fan-shaped beam of X-rays. The detector will take snapshots called profiles. Typically, about a thousand each time around. So with each complete rotation, we'll get one cross-sectional slice."

Opaline's tone had become a little less kindergarten-teacher sweet.

"The computer will use digital geometry processing to generate three-dimensional images of the inside of the body from the series of two-dimensional images taken around our single axis of rotation. Get it?"

"I do. Thank you."

"You ready?"

I nodded.

"Let's do it."

Forty-three minutes later, we were all in the ante-room with Mrs. Tong seated at the workstation, the rest of us bunched around her. While enter-ing instructions, she'd explained how the data produced by the scanner would be manipulated through a process known as windowing to dem-onstrate various bodily structures based on their ability to block the X-ray beam. She said that although images generated were historically in the axial or transverse plane, orthogonal to the long axis of the body, modern scanners now allowed data to be reformatted in various planes or even as volumetric—three-dimensional—representations.

First we'd viewed two-dimensional images produced, according to Mrs. Tong, by MPR, or multi-planar reconstruction. Slice by slice, we'd moved from the window-seat baby's head to its toes, interpreting pictures that resembled abstracts by Miró.

We'd noted that the skull was deformed due to collapse of both parietal bones. We'd seen that the auditory canals were well defined, that the tiny ossicles—the maleus, incus, and stapes—were present in the middle ear. Leclerc had pointed out the cochlea and vestibule of the inner ear, the labyrinthine segment of the facial nerve canal, the pyramidal process, and other anatomical features.

I'd measured the *pars squama* and the *pars basilaris* of the occipital bone and the lengths of the femoral and tibial shafts.

We'd all agreed. The fetus was full-term.

"Switch to three-dimensional?" Mrs. Tong asked.

"Yes," Leclerc said.

"These images will be produced using the volume-rendering technique and maximum-intensity mode," Mrs. Tong said.

No abstracts now. The baby appeared in detailed shades of gray and white, angled down, tiny limbs V'ed inward like two sets of wings.

Leclerc used a finger to point out the obvious. "Remnants of the cerebral hemispheres, cerebellum, pons, medulla oblongata, spinal cord." His finger moved from the skull to the thorax. "Esophagus, trachea, lungs. This is the heart, though I can't make out the separate cardiac chambers." He indicated the abdomen. "There's the stomach, the liver. The rest of the organs are unrecognizable."

"Is that a penis?" Pomier's voice sounded husky.

"It is."

"I see no skeletal malformations or trauma," I said.

Leclerc and LaManche agreed, then exchanged comments about a few anatomical landmarks.

I didn't really hear. My attention had shifted to an area of radio opacity in the trachea, partly obscured by superimposition of the tiny jaw.

"What the flip is that?"

7

LaManche nodded as though I'd answered a question, not asked one. Obviously, he saw it, too.

"I noticed that earlier, thought the cloudiness was an artifact," Leclerc said. "Now I'm not so sure."

"Is there any way to visualize the area more clearly?" I asked.

Mrs. Tong went back to 2-D, and we viewed the infant's neck in slices. It didn't help much. The radio opacity appeared centered in the trachea or esophagus. Beyond that, we could make out little detail.

"Perhaps dust or sediment filtered in through the mouth following decomposition," LaManche suggested.

"Perhaps." I didn't believe it. The white glow was intense, suggesting solidity.

For a full minute we all stared at the monitor. Then I made a decision. "May I borrow a scalpel and forceps?"

"Of course." Leclerc hurried off, reappeared in moments, and handed the instruments to me.

As the others watched, I returned to the scanner and unpocketed and snapped on gloves.

Forgive me, little one.

While steadying the baby with my left hand, I drew the scalpel blade across the shriveled little throat with my right.

The papery tissue split with a soft pop. Laying the scalpel aside, I picked up and inserted the forceps. Three quarters of an inch down, they met an obstruction.

I separated the tines, closed them, and gently tugged. The mass didn't budge.

Barely breathing, I opened the tips wider, wiggled them deeper, and pulled again.

The obstructing object yielded its grip on the trachea and slid upward with a dry scratching sound. Advancing by millimeters, I teased it through the incision and dropped it onto my palm.

Dingy white. Gauzy and crinkled.

I poked at one edge with the tweezers. A filmy layer lifted, revealing a dotted perforation.

Sweet mother of God!

A cerebral flare exploded, an image too horrible to contemplate.

I had to stand a moment, fighting the ice in my chest, the burning behind my lids.

When I'd regained my composure, I looked again at the baby.

I am so sorry. So very, very sorry.

One deep breath, then I rejoined those waiting behind the glass.

Wordlessly, I uncurled my fingers, revealing the horrific thing in my hand. Everyone stared, puzzled.

LaManche spoke first. "Wadded toilet tissue."

I could only nod.

"Forced down the child's throat to stop his breathing."

"Or crying."

That was it for Mrs. Tong. She began to weep. Not big blubbery sobs but hiccupy whimpers. As the others stood in awkward silence, I placed a hand on her shoulder.

She turned her head and gazed up at me over one shoulder. "Someone killed this little angel on purpose?"

My look was answer enough.

In a low and very even voice, I said to LaManche, "Detective Ryan will want to know."

"Yes. Please transmit this information to him."

As I hurried through the door, Leclerc asked Mrs. Tong if she would like to go home.

"Not on your life."

The corridor was deserted. Ignoring the hospital's no-cell-phone policy, I scrolled to and tapped Ryan's private number on my iPhone. His mobile rang, then rolled to voice mail.

Damn.

I left a message: "Call me back. Important."

I looked at my watch. Eleven-ten.

I walked to the end of the hall. The place was a ghost town.

I walked back toward X-ray. Checked the time again.

Eleven-fourteen.

I paced. Eleven-twenty-two.

Where the hell was he?

I was about to give up when Ryan finally called. I launched right in. "At least two of the babies were full-term. We'll know about the third one shortly."

"Any medical problems?"

"No. The window-seat baby is a boy." I told him about the bunched-up toilet paper.

For a long moment only background noise buzzed across the line. Voices. Clinking glassware.

"That it?" Clipped. Ryan was fighting to check his emotions, as I had.

"We're scanning the bathroom-vanity baby now."

I waited for a response, got none.

"Anything on your end?" I asked.

"Trees ID'ed the mug shot. Ditto the ER doc and the landlord. It was Ruben at the hospital and Ruben living in the apartment in Saint-Hyacinthe. Paxton says—"

"He owns the building."

"Right. Paxton now says he originally rented to Smith. Then Smith sort of dropped out of the picture.

As long as Rogers kept ponying up the bucks, he didn't ask questions."

"Anything new from Edmonton?"

"The RCMP sergeant I talked with this morning is arriving in Montreal tonight. We'll meet tomorrow morning."

Normally, Ryan would have invited me to join them. It was my case, too. He didn't.

"What time?" I asked.

"Eight."

"I'll try to drop by."

Back in X-ray, the scans of LSJML-49276 had been completed, and everyone was again gathered at the workstation. Mrs. Tong's eyes were puffy, and her face had that blotchy after-crying look.

The image on the screen was in 2-D, an axial slice at the level of the chest. Leclerc was talking. "Air is present in both major bronchi and the esophagus. Both lungs appear aerated."

Mrs. Tong hit some keys to bring up views of the abdomen.

Leclerc continued his monologue. "Air in the stomach."

"So the baby was breathing and swallowing," Pomier said.

"Perhaps." LaManche's saggy eyes looked weary in his saggy face. "Air can also be present due to decomposition. At autopsy, we will take samples for toxicological testing."

LaManche didn't have to elaborate. I knew that inhaled air would contain high levels of nitrogen and some oxygen, while gases resulting from decomposition would be mostly methane.

I also knew that, upon removal of the breastplate following the Y-incision, billowing of the lung parenchyma would indicate air in the lobes. And that, when placed in water or formaldehyde, aerated lungs would float.

Mrs. Tong didn't need to hear any of that.

We analyzed the baby girl as we had the mummified boy. I measured her long bones and the basal parts of her occipital bone. We all observed her skeletal maturation and condition.

And came to the same sad conclusion.

LSJML-49276 was a full-term female infant exhibiting no malformation or skeletal trauma.

At one-forty a.m. we tucked the babies back into their tubs and bags for the return trip with Pomier to the morgue.

I arrived home at two-ten. Was asleep by two-fifteen.

Church bells blasted me awake. I swept my iPhone to the floor, trying to stop the bonging.

The digits on the screen said seven a.m.

I tried to recall why I'd set the alarm.

Ryan. Edmonton. RCMP. Right.

Groggy, I dragged myself to the bathroom, the

closet, the kitchen. The pantry produced very old Frosted Flakes, the freezer ground coffee. The combo helped some. But when I've logged under five hours, caffeine and sugar can accomplish only so much.

Thirty minutes later, I was swiping my card at Wilfrid-Derome. OK. There are advantages to rising early. Parking was a snap.

After dumping my purse, I descended to the fourth floor and entered a door marked *Section des crimes contre la personne*.

The squad room contained about a dozen desks. Each held the usual cop stuff—phone, manila folders, mounded in- and out-baskets, gag trophies and mementos, mugs of half-drunk coffee.

A supervisor's office was off to the right, and a copy room. Doors leading to interview rooms were to the left.

Only a few detectives were present, those who were running leads by phone or computer, one in a suit who I assumed was preparing for court. I wound my way toward the back corner.

"Hey, Rochette, today Tuesday?" asked a voice behind me. It was a detective named Chestang. "That mean rosebuds?"

"It's Wednesday." Like Chestang, Rochette was speaking loudly for my benefit. "Polka dots."

Today's teasing stemmed from an incident in which I'd been dragged from a fire and deposited bum-up. My leopard-skin panties had saluted the world.

Though the episode had occurred several years earlier, it was still the top choice for source material.

Ignoring the witty repartee, I continued on course.

Ryan was at his desk, one haunch resting on the edge. A man sat opposite him. No yellow-striped pants or gray shirt, but I assumed he was the Mountie from Edmonton.

And no. He wasn't wearing red serge, jodhpurs, and a Stetson. That garb is strictly ceremonial.

A word about the Royal Canadian Mounted Police, RCMP, or in French, the Gendarmerie royale du Canada, GRC. The world calls them Mounties. Internally, they refer to themselves as the Force. Too many *Star Wars* movies, you say? Nope. The tradition goes back much further.

The RCMP is unique in that it functions at the national, provincial, and municipal levels, providing federal policing services to all of Canada and, under contract, to three territories, eight provinces, more than 190 municipalities, 184 aboriginal communities, and three international airports.

While the two most populous provinces, Ontario and Quebec, maintain their own provincial forces, the Ontario Provincial Police and the Sûreté du Québec, all the others rely on the RCMP to some extent. In the three territories, Yukon, Nunavut, and the Northwest Territories, the Mounties are the only game in town.

Confusing? To complicate matters further, some

large cities, such as Edmonton, Toronto, and Montreal, have their own municipal police departments.

Just think of the FBI, state troopers, the sheriff's department, city cops. Same deal.

Ryan's visitor was sitting with his back to me, elbow cocked over the arm of the chair. Graying temples suggested some mileage.

Hadn't Ryan said the guy was a sergeant? So the Force wasn't fast-tracking him into the OCDP, the Officer Candidate Development Program. I wondered if he'd plateaued in his career. If, like many NCOs, he'd grown resentful of the "white shirts," as the noncommissioned called the commissioned officers.

Whatever. Though unimpressive if working at headquarters in Ottawa or at a divisional HQ, sergeant was a decent enough level for a member in the field.

So why was Ryan looking at the guy like he was barf on the sidewalk?

Drawing close, I took in more detail. Though of average height, the sergeant was powerfully built, with arms and a chest that stretched his shirt to the limit.

Ryan said something I didn't catch. His visitor responded, tilting his head so that his chin went forward and up.

The odd mannerism jostled a gaggle of cells where a memory was stored.

I slowed. No way.

The sergeant reached out and placed a Styrofoam cup on Ryan's desk. His left hand flashed into view for a moment.

My pulse went off the map.

8

For a moment I considered retreat. Flight back upstairs to my lab. But my higher centers were already lobbing words like "professional" and "adult."

Sergeant Oliver Isaac Hasty. Other than deeper laugh lines and the graying-temples thing, he hadn't aged a bit. No loosening of the jaw. Not an extra ounce of fat.

Ollie had been a corporal back then, on temporary-duty assignment to the FBI Academy in Quantico. Behavioral science training or some such. I'd been teaching a body recovery workshop to special agents.

Ollie and I met over beers in the Boardroom. He was Canadian. I was considering an offer to consult to the LSJML in Montreal. All that week he'd provided insight into my strange neighbors to the north.

The chemistry was blistering, no denying that. But I found Ollie's view of himself something of a put-off.

No matter the topic, Corporal Hasty was an expert, and others knew little.

When the course ended, I headed home to North Carolina, libido frustrated but self-esteem intact. When his training concluded, Ollie drove to Charlotte to visit. No invitation. In Ollie's world, rejection was not an option.

My marriage had just imploded, and I was still shattered by Pete's betrayal. And living alone for the first time in two decades. Horny divorcée-to-be. Brawny Mountie. Eros can be denied only so long. Though I wasn't nuts for Ollie, for a solid week our slap-and-tickle burned down the house.

So what happened? you ask.

Ollie was twenty-nine. I was, well, a wee bit older. I lived in Dixie. He lived in Alberta, damn far away. Neither he nor I wanted to go steady, so no future get-togethers were planned.

We exchanged brief letters and phone calls for a while; no e-mail back then. Eventually, predictably, the thing just died.

And here he was. Sitting face-to-face with player number two in my very short lineup of postmarital lovers.

Hearing footsteps, both men looked my way.

"Dr. Brennan." Ollie rose and spread both hands, the left missing most of its fourth digit.

"Sergeant Hasty." Ignoring the invitation to hug, I extended a palm. As we shook, I tried to recall how the finger was lost. Weird, but that's where my mind went.

"I understand you two know each other." Ryan remained butt-leaning on the desk.

"Dr. Brennan and I met in Quantico." Ollie's liquid brown eyes held mine. "When was that?"

"A long time ago." I willed my cheeks not to flame.

"Dandy," Ryan said. "Shall we discuss Annaliese Ruben?"

As I slipped past Ollie and took a chair to his left, I wondered what Ryan knew. Had our long-ago dalliance come up in the course of conversation about Annaliese Ruben? Surely Ollie would not be so crass.

Was Ollie's history with me the source of Ryan's current coolness? Ridiculous. At best it had been an episode of catch-and-release, old news by the time I came to Montreal. And Ryan and I had pulled the plug on our relationship over a year ago. He couldn't be so childish as to harbor a grudge about a fling that happened before he and I met. Could he? Besides, if he knew, it would have been very recent news to him, his iceberg demeanor already in place.

"Let's," said Ollie.

"How about we start with why you're here," said Ryan.

"Two reasons. First, there's an outstanding warrant on Ruben. You say she's here in Quebec. Second, Ruben is an HRP reported missing from my turf. As a member of the Project KARE task force, I have to follow leads on MPs who fit that profile."

Without waiting for a response, Ollie snapped open the brass clasps on his briefcase, withdrew a folder, and flipped its cover. I noticed that the file held two thin pages.

Worrisome thought. Had Annaliese Ruben's disappearance been investigated at all? Cared about?

"The report was filed as a front-desk walk-in," Ollie began. "Reporting party was Susan Forex, street name Foxy."

"Odd move for a hooker," Ryan said.

"Foxy's an odd chick."

"You know her?"

"I do. But Foxy's bellying up wasn't all that strange. The ladies in Edmonton are scared shitless."

"Rock and a hard spot. Cops or crazies."

Ollie gestured agreement. "A rookie named Gerard took Forex's statement. Forex claimed Ruben was boarding at her house. According to the summary, Ruben had a date to see a john she described as a big spender. The meet was to be at the Days Inn downtown."

Ollie was plucking relevant information out of the file.

"Ruben never came home. Four months later, Forex decided to report her missing."

"Took her a while to get worried," Ryan said.

"How long were they roommates?" I asked.

"Maybe half a year."

"Did anyone follow up?"

"Wasn't much to follow. Street people change addresses like the rest of us change socks. And most won't give the cops squat. A prossie named Monique Santofer was also living with Forex at the time. Both were questioned, a few others. No one knew spit."

Ryan and I said nothing. We both knew the reality.

After those queries, the file had probably circulated within the detective bureau, created no blip on anyone's screen. From there, it had gone to a centralized missing persons division where far too few detectives were responsible for the impossibly large number of persons reported missing each year. Eventually, it had become buried in a stack of others like it.

But somehow, thankfully, it had found its way to Project KARE.

"Why do you think Forex made the effort?" I asked.

"Edmonton is a killing field for these women. Many are so scared they're voluntarily giving DNA samples so their bodies can be identified if they're killed."

"The numbers are that high?"

"At least twenty women have been murdered since 1983. More are missing, maybe dead. And you know that asshole Pickton's not far from anyone's mind."

Ollie was referring to Robert William "Willie" Pickton, a Port Coquitlam, British Columbia pig farmer convicted in 2007 of killing six women and charged in the deaths of twenty more. Many of Pickton's victims were prostitutes and drug users from Vancouver's downtown east side.

I didn't work the case, but colleagues did. Excavation began when remains were discovered on Pickton's property in 2002. The media went batshit, and a court-ordered ban on publication and broadcasting was imposed. Rumors ran wild. Bodies allegedly were left to decompose, fed to the pigs, ground up and mixed with pork from the farm.

Only when the trial began did details emerge. Hands and feet stuffed inside bisected skulls, remains dumped as trash or buried near the slaughterhouse, bloodstained women's clothing in Pickton's trailer.

Inexplicably, a jury found Pickton innocent of first-degree but guilty of second-degree murder in the deaths of six women. He was sentenced to life in prison, with no possibility of parole for twenty-five years—the maximum for second degree permitted under Canadian law.

At an estimated cost of $70 million, Pickton's was the largest serial killer investigation in Canadian history. In 2010 the remaining twenty murder charges were dropped, ending any prospect of future trials. Prosecutors apparently concluded that since Pickton had already received the maximum possible sentence, further expense was not warranted.

A sad footnote. With the lifting of the media ban in 2010, the public learned that Pickton had been charged in 1997 for attempted murder in connection with the stabbing of yet another sex worker. The clothes and rubber boots he was wearing when arrested lay forgotten in an RCMP storage locker for seven years. When finally tested in 2004, they revealed DNA from two of Vancouver's missing women.

Too late for a boatload of victims.

Ollie's voice brought me back.

"—it's not just Vancouver. Women have vanished or turned up dead along Yellowhead Highway 16 in BC. You know what they call that stretch now? The Highway of Tears. There are websites and magazines dedicated to it. And the RCMP has expanded the list of MPs and broadened the area they think that killer may be working. Who knows how many other victims are out there lying in ditches or shallow graves?" Ollie's tone suggested both frustration and compassion.

"Thus Project KARE," I said.

"I've been with the task force for two years. We're committed to finding and caging these degenerates."

"It's an RCMP initiative, right?"

"Not anymore. In Alberta we've said enough is enough. In addition to members of the RCMP Major Crimes Units in Edmonton and Calgary, the task force now includes investigators from the Edmonton PD and other detachments having jurisdiction. These women need protection. The predators have to be stopped."

Just as the death of babies disturbed Ryan, the slaughter of those on society's fringe distressed Ollie. I remembered hearing the same passion in his voice years ago. It was one of the few things I'd liked about him.

"But it seems Ruben is not a victim," I said.

"Tell me what you know." Ollie pulled pen and notebook from his briefcase.

I listened as Ryan laid out the facts. The ER visit by Amy Roberts. The apartment in Saint-Hyacinthe occupied by Alma Rogers. Ralph Trees's girlfriend, Alva Rodriguez. The babies. The fingerprint. The CPIC hit for Annaliese Ruben.

"And now Ruben is off the radar," Ollie said.

"Yes," Ryan said.

"You think she's left the area?"

"Queries at the airport, bus and train stations, and rental car agencies came back negative. Ditto for taxis."

"You pull the hospital security cameras?"

"She arrived and departed on foot. Approached from the direction of the apartment, which was under a mile away. Left heading the same way."

"What about local stores, libraries, anywhere else they might have caught her?"

"Nothing."

"Ruben have friends or relatives locally?"

"Other than Trees, the landlord, and one snoopy neighbor, no one seems to know she existed."

"She wasn't working the streets?"

"Not that anyone knows, but she had to have some means of support."

"Meaning she has no arrest record in Quebec."

"Zip. Maybe the learning curve in Alberta paid off."

"You checked likely aliases?"

Ryan just looked at him.

"The Edmonton PD nailed Ruben twice for soliciting," Ollie said. "She vanished right after the second pop."

"In 2008," I said.

"That skews right with the landlord's time line," Ryan said. "Paxton claims Ruben and a guy named Smith took occupancy about three years ago."

"He retain contact information for Smith?"

"Not even a first name."

"What could he tell you?"

"They were grand tenants. Didn't complain about the plumbing. Paid cash in advance."

"Where's Smith now?"

"In the wind."

"You try running him to ground?"

"Hadn't thought of that."

Ollie's lower lids pinched up slightly at Ryan's sarcasm. "Smith have a job? A car? A cell phone?"

"You want to run Smith, first name unknown, age unknown, physical description unavailable, be my guest." Ryan flapped a hand at one of the computer terminals behind him.

There was a moment of tense silence. I broke it.

"You think Smith could be the high-rolling john Ruben intended to meet at the Days Inn? Maybe he talked her into heading east with him?"

"Nice of her to drop a line to the loving roommates back home." Ryan shook his head in disgust.

"Did Forex ever get a look at this john?"

"No."

"Where are Forex and Santofer now?" I asked Ollie.

"Santofer OD'd last year, so she's out of the picture. Forex is still living at the same address. She owns the place."

"You got surveillance on it?" Ryan asked.

"Hadn't thought of that." Ollie shot Ryan's sarcasm right back at him.

"Any reason to suspect Ruben might have returned to Alberta?" I asked. "That may be her pattern. Leave town when things get hot. She knows people in Edmonton. It's within her comfort zone."

"Right." Ryan snorted. "She motored west in her unlicensed Boxster. Or hired a limo and driver to take her cross-country."

"She could have hitchhiked." Terse. Ryan's attitude was grating on me, too.

"If so, we'll nail her. Every cop shop in Canada has her mug shot."

"She has a dog." Why the hell did I keep dwelling on that?

"People thumb it with pets." Ollie's eyes were hard on Ryan.

Ryan spoke without smiling. "Charley the poodle."

"Steinbeck didn't hitchhike," I snapped. "He had a trailer."

Ollie looked from Ryan to me, alert to an undertone he didn't understand and didn't like. He was about to speak when the mobile on his belt buzzed. He yanked it free and checked the caller ID. "Gotta take this." Rising to his feet.

Ryan arced an arm toward the interview rooms.

Ollie circled the desk and disappeared through the first door.

Tense moments passed during which Ryan stared at his shoes. Finally, I could take it no longer. "Do you have a problem with me, Detective?"

Ryan pushed from the desk to pace away. Paced back. Finally, "Let's just close this case."

I was opening my mouth to ask his meaning when Ollie reappeared. His expression suggested good news. "You may have been dead-on, Tempe."

Ryan tensed at Ollie's use of my first name.

"She's in Edmonton," Ollie went on.

"Ruben?" I was stunned.

"She was just spotted at a Tim Hortons a few miles east of downtown. The place is about a kilometer off the TransCanada."

"Now what?"

"Now the party moves to my town."

9

"I've got someone booking flights." Ollie turned to me. "Can you be at the airport by eleven?"

"Me?" I didn't bother to hide my surprise.

"Ruben whored in Edmonton, too. You think her mothering instincts were better out west?"

"The local ME must have experts he calls on."

"That office is having some issues."

"The SQ won't pick up her expenses," Ryan said.

"The RCMP will. I'll run her through as a temporary CM. Civilian member."

"I know what the term means." Ryan gave Ollie a smile that carried zero warmth.

"So." Ollie's eyes held mine levelly. "Are you in?"

My mind played a flash reel of squirming eyes, tiny mummified hands, wadded tissue. I checked my watch, then nodded.

"If you can't get away, Detective, I understand." Ollie spoke without turning to Ryan.

"I'll see you at the airport," Ryan said.

Upstairs, there were no new anthropology cases. After clearing my sudden change of plans with LaManche, I headed out.

I'd just entered my condo when my iPhone sounded. The noon flight was full, so we were booked on the one o'clock. I used the extra hour to shower, print my boarding pass, and place a courtesy call to the ME in Edmonton. He thanked me and said his facility would be at my disposal, should I need it.

At twelve-twenty, I met Ryan and Ollie at the gate at Pierre Elliott Trudeau. Air Canada flight 413 was posted as delayed. Our new departure time was one-fifteen. I took little comfort in that estimate. The attendant said it was a mechanical issue. Right.

We finally took off at three-forty-five. Which meant we missed our connection in Toronto. Luckily, the next flight to Edmonton left at five. Following a sprint through the airport, we made it. The joys of modern aviation.

Ryan has many fine qualities—intelligence, wit, kindness, generosity. As a traveling companion, he's a pain in the ass.

Ollie's presence did nothing to improve Ryan's disposition. Or maybe it was me. Or the *croque-monsieur* he ate in the coffee shop. The atmosphere in our little band was as friendly as that at a drug raid.

Ollie offered transport upon landing, but Ryan insisted on renting a car. Though Ollie suggested I accompany him, I felt it more diplomatic to remain with Ryan.

With no reservation, the rental process took over an hour. I didn't ask why.

Edmonton is Canada's answer to Omaha. Solid, unassuming, and surrounded by a whole lot of nothing. It's a place that makes you think of sensible shoes.

We saw a lot of the city en route to RCMP K Division headquarters. At first I offered directions based on GPS maps I pulled up on my phone. Ryan neither acknowledged nor followed my suggestions. Eventually, I gave up and focused on the world sliding past my window. The view involved a whole lot of brick.

It was nine-forty when we finally turned onto 109th Street. My stomach was whining that I should have had a sandwich with Ryan. I ignored it.

After presenting ID and explaining our destination to a commissionaire who maintained an attitude of near-terminal severity, Detective Sunshine and I were issued clip-on badges stamped with very large T's. Feeling decidedly temporary and untrusted, we followed a corporal onto an elevator and ascended in silence. At an office marked *Project KARE*, our escort indicated that we might proceed on our own.

Ryan opened and held the door for me. I pointedly waited for him to go first.

The setup looked a lot like Ryan's home base at

Wilfrid-Derome. Not that the RCMP would call it a squad room. Here it was an office. No matter. Like the crimes that necessitate their existence, such spaces share a depressing uniformity no matter the locale. Same in-boxes, foul coffee, and memorabilia.

At ten p.m. the place was deserted.

Ollie's desk was off to one side. He was at it, shoulder-cradling a phone. On hearing the door, he looked up and gestured us to him.

As we approached, Ollie foot-dragged a chair into position beside one already facing his desk. He did not look happy. Ryan and I sat.

Ollie's end of the conversation continued staccato. "When? Where?" Finally, "Shit. Keep on it."

The receiver smacked home with a crack.

"They lost her."

Ryan and I waited for elaboration.

"Ruben hung around the Tim Hortons until noon. Then she walked to Northlands."

"What's Northlands?" I asked.

"I guess you'd call it an entertainment complex. Sports events, horse racing, rodeos, slots, trade shows."

"Modern opiate for the masses," Ryan said.

"That's one way to look at it."

I remembered. Ollie liked horse racing and rodeos.

"Rich pickings for the sex trade," Ryan said.

"It's a problem area." Terse. Ollie was winging a pen up and down in his fingers. Its tip struck the blotter with agitated tics. "Ruben slept on a bench in Borden Park for most of the afternoon. At five she went back to the donut shop. At seven she walked to Rexall Place."

"Why didn't they bag her?"

"Those weren't their orders."

Ryan was about to snipe again. I cut him off. "What's Rexall Place?"

Ollie looked at me, then did the little chin-up thing. "Hello? The Edmonton Oilers?"

"It's a sports arena." Ryan's tone was totally flat.

"And sometime concert hall. Nickleback is playing tonight."

"That's where your guys lost her."

"I guess I'm not communicating very well, Detective. Nickleback is an Alberta group. There were thousands of people milling around the grounds."

"Takes skill to keep a tail in a crowd," Ryan said.

"We'll find her." Frosty.

"Faster than you lost her?"

Ollie's pen stopped moving.

I shot Ryan my squinty-eye look. "Sounds like Ruben was trying to make contact with someone," I said.

"Probably," Ollie agreed.

"Susan Forex?"

"I'm waiting for word on her whereabouts."

"Did Ruben have a pimp?" Ryan asked.

"A twisted little prick name of Ronnie Scarborough. Goes by Scar. Guy's got the charm of a dirty needle."

"Meaning?"

"He's ugly, he's violent, and he has a short fuse."

"A bad combination."

"Scarborough's handle doesn't come from his name. He once put a scar on a girl's face the size of my hand. Used a hot poker."

"Think Ruben might attempt to hook up with him?" I asked.

"I think she'd try Forex first. But who knows."

"What now?" I asked neither of them in particular.

"Now we wait for my guys to sniff Ruben out. I've booked two rooms at the Best Western. That's about a block from here. You want to check in or grab something to eat?"

"I'm famished," I said.

"Gourmet or cheap?"

"Quick."

"Burgers all right?"

"Perfect."

At ten-thirty p.m. the Burger Express hosted only two other customers: an old geezer I suspected might have cadged his meal, and a teen with a backpack and no visible eyes.

The kid manning the counter looked like an escapee from rehab. Scuzzy teeth. Ratty hair. Nightmare acne.

Didn't diminish my appetite. I ordered the mastodon burger. Or whatever the colossus was called. Onion rings. Diet Coke.

As we ate, Ollie filled us in on Susan Forex.

"She was collared twice after filing the report on Ruben. Once as part of a general sweep—that time she skated. Once for soliciting—that bought her a year of probation."

"Then straight back to the life." Ryan sounded disgusted.

"Something like that." Ollie's tone could have frozen peas.

"Guess she missed the constant round of parties and gallery openings."

"Forex is different from most girls on the stroll."

"Meaning?"

"Forget it."

Ryan turned to me. "Coffee?"

"No, thanks."

I was already regretting my menu selections. And the speed with which I'd ingested the damn things.

Ryan left to score caffeine. Perhaps to light up. Though he'd kicked cigarettes years back, recently I'd smelled smoke on his clothes and hair. That along with the uncharacteristic surliness meant he was edgy as hell.

We were shoving waxy wrappers back into grease-stained bags when Ollie's mobile buzzed. While he took the call, I crossed to an overfilled trash bin and mashed our contribution into the mix.

When I returned to the booth, Ollie looked like a kid who'd found his lost puppy after a very long search.

"Forex is at a bar over near the Coliseum."

"Is Ruben with her?'

"She's alone. And working."

"You're thinking surprise visit?"

"Popping in during business hours might make her more forthcoming."

We both smiled, then I started toward the door. Halfway there, a hand caught my arm. I turned.

Ollie was wearing that face men don when they're about to go macho.

"You often think about"—he gestured from his chest to mine—"us?"

"Never."

"Sure you do."

"There was no," I hooked finger quotes, "us."

"We had a hell of a time."

"Mostly you were a jerk."

"I was young."

"And now you're a wise old sage."

"People change."

"You got a girlfriend, Ollie?"

"Not currently."

"Why's that?"

"Haven't found the right one."

"The love of your life."

Ollie shrugged.

"We should go," I said.

"Don't want to keep Detective Douchebag waiting."

"What's that supposed to mean?"

"The guy's not the best company."

"You deliberately provoke him."

"He's an asshole."

"Ollie." I drilled him with a look that said I meant business. "Did you discuss"—I mimicked his gesture—"us with Detective Ryan?"

"I may have mentioned that I knew you." The flicker in his gaze was all the tell I needed.

"You unprincipled bastard."

Before I could react, Ollie pulled me close and pinned my body to his chest. "When we wrap this up, you know you're going to want me," he whispered in my ear.

Pushing hard with both palms, I disengaged. "Never gonna happen."

I whipped around, hot-wired with revulsion.

Ryan was standing outside the door, staring in through the glass. In the garish neon, his face looked drawn and gaunt.

Shit. Shit. Shit.

Uncertain how much he'd seen, I gave a thumbs-up and smiled brightly. Good news!

Ryan walked into the shadows, features so tight, they looked painted on his bones.

10

Ollie drove. I rode shotgun. Ryan sat in back.

A light rain had begun to fall. As we wound through the city, a kaleidoscope of blurred color and shadow slipped past my window. The wipers beat a slow metronome on the windshield.

Ten minutes out, Ollie turned onto a street lined with bars, strip clubs, and fast-food joints, all lit and open for business. Fragmented neon glistened on the pavement and splashed across signs, cars, and taxis.

A few small businesses elbowed for position: an auto supply outfit, a pawnshop, a liquor store. Their windows were dark and barred against vandalism and theft.

A handful of men in sweatshirts and windbreakers moved in both directions, heads down, shoulders hunched. Here and there smokers lingered in doorways, enduring the wind and damp for a nicotine fix.

Ollie pulled to the curb in front of a two-story brick building with *XXX Adult Store* painted on one side. In addition to the world's largest collection of movies and images, the enterprise offered twenty-five-cent peep shows twenty-four/seven.

"Your heart's desire right here, for a price." Ollie swept a hand across the squalid scene around us. "Drugs. Women. Boys. Weapons. You want a hit man, you can probably find that, too."

"How about Susan Forex?" I said.

"Let's see what we can do."

Ollie punched a number on his speed dial and put the phone to his ear.

I heard a voice on the other end but couldn't make out the words.

"In front of the triple-X," Ollie said after several seconds.

Pause.

"How long?"

Pause.

"Anything on Ruben?"

Pause.

"Call me the minute you do."

Snapping the lid, he said, "Lucky break. The lady's not having a profitable evening."

We all got out. As Ollie *wheep-wheep*ed the locks, I slipped on a jacket I'd pulled from my roll-aboard.

The air smelled of fried food, gasoline, and wet concrete. Muffled music pulsed from a building to our right, boomed as a patron emerged, grew muted again when the door swung shut.

Ollie led us fifty yards north to a stucco box whose sign identified it as the Cowboy Lounge. The neon cowgirl wore nothing but a ten-gallon hat.

"I do the talking." Ollie aimed that at Ryan. "She knows me. I'm less threatening."

Ryan said nothing.

"You good with that, Detective?"

"I'm good with that, Sergeant."

Ollie entered. I followed. Ryan brought up the rear. We all stopped a few feet inside the entrance.

The first thing to hit me was the smell, a noxious blend of stale beer, cigarette smoke, reefer, disinfectant, and human sweat. The stink invaded my nose as my eyes adjusted to the gloom.

To the left, the crack of pool balls drifted from a room set off by swinging half-doors. The bar was straight ahead, a carved wooden affair with an ornate mirror behind and stools in front.

At midbar, a plaid-shirted man drew beer from a long-handled tap. He had moles on his face and jittery eyes that landed on us a nanosecond, then moved on.

A dozen mismatched tables filled the space to the right. Framed posters covered the walls around them—Gene Autry, John Wayne, the Cisco Kid.

Willie Nelson wailed from a jukebox beyond the tables. A player piano sat beside it, cover cracked, wooden case a battlefield of cigarette burns.

I guessed the original idea had been Wild West saloon. Instead, the place looked like a rundown roadhouse in Yuma. With lousy lighting.

Half the tables and all of the bar stools were full. The clientele was mostly male, mostly blue-collar. The few women present were definitely rough trade—brassy hair, tattoos, couture designed to advertise flesh.

Moving among the tables was a waitress in red bustier and tourniquet-tight size-sixteen jeans. Her hair was fried, her makeup cheap and overdone.

Ollie tipped his head toward a tall, angular woman at the left end of the bar. "Looks like our gal's the pick of the litter tonight."

I appraised Susan Forex. Her hair was long and blond, her peasant blouse artfully draped to reveal one shoulder. A denim micromini, cinch belt, and ankle-strapped stilettos completed the look.

Forex was talking to a dumpling in western boots and a thousand-gallon Stetson. Stetson had a beer. She was drinking what appeared to be whiskey on the rocks.

Leaning as close as the hat would allow, Stetson spoke into Forex's ear. She ran a long red nail up his forearm. Both laughed.

We crossed the room, senses alert to danger.

The bartender watched, eyes bouncing from us to the door, to the waitress, to the tables, to his charges at the bar. A few other eyes rolled our way. Most didn't.

"Hello, Susan."

Forex swiveled at the sound of her name. When she saw Ollie, her smile collapsed.

"Friends of yours?" Stetson peered around Forex toward us, a drunken grin splitting his doughy face.

"Beat it." Forex flicked a dismissive wrist at her would-be john.

"Darlin', you and me are gonna—"

Forex rounded on him. "Get the hell out of here."

Stetson's face crumpled in confusion, tensed when he grasped that she was blowing him off. "Pay for your own drink, bitch."

With that witty retort, Stetson shoved from the bar stool. Standing straight, including the hat, he was maybe my height.

Ollie waited until Stetson was out of earshot. Which wasn't long. Stompin' Tom Connors was now singing about a Sudbury Saturday night.

"We're not here to hassle you, Foxy."

Forex rolled her eyes and crossed her legs. Which were spectacular.

The bartender closed some distance but kept his gaze on everything but us.

Ollie got right to it. "You filed a missing persons report on Annaliese Ruben."

Forex went totally still. Bracing for bad news? Preparing a lie to protect her friend?

"You OK, Foxy?" The bartender spoke just loud enough to be heard above the music.

"I'm good, Toffer."

"You sure?"

"She's sure." Ollie badged him.

Toffer backed off and became very busy wiping the bar.

Up close I could see that Forex's hair was dark down close to her scalp. Though yellowed, her teeth were even and perfectly straight, suggesting a childhood affluent enough to include braces. Her skin was smooth, her makeup skillfully applied. In that light, she could have been thirty or fifty.

"We think Ruben was living in Quebec the past three years," Ollie continued. "Word is she's back in Edmonton."

"Good. The little punk stiffed me on her share of the last month's rent."

As Ollie questioned Forex, I checked out two men sitting a few stools over. Their body language told me both were listening. One guy was large, with wild black hair and dark little eyes that looked like raisins. The other was smaller, with leather wristbands on arms inked with jailhouse tattoos.

"Come on, Foxy. You know where she is." Ollie seemed unaware of the interest our conversation was drawing. "She dimed you, right? Asked for a place to crash?"

"I love a good spring rain, don't you, Sergeant?"

"Or did she call Scar?"

"Who?"

"You know who I'm talking about."

Forex picked up her drink and swirled the ice. I noticed that her fingers were well manicured and free of nicotine stains.

"Help me here, Foxy."

"Ruben was too young to be living on the streets. I took her in. Doesn't mean I bought the rights to her life story."

That didn't tally with the statement of the ER doctor in Saint-Hyacinthe.

"I thought she was older," I said.

Forex's eyes crawled to me. For a moment she said nothing. Then, "Nice jacket."

"Ruben self-reported her age as twenty-seven," I pressed.

"The kid was barely old enough to shave her legs. Should have been in school. But I get why that wasn't her thing."

"Why's that?"

Forex snorted. "You've seen her?"

"A picture."

"So we both know she won't be America's next top model." The naked shoulder rose, dropped. "Kids can be vicious."

In the corner of my eye, I saw Raisin Eyes elbow his buddy. His face looked icy green in the glow of a neon frog shouting, *Let's party!*

"Where was Ruben living before she moved in with you?" Ollie still seemed unaware of the pair down the bar. Not so for Ryan. Ever so subtly, he tipped his head left. I nodded.

"What am I, her Facebook pal?" Forex said.

"Why would Ruben lie about her age?" I asked.

"Gee." Forex widened her eyes at me. "Why would a kid on the run do that?"

Good point. Stupid question.

"On the run from what?" Ollie jumped on Forex's phrase.

"Hell if I know." Forex's tone said she'd be making no further slips.

"We'd like to get to Ruben first," Ollie said. "Stop her from reaching out to Scar."

"Are you listening to me? The kid was only at my place a few months. I hardly knew her."

"You cared enough to report her missing."

"I didn't want trouble."

"I know your pattern, Foxy. Ruben isn't the only kid you've taken in."

"Yeah. I'm Mother frikkin' Teresa."

"Monique Santofer." Ollie's voice sounded gentler. "How old was she?"

Another shrug.

"What happened with Santofer?"

"I found her wired to the eyes and threw her ass out."

"That your policy? No drugs?"

"My pad. My rules."

"Let's try again. Where'd Ruben live before she moved in with you?"

"Buckingham Palace."

"She leave anything behind?"

"A pile of junk."

"You still got it?"

Forex nodded.

"Might be we'll need to take a turn through your place." Ollie's tone was again cop-hard. "I know you won't mind."

"Damn right I'll mind."

Ollie smiled. "Life's a cesspool of disappointment."

"You got a warrant?"

"You know I can get one."

"You do that."

"Take that to the bank."

Forex's eyes narrowed. "There's more to this than you're letting on."

"Sounds like you've got some trust issues."

"Said the cat to the mouse."

"Squeak, squeak." Ollie winked.

I felt my face make the same grimace as Forex's.

Ollie pulled a card from his wallet. "Call if you hear from Ruben."

Forex drained her glass and smacked it down on the bar. "Shit."

"You're a star, Foxy."

"What I am is too old for this crap."

With that, Forex grabbed her purse and walked out in her treacherous high heels.

Turning one shoulder, I whispered to Ollie, "Did you bring Ruben's mug shot?"

Face neutral, he pulled the printout from a pocket and handed it to me. As Ryan and Ollie watched, I moved down the bar to Raisin Eyes and his buddy.

"I couldn't help noticing your interest in our conversation." I held up the mug shot. "Either of you know this girl?"

Both faces stayed pointed at their beers.

"See that gentleman over there? He's a cop. An overachiever. Gets off on busting people. You know, just in case they might have done something wrong. Believes in preventive policing."

Raisin Eyes swiveled on his stool, sending a tidal wave of body odor rolling my way. I waggled the printout. He made a show of studying the image.

"Word on the street is she might have worked out of here," I said.

"Doing what, selling Popsicles? Chick looks like a fucking ice-cream truck." Raisin Eyes laughed at his own joke. "What do you think, Harp?"

Harp sniggered. "Eskimo Pie all the way."

"Do either of you recognize her?"

"I don't recognize Popsicles. I suck 'em." Oily grin. "How about you? You got a stick up your cheeks so's I can get a good hold?"

Raisin Eyes never knew what hit him. Shooting past me, Ryan arm-wrapped the guy's throat and hyper-rotated his elbow up and back in one lightning move. The more Raisin Eyes twisted, the more Ryan tightened the armlock.

Harp bolted for the door. Toffer started in our direction.

"Let's not make any bad decisions here," Ollie warned.

Toffer held position, fingers curled into fists at his sides. A few patrons headed for the exit. Others watched, pretending not to. Ollie joined us but did not intervene.

"You're breaking my arm." Raisin Eyes's face was the color of claret.

"Apologize to the lady."

"She's the one—"

Ryan increased the pressure.

"Sonofabitch. Whatever."

"I'm running out of patience." Ryan's tone was dangerous.

"Fuck. I'm sorry."

Ryan released his hold. Raisin Eyes flopped forward, left hand rubbing circles on his right shoulder.

"Name?" Ryan demanded.

"Who the fuck's ask—"

"I am." Forged steel.

"Shelby Hoch."

"That's a good start, Shelby."

Ryan gestured for me to hold up the printout. I did. Ollie continued to watch in silence.

"Let's start over," Ryan said. "You know this lady?"

"I seen her around."
"When?"
"Last night."
"Where?"
Hoch hooked a thumb at the red-bustier waitress.
"Leaving a motel with shit-for-brains."

11

We turned as one.

The waitress was staring at us from among the tables, face white, lips geranium-red. Like many large animals, she could move fast when frightened. Slamming down her tray, she bolted for a door to the right of the bar.

Ollie, Ryan, and I shot after her.

The door opened onto an alley. When I came through it, the woman was doubled over and gasping from her short sprint, and bad cop/good cop roles had already been chosen. Ollie held one plump arm. Ryan had a reassuring palm on her back.

Rain was falling in earnest now, drumming the Dumpsters and the cases of empty beer bottles stacked beside them. A soggy plastic bag was moving with the wind against the back of the building, puffing up then flattening against the wet brick.

We waited for the woman to catch her breath. In the

salmon glow of a streetlight, her flesh looked pale and soft with fast-food fat. Black underwear bunched out from the waistband of her overstuffed jeans.

Finally, the woman straightened. Still breathing hard, she dug Marlboros from a back pocket, shook the pack, and pulled a cigarette free with her lips.

Ryan withdrew his hand. "You all right?"

Slipping matches from the cellophane, the woman cupped her fingers, lit up, and drew smoke into her lungs, all the while keeping her eyes down.

"Why the rabbit act, sunshine?" Bad-cop Ollie. "You got something to hide? Something we should know about?"

The woman exhaled, creating a silvery cone beneath each nostril.

"I'm talking to you."

The cigarette tip flared again, bathing the clown face in a soft orange glow.

"You got a hearing disorder?"

The woman exhaled as before, then, eyes still averted, tossed the match.

"That's it." Ollie yanked cuffs from his belt.

Good cop raised a "hold it" palm toward bad cop.

"What's your name, ma'am?"

"Phoenix." Barely audible.

"May I ask your first name?"

"Phoenix Miller. Everyone just knows me by Phoenix."

"One of my favorite towns."

"Yeah. I heard Arizona's pretty."

"I'm Detective Ryan. My gruff friend here is Sergeant Hasty."

Phoenix flicked her Marlboro with a ragged thumbnail. The ash dropped and dissolved in the oil-iridescent puddle at our feet.

"We'd like to ask you a couple of questions, Phoenix."

"About what?"

"A gentleman at the bar says he saw Annaliese Ruben with you last night."

"Shelby Hoch ain't no gentleman. He's a foulmouthed slug."

"Thanks for the insightful character analysis." Ollie, Prince of Sarcasm. "Annaliese Ruben?"

"Why do you want her?"

"I'm her dentist, and I'm worried she's not flossing her teeth."

"No, you're not."

"Hoch says he saw the two of you at a motel. What hot-sheet palace would that be, sweetheart?"

Phoenix studied the Marlboro as if it might provide guidance. It trembled in her fingers.

"Your girlfriend still there?"

"How would I know?"

"Birds of a feather."

"I'm out of the life."

"Right." Ollie snorted. "You quit rolling down your panties for twenty bucks and some flake."

The lipsticked mouth opened, but nothing came out. In the surreal light, it looked like a round dark hole.

"We're not interested in your personal life," Ryan said. "We want to find Ruben."

"She in trouble?" For the first time, Phoenix allowed her eyes to make contact with those of another.

"We want to help her." Ryan held her gaze as he sidestepped the question.

"She's just a dumb kid."

"Selling poontang out of Motel Sleaze." Ollie.

"I'm telling you. It's not like that."

"What's it like?"

"I clean. They comp me a room." As she spoke, Phoenix kept looking to Ryan for reassurance.

"You live at the motel?"

She nodded.

"Which one?"

"The Paradise Resort."

"Hundred and Eleventh Street?" Ollie asked.

"You won't mess me up, will you? I need that room." Phoenix's eyes bounced from Ryan to Ollie and back. "It's a good gig."

"Is Ruben still there?" Ryan asked.

"Better not be. I told her she could only stay one night."

"Because of the dog?" The question was out before I knew it was forming. Was I obsessed?

The mascara-laden eyes shifted to me. "Mr. Kalasnik

don't allow no pets. He's the owner. Who are you?"

"How did Ruben find you?" Ryan asked.

"Everyone's hip that I work at the Cowboy."

"Why you?"

"The kid don't have a whole lot of options."

"Is there anyone else Annaliese might contact?" Ryan asked.

"I don't know."

"Does she have family in Edmonton?"

"I'm pretty sure she's not from here."

"From where?" Ollie.

"I don't know."

"When did she first come to Edmonton?"

"I don't know."

"I'm hearing that a lot."

"We didn't talk about her past."

"But you were going to turn her life around."

"I never said that."

"You and Foxy make quite a tag team." Bad cop was doing his best to provoke, hoping for an outburst that might be revealing. "Saint Susan and Saint Phoenix."

"God knows I ain't no saint. But I've been around a long time. Seen it again and again." Phoenix wagged her head slowly. "I've had a belly full of little girls should be worrying about algebra and zits; instead, they're off the bus and straight into the life."

I knew exactly what she meant. Every day teens from Spartanburg, St-Jovite, or Sacramento head to Charlotte, Montreal, or L.A. to be models or rock stars or to escape abuse or boredom or poverty back home. Every day pimps cruise the bus and train stations, watching for backpacks and hopeful faces. Like the predators they are, these animals swoop in, offering a photo shoot, a party, a meal at Taco Bell.

Most of these kids end up junkies and whores, their Hollywood dreams becoming hellish realities of dealers and daily fixes and paddy wagons and pimps. The unluckiest arrive toes-up at the morgue.

Every time I see one of these children, I go numb with anger. But I have come to understand. Though I despise the human destruction, the carnage, I am powerless to stop it. Nevertheless, I care. I feel grief and always will.

I refocused on Phoenix.

"—three years go by. I figure Annaliese either got herself killed by one of these women-hating sickos, or else she got out." Phoenix picked tobacco from her tongue and flicked it. "Two days ago she shows up looking like a train wreck, asking for a place to crash. Leaving her on the street was like throwing raw meat to wolves. If taking her in's a crime, arrest me."

"Is she still at the Paradise Resort?"

Phoenix shrugged.

"Annaliese needs more help than you can provide." Ryan brought sincere to a whole new level.

"My shift don't end until two. I gotta have those tips."

Ryan looked at Ollie, who dipped his chin.

"We only need permission to enter your room," Ryan said.

"You won't take nothing?"

"Of course not."

"Mr. Kalasnik don't like no kind of fuss."

"He'll never know we were there."

A car horn sounded. Another honked back. Down the alley, the plastic bag broke free and spiraled upward with a soft snap.

Phoenix made her decision. Unhooking a chain from her belt loop, she detached one key and held it out to Ryan.

"Number fourteen. All the way down on the end. Leave it in the room. I got another."

"Thank you." Ryan's smile was damn near priestly.

"Don't hurt her."

The Marlboro hit the wet pavement in a shower of sparks. Phoenix crushed it with the heel of one boot.

For several years Edmonton enjoyed the dubious distinction of having the highest homicide rate of any major Canadian city. In 2010 she slid to number three. Winding through the dim post-midnight streets, I wondered if E-town's ratings slump had caused her citizenry to question the burg's official nickname: City of Champions.

En route to the Paradise Resort, we discussed Susan Forex. Or tried to. Mostly the men sniped at each other.

"She's holding back," Ryan said.

"Gee. Why would that be?"

"Probably writing her memoirs. Thinks a spoiler might lower the value of the property."

"She's covering her ass," Ollie said.

"But is it that simple?" I asked.

"What do you mean?"

Unsure, I thought for a moment. Didn't help. "Susan Forex and Phoenix Miller both tried to protect Annaliese Ruben," I said.

"Must admire her mothering skills." Ryan's tone was acid.

"Even hookers hate baby killers." Ollie's way of agreeing.

"So why help her?" I asked.

No one had an answer to that.

"Can you really get a search warrant for Forex's house?" I asked Ollie.

He shook his head. "Slim chance. I'd have to convince a judge that I think Ruben is there, that she's the subject of a felony investigation in Quebec, that she's on the run, and that we don't have time to get an arrest warrant from Quebec."

Phoenix Miller's home sweet home was a two-story L-shaped affair with outdoor walkways accessing maybe thirty rooms. An enormous sign proclaimed *Paradise Resort Motel* in mile-high letters. A flashing arrow pointed would-be guests to a covered portico. Below it, the office door was flanked by planters luxuriant with dead vegetation.

Clearly, the place offered neither of the delights promised by its name. *Total Dump* would have been a more appropriate moniker. Perhaps *Last Resort*.

A few cars and pickups occupied a swath of concrete fronting the building. Off to the left, beyond them, were several campers and an eighteen-wheeler.

Most motels, you'd hesitate before staging a stealth strike at one in the morning. The Paradise Resort was not one of them. Office dark. No security. Not a soul in sight.

We fell silent as Ollie cruised the L. Room fourteen was at the end of the arm tangential to 111th, its entrance obscured by an iron and concrete staircase shooting to the upper level. No vehicle waited out front or at the adjacent unit.

Ollie cut the headlights, pulled into the slot facing room thirteen, and killed the engine. We got out and quietly closed our doors.

Music floated from a Mexican restaurant across a small service road fifty yards beyond the motel. Traffic whooshed in a steady stream over on Highway 16.

We approached Phoenix Miller's room in single file. Ollie positioned himself to one side of the door. Ryan took the other, gesturing me behind him with one hand.

I noted no yellow glow beneath the door or rimming the drapes, no flickering blue radiance from a TV.

Ollie knuckle-rapped to announce our presence.

No answer.

He knocked again.

Not a sound.

He pounded with the heel of one hand.

Nothing but mariachis and the whoosh of cars and trucks.

Ryan stepped forward and inserted the key.

12

The room was dark and still.

We all paused, listening for sounds of a human presence. My nose took in disinfectant and the Meadows & Rain Febreze I use at home.

Beside me, I felt Ryan palm the wall. A switch clicked, then sallow yellow light flowed from an overhead globe double-tasking as a crypt for dead insects.

Unit fourteen was approximately the size of my bathtub. The walls were peach, the thin brown carpet stained and cigarette-burned.

My eyes circled clockwise. To our left, a battered bureau held a clunker TV with a foil-wrapped antenna. Beyond the bureau, a metal rack housed a paltry collection of garments, some on hangers, some stacked in piles on shelving below.

The bed sat opposite the door, neatly made with a red-and-white floral spread that looked like a dorm-room special from Target. A square red throw was carefully positioned on each pillow.

Beside the bed, in the room's far left corner, a red plastic lamp occupied a white plastic nightstand. Above the bed's wall-bolted headboard hung a cheaply framed print of a bowl of red tulips.

Ahead and to the right was a closed door I assumed led to a bath. Beside the door, in the room's far right corner, a built-in cabinet held a microwave oven, a hot plate, and a mini-fridge.

A white plastic kitchenette set occupied the space below the room's only window, to the right of the entrance. Miniature cacti filled a small ceramic pot at the table's center. A red cushion covered the seat of each chair.

I felt hollow inside. Though the furnishings were cheap and shabby, it was clear that a caring hand had tried its best. The bedspread and matching pillows. The lamp. The plastic furniture. The plants. The cushions. Though barely making enough to survive, Phoenix Miller had worked to brighten the depressing little space.

"Annaliese Ruben?" Ollie called out.

Nothing.

"Ms. Ruben?"

No response. No sounds of movement.

As at the main entrance, Ryan and I moved to one side of the closed door, Ollie to the other. Ollie reached out and turned the knob.

The bathroom was impossibly small, the fixtures crammed into a space little bigger than a locker. Fully open, the door blocked access to the tub.

Cosmetics and body lotions lined the back of the toilet. A pink nightshirt hung from a hook beside it. Red and white towels filled a bar on one wall, carefully draped and alternating by color. The plastic shower curtain was, of course, red. The tile was spotless, the mirror and sink immaculate.

"Tidy lady." Ollie's words were edged with condescension.

"She's doing what she can to make this a home," I said.

"Tough job in this shithole."

Ollie opened the medicine cabinet and started poking through the contents. The move annoyed me. "We came to find Annaliese Ruben. She's not here. Let's go."

"You in a hurry?"

"Miller is not our concern. There's no reason to invade her privacy."

Ollie shot me an über-patient smile but closed the cabinet.

As I rejoined Ryan in the main room, I heard the sound of the shower curtain being pushed to one side.

"Now what?" I asked when Ollie reappeared.

He checked his mobile, apparently found nothing of interest. "Now we get some sleep. In the meantime, I'll put eyes on this place and on Miller."

"Someone should canvass out here tomorrow, talk to the owner," Ryan said.

"Hadn't thought of that, Detective."

Ryan's jaw did that clampy thing, but he said nothing.

Ollie crossed to the makeshift closet, flipped through the hanging clothes, toed the stacks, then knelt on one knee to peer under the bed.

"Check the microwave?" Ryan tossed the key not so gently onto the bureau.

Ollie ignored the sarcasm. "Let's roll."

We all trooped out.

At the Best Western, Ryan registered and disappeared.

"I'll walk you to your room," Ollie said when I had my key.

"No, thanks."

"I insist."

"I decline."

"It's a tough town."

"I'm inside a hotel."

Ollie raised the handle on my carry-on. I reached for it. He swiveled the thing into pulling position and gestured for me to proceed.

Seething, I set out across the acre of lobby. Ollie followed, wheels clicking on the tile. I unlocked my door in icy silence.

"Let's shoot for eight tomorrow," Ollie said.

"Phone if anything breaks."

"Yes, ma'am."

Ollie made no move to release my suitcase. Yanking the handle from his grasp, I took two steps backward and slammed the door.

The room was typical North American Motel. King bed, dresser, desk, upholstered chair. The drapes and bedding featured appropriately paired selections from the green quadrant of the color wheel. A framed print was bolted to each of the walls. Though the decor would never inspire coverage in *Architectural Digest*, the place was light-years upmarket from the Paradise Resort.

Not that it mattered. Face wash. Swipe at the teeth. I was out.

Minutes later, the Irish National Anthem blasted me awake. I shot a hand toward the nightstand. As my iPhone hit the carpet, the boys kept singing.

Groping in the dark, I found the phone and clicked on.

"Brennan." Trying to sound alert. Pointless. It was the middle of the night.

"I hope I didn't wake you?" The caller was female and speaking French. "It's Simone Annoux."

My semiconscious mind fumbled with the name. Came up blank.

"In the DNA section."

"Of course, Simone. What's up?"

As I switched the call to speaker, I noticed that the digits said six-twenty. Eight-twenty in Montreal. I'd been asleep almost four hours. I lay back and placed the phone on my chest.

"You submitted samples from an infant death case in Saint-Hyacinthe? When we talked, you mentioned that identity was an issue?"

Simone is a tiny woman with carrot hair, thick glasses, and the assertiveness of an earwig. Her excessive timidity results in the phrasing of most of her comments as questions. Drives me nuts.

"Yes."

"We tried something a bit controversial. I hope that's all right?"

"Controversial?"

"I thought you would want to know?"

"What did you try, Simone?"

"Are you familiar with BGA?"

"Ben Gurion Airport?"

"Biogeographical ancestry."

"Tony Frudakis," I said.

"Yes. And others. Though I believe Dr. Frudakis has abandoned this avenue of research?"

In the early 2000s, women were being murdered in Baton Rouge, Louisiana. Based on an FBI profile and one eyewitness statement, investigators sought a young white male as the serial killer. With no success. Frustrated, they turned to a molecular biologist named Tony Frudakis.

At that time DNA from a crime scene or victim could be used only for comparison to samples in CODIS, the

Combined DNA Index System, a database containing approximately five million profiles. If investigators had a specimen but no suspect, they could run it through the database to see if it matched a sample on file.

While CODIS is good at linking unknown suspects to individuals already entered due to criminal activity, it's useless for predicting ancestry or physical characteristics. And that's no accident. When the National DNA Advisory Board selected the gene markers—the DNA sequences having known locations on chromosomes—for use in CODIS, they deliberately excluded those associated with physical characteristics or geographic origins. Couldn't risk offending any ethnic group. No comment on that political reasoning.

DNAWitness, the test Frudakis developed and used in the Baton Rouge case, employed a set of markers selected precisely because they *did* disclose information about physical traits. Some were found primarily in people with Indo-European roots, others mainly in people of African, Native American, or South Asian heritage.

Frudakis told the Louisiana Multi-Agency Homicide Task Force that the perp they were seeking was 85 percent sub-Saharan African and 15 percent Native American. The Baton Rouge serial killer, linked by DNA to seven victims, turned out to be a thirty-four-year-old black man named Derrick Todd Lee.

"—distribution of these genetic markers has been

associated with broad geographic regions, resulting in the recognition of BGA and the use of the markers as a major genetic component in the dissection of race. But you have to keep in mind that the diversity of these markers was complicated over the eons by historic events—population migrations, for example."

While I'd been thinking about Frudakis, Annoux had gone into lecture mode. I heard no question marks when she talked science.

"People move around," I said.

"Yes. Paleoanthropologists believe all modern humans are descended from populations that migrated out of Africa some two hundred thousand years ago. First they settled in the Fertile Crescent. Gradually, groups splintered off in every direction; eventually, some crossed the Bering Strait to America. With distance came reproductive isolation resulting in divergence of the gene pools."

"What does this have to do with the baby?" It was way too early for discourse on evolutionary molecular biology.

"BGA markers can be used to determine what percentage of an individual's DNA is shared with Africans, Europeans, Asians, or Native Americans. The technique has been used in a number of high-profile criminal investigations. Shall I explain the process?"

"Keep it short."

"The test examines for the presence of one hundred and seventy-five SNPs called AIMs, or ancestry informative markers. Are you with me?"

An SNP, or single nucleotide polymorphism, is a DNA sequence variation in which a single base varies between members of a species or between paired chromosomes in an individual. In mega-oversimplified terms, it means there are multiple forms of a "gene." Millions of SNPs have been cataloged in the human genome. Some are responsible for diseases, such as sickle cell. Others are normal variations.

"Yes," I said.

"Compared to other animal species, the genetic diversity exhibited by *Homo sapiens* is minuscule. That's because our common links are so recent. We're ninety-nine-point-nine percent identical at the level of our DNA. It's that little bitty one tenth of one percent that makes us different."

I heard a series of beeps, checked the phone screen. Ollie. Already? Though curious, I hit ignore.

"—according to Frudakis, and others agree, about one percent of that one tenth of one percent differs as a function of our history. His method mines that point-oh-oh-one percent to find distinctive differences that determine genetic ancestry. Several companies are now doing this type of analysis, some for genealogical purposes, others to aid in forensic investigations. Sorenson Forensics has a program called LEADSM. I have a very dear friend there who—"

"The Saint-Hyacinthe baby's genetic markers were compared to those found in specific reference populations?" I was eager to finish the call and get back to Ollie.

"Yes? The results suggest she is seventy-two percent indigenous American and twenty-eight percent Western European."

That got my attention. "The baby's parents are aboriginal?"

"One or the other might have been categorized as such. Race is such a complex—"

"Thank you so much. This is really very helpful. Sorry, but I have to take another call."

I disconnected and dialed Ollie. He answered on the first ring.

"It's Brennan. You phoned?"

"Good morning, starshine. Sorry to wake you."

"I was up." I told him about Annoux's report. "The approach is a bit controversial."

"Why's that?"

"Racial DNA profiling?"

"Right. So Ruben is Indian."

"Native American. She or the child's father."

"Or both."

"Yes. Why did you try to reach me?"

"I have good news."

"You netted Ruben?"

"Not that good. I just got a call from Susan Forex. She's unhappy with her latest boarder and wants her gone."

"Why not simply kick her out?"

"The lady refuses to budge."

The implication struck home.

"Better than a warrant," I said.

"Better than a warrant," Ollie agreed.

13

In the late eighteenth century, spurred by competition in the fur trade, the Hudson's Bay Company expanded westward into the Canadian interior, establishing a string of posts along the major rivers. One was built on the North Saskatchewan, at what is now Edmonton. E-town was also a player in the Klondike gold rush of the 1890s, and in the post–World War II oil boom.

Today Edmonton is the capital of Alberta province. She has an impressive legislature building, a university, a conservatory, a living-history museum, and a gazillion parks. These attractions draw thousands of tourists. But nothing can compete with the mall.

Encompassing over six million square feet and containing more than eight hundred stores, West Edmonton Mall is North America's largest and the fifth largest in the world. And the big gorilla isn't all about shopping. The complex also has a giant water park, a man-made lake, a skating rink, two mini-golf courses, twenty-one movie theaters, a casino, an amusement park, and countless other delights.

Susan Forex lived a stone's throw away. A very short throw.

Ollie, Ryan, and I pulled into the neighborhood at seven-forty-five. Ollie had purchased coffee and donuts, and we'd breakfasted in the car. I dislike jelly-filled, which most of them were, so I shamelessly grabbed all three chocolate-glazed.

High on sugar and caffeine, I checked out the 'hood. The houses were closely packed and all of a type, some fronted by large porches, others having little more than a stoop. Each had a flower bed or shrubbery hiding the foundation and a small patch of lawn running to the sidewalk. Here and there a bicycle or pull toy lay abandoned in the grass.

Ollie slid to the curb in front of a two-story number with gray siding and black shutters. The front steps were on the left. A covered porch ran sideways, across the front.

"Very Brady Bunch."

I couldn't disagree with Ollie's take. The setting wasn't what I'd expected.

"Pretty lady likes to get away from the job," Ollie added.

"Most of us do," Ryan said.

"Bet the neighbors are clueless about her line of work."

"You talk cop shop over the backyard fence?" Ryan's tone was totally flat.

"I live in a condo."

"You get my meaning."

"My job isn't sucking off johns in an alley."

"*Mon Dieu,* we're judgmental."

"My bad. Forex probably organizes the annual homeowners' picnic."

"She might."

"Only if it's held during daylight."

"The beauty of self-employment. You control your own hours."

"Nice image. Forex and the prossie posse serving up coleslaw."

I'd had my fill of the hostile repartee. "What do you know about this boarder?"

"Her name's Aurora Devereaux. She's new in town and so far has managed to stay under the radar."

"Did you run the name?" Ryan asked.

Ollie palm-smacked his forehead. "Wish I'd thought of that."

"You're a real asshat." Ryan's words were ice.

That did it.

"We're treading on the edge of my patience here." I glared from Ollie to Ryan in the backseat. "I don't know what the problem is, but you both need to dial down the attitude."

Ollie mouthed the word "hormones."

"Devereaux?" Resisting the urge to smack him.

"It's a shiny new alias, one of several. The lady's real name is Norma Devlin. She's twenty-two, from

Calgary, landed in Edmonton four months back.
Calgary PD says her jacket's pretty crowded, most of
it juvie, so it's unavailable without a warrant. Mostly
petty shit, shoplifting, soliciting, disorderly. Lot of
probation, no jail time."

"Whatever Devereaux did to anger Forex, it wasn't
prostitution," I said.

"Nope." Ollie disengaged his seat belt. "Let's do us
some evicting."

Forex answered the bell in seconds. She was dressed
in jeans and an untucked blue cotton shirt. With her
hair pulled back and sans makeup, she looked years
older than she had in the Cowboy. And tired. She also
looked like she'd just dropped her kid off for soccer.

"It took you long enough." In a loud whisper.

"Good morning, Foxy. We're good. And yourself?"

Forex's eyes flicked past Ollie and did a quick scan
of the street. Holding the door wide, she stepped back.

"You're asking us in?" Ollie wanted an explicit
invitation.

"Yes." Hissed.

"All of us?"

"Yes." She made a fast scooping gesture with one
hand.

Ollie entered. Ryan. Yours truly. Forex quickly
closed the door behind us.

I looked around. We were standing in an
overfurnished parlor that L'ed into an overfurnished
dining room. Dark, heavy carved stuff like my

grandmother had. The carpet was moss, the sofa aqua and green stripes, the wing chairs a shade of turquoise that didn't really blend.

A staircase rose on our left, two steps to a landing, then a right turn and up. The usual framed pictures of babies and graduates and brides angled up the wall above the banister.

Straight ahead was a kitchen. In an alcove I could see a Mac computer, its screen filled with a spreadsheet. Ledgers and printouts filled the countertop to either side. Black loose-leaf binders crammed a shelf above.

I noticed that Ollie was also eyeballing the workstation.

"Doing a little payroll?" he asked.

"I keep the books for a couple of businesses. It's perfectly legal."

"That what you tell the neighbors? You're an accountant?"

"What I tell the neighbors is none of your business."

"You've got skills. Why turn tricks?" Ollie sounded sincerely curious.

"Because I like it." Defensive. "Now. Are you going to get that bitch out of my house?"

"Tell me why you want her gone."

"Why? I'll tell you why. I took her in, and she violated my trust."

"Aurora Devereaux."

"Yes. I opened my home. Charged her next to nothing."

"She's not paying the rent?"

"It's not that. I made my rules clear. You live in my house, you're frickin' Doris Day. No men. No booze. No drugs." Forex's face was going deeper red with every word. "How does she thank me? She gets coked to the eyeballs night after night. Once maybe I can overlook. We all make mistakes. But this little miss is a hard-core junkie. Here, under my roof, she's shooting up or snorting or tweaking or whatever the hell she does."

Ollie tried to ask a question, but Forex was rolling.

"I get home from the Cowboy, you know what she's doing? Sitting bare-ass naked in my backyard." A palm smacked the blue cotton. "Singing! It's goddamn two in the morning, and she's doing strip karaoke outside my house!"

"Singing what?" Ollie asked.

"What?" Exhaustion and frustration were turning Forex's voice shrill.

"Just wondering about her musical selection."

Forex's head thrust forward, causing the tendons in her neck to go taut. "What the flip does it matter?"

"I always do 'Fat Bottom Girls.'"

Forex threw up both hands. "She fucking hates me!" Hitting hard on the verb and elongating the *e*.

Ollie didn't get the reference. "You gotta grow thicker skin, Foxy."

"Puddle of Mudd," I said.

Three faces swiveled my way.

"They're out of Kansas City. The song may actually be titled 'She Hates Me.' With the expletive implied."

"Are you three for real?" Forex dropped her arms. "I've got a headcase doing blow au naturel on my lawn, and you morons are playing *Name That Tune*?"

I glanced at Ryan. Though he turned away, the ghost of a smile played on his lips.

"Did you ask Devereaux to leave?" Now Ollie was all business.

"Right after I ordered her to cover her puffy white ass. She cussed me out, slammed into her room, and locked the door. That's why I called you."

"Is she still in there?"

"The door's still locked."

"You don't have a key?"

"I like my face arranged as it is."

"OK. Here's what's going to happen. While we roust Devereaux, you're going to disappear. No commentary. No interference. No input of any kind."

"That ungrateful—"

"We're outta here." Ollie turned toward the door.

"OK. OK." Forex snagged his arm. "Her room's in back, above the garage."

"Same crib Annaliese Ruben used?"

"Yeah, yeah, I get it. Never a free lunch." Forex removed a key from an end-table drawer and tossed it to Ollie. "No need to mess the place up. Anything Annaliese left is in a duffel in the closet."

Forex led us into the kitchen to a back door that

opened onto a small patio overlooking a nicely kept lawn.

"Devereaux own a firearm?" These were the first words Ryan had spoken since entering the house.

"Not that I know of. It's against my rules. But what the hell? Her Highness ignores them."

As we filed out, Forex called to our backs, "Watch yourselves. Coming off the junk, she'll be mean as a snake."

Cars entered the garage from an alleyway in back, people from a door in the side facing the house. We followed a trail of concrete pavers to the latter.

The door was unlocked, so we went in. The interior smelled of oil, gasoline, and a hint of rotting garbage. A silver Honda Civic occupied most of the space. The usual garden tools, recycling tubs, and rollout trash bins lined the walls. Directly ahead, through a tiny storage room, a set of stairs ascended to a second story. We quietly climbed them. At the top, we assumed our back-to-the-wall formation, then Ollie knuckle-rapped the door.

"Ms. Devereaux?"

No answer.

"Aurora Devereaux."

"Kiss off." Muffled and slurry.

"It's the police. Open up."

"Go away."

"That's not going to happen."

"I'm not dressed."

"We'll wait."

"You want to peep my tits, it'll cost twenty."

"Put on some clothes."

"You got a warrant?"

"I'd like to keep this friendly."

"If you've got no warrant, you can kiss my patootie."

"Your call. We talk here or downtown."

"Screw you."

"Actually, you're the one who'll be screwed. I've got witnesses say you've been turning tricks."

"Big fucking—"

"—deal," Ollie finished. "That's not why we're here."

"Yeah? Then how'd I get so lucky?"

"Buddy heard you singing, asked me to drop off a recording contract."

An object smacked the door, then ricocheted onto the floor. Glass shattered.

Ollie looked at us, one brow cocked. "I'm coming in now," he said.

"Suit yourself. I've got plenty more lamps."

Ollie inserted and turned the key.

Nothing hit the door. No footsteps pounded the floor.

Turning his body, Ollie palmed the door open and stepped sideways as far as he could. Ryan and I drew farther back against our wall.

Aurora Devereaux sat propped among pillows and a chaos of bedding.

I fought to keep the shock from my face.

14

Devereaux had astonishing blue eyes and bottle-blond hair that started low on her forehead. Her dark brows arched high, then plunged to form a hairy patch over the bridge of a nose that was short and ended in upturned nostrils. Her thin lips were parted, revealing wide-spaced and very crooked teeth.

I recognized the combination of traits. Cornelia de Lange Syndrome, or CdLS, a genetic condition caused by a gene alteration on the fifth chromosome.

Inexplicably, I flashed on a name I hadn't thought of in almost four decades. Born six days apart to women living in Beverly on Chicago's South Side, Dorothy Herrmann and I were inseparable from the time we could walk until my relocation to North Carolina at age eight. We called each other Rip and Rap. Dorothy peoples all of my earliest childhood memories.

Dorothy's younger sister, Barbara, had CdLS. In the old snapshots, Barbara is among us neighborhood kids, wearing a Christmas sweater too long for her arms, dressed as Bo Peep for Halloween. Always her face is split by a smile, shame over her odd features and her jack-o'-lantern teeth far in the future.

Except for the bad bleach job and the bad attitude, Barbara Herrmann would have grown to be Aurora Devereaux's twin. Had she lived.

I was at university when I learned of Barbara's suicide. Dorothy and I had kept in touch, but caught up in my own self-centered teen world, I'd been oblivious to hints of her sister's growing depression. Or, wanting life to be rosy, I'd chosen to ignore them. Barbara was happy, always smiling. Nothing was wrong.

Should I have acted? Might visits, letters, phone calls have prevented Barbara's death? Of course not. Her own family had been unable to do that. Still, my insensitivity haunts me.

Devereaux sat with her tiny hands resting on her upraised knees. From the length of her torso and legs, I put her height at that of your average middle-schooler.

Like Barbara Herrmann, some CdLS individuals have subnormal mental ability. Based on the exchange with Ollie, I doubted that was the case with Devereaux.

"We're coming in now." Ollie's voice had lost some of its tough cop tone. I could tell from his face that he, too, was shocked. Ditto Ryan, though he hid his reaction better.

Devereaux watched in silence as the three of us

stepped from the top riser and circumvented the shattered lamp lying on a rectangle of tile inside the door.

The room was maybe twelve-by-twelve. In addition to the daybed, it held a wooden table and two captain's chairs, a dresser, and shelving filled with a scramble of clothes, purses, toiletries, and magazines. The wall-mounted TV looked like something you'd see in a hospital.

The right side of the room was a kitchenette with an undersize fridge, a sink, and a stove arranged shotgun-style along one wall. Its floor was done in the same tile as the entrance, setting the space off from the carpeted living/sleeping area. The sink and small counter were heaped with dirty dishes and utensils, open cans, and the remains of fast-food meals.

From the kitchenette, a short corridor led to a closet and a bath. Both doors were open, and both overhead lights were on. The rooms looked like bombsites, with garments, linens, makeup, laundry, footwear, and a mix of unidentifiables jumbled on the floors and draped on the fixtures or hung haphazardly from doorknobs, towel and closet bars, and the shower rod.

Ollie plucked a shiny green robe from a chair and tossed it onto the bed. Devereaux ignored it.

"Foxy's not happy," Ollie began.

"Bitch never is."

"Says you had a groovy high going last night."

Devereaux raised a palm and one bare shoulder. *So?*

"Foxy wants you out."

"Foxy wants a lot of things."

"Do you have a lease?"

"Sure. I keep it in the safe-deposit box with my estate planning papers."

"Then you have no legal right to stay."

Devereaux said nothing.

"Time to go, Aurora." Ollie sounded almost sympathetic.

Devereaux snatched a small plastic bottle from the bedside table. Raising her chin, she inhaled antihistamine into one nostril, then the other.

While waiting out the noisy process, I took in more detail. The place was devoid of personal items. No photos, fridge magnets, knickknacks, or macramé plant holders.

In addition to the antihistamine, the bedside table held a half-empty bottle of Pepto and a mound of bunched tissues. Recalling another symptom of CdLS— gastroesophageal reflux disease, a condition that can make eating unpleasant—I felt a wave of compassion for the childlike woman in the bed.

As Devereaux blew her nose with a thoroughness I had to admire, I edged toward the hall for a closer look at the closet, being as discreet as possible. My movement wasn't lost on our hostile hostess.

"Where the hell's she going?"

"Never mind her," Ollie said.

"The fuck, never mind. I don't like strangers sniffing through my undies."

"Ms. Forex left a duffel in the closet," I said. "We have permission to search it."

The neon blues jumped to me. Their lashes were curly and perhaps the longest I'd ever seen.

"*Ms. Forex,*" delivered as a full-on sneer, "has the brainpower of a salami sandwich."

"She was kind to you."

The heavy brows winged up in surprise. "That what you call it? Kindness? I was her latest pity project."

"Pity project?"

"Take in the flawed and make their lives bliss."

"Was Annaliese Ruben flawed?" My compassion was losing out to dislike.

"She wasn't Miss America." Devereaux snorted, an ugly antihistamine-wet sound.

"You knew her?"

"I heard about her."

"Where's the duffel?" Curt. Ollie was fast losing patience.

"No clue."

"Give it the old college try, Aurora."

"You've got no warrant, you don't get shit."

"I'm trying to appeal to your good side, kiddo."

"I don't have a good side."

"Fair enough. Let's try another angle. I've got a landlady reporting illegal substances on her property. How about we toss the place, starting with this?"

Ollie lifted a shoulder bag from the floor beside the bed. The thing was metallic, with enough fringe to embarrass Dale Evans.

Devereaux arched forward at the waist and shot out an arm. "Give me that!"

Ollie held the purse just out of her reach.

"You bastard."

Smiling, Ollie swung the bag like a pendulum.

"Bastard!"

Ollie pointed to the robe.

"Turn around!"

Ryan and I did. Ollie did not.

I heard movement, the swish of fabric, then a thumpy jangle as the purse hit the bed.

"Excellent."

On hearing Ollie's comment, Ryan and I turned back.

Devereaux was sitting sideways, lower legs over the edge of the mattress, toes not touching the carpet. She was wearing the robe and the same fuck-you pout.

Ollie repeated his question. "Where's the duffel?"

"Closet shelf."

"I believe you have some packing to do?"

"I'd rather eat dog shit than spend one more day in this dump!"

Bag pressed to her chest, Devereaux scooched forward and dropped from the bed. Grabbing shorts and a top from the mess on the shelving, she strode to the bathroom and slammed the door.

Ryan, Ollie, and I were right on her heels.

The closet was a miniature walk-in with a long head-high bar on one wall and shorter double bars on the other. Dresses, tops, and skirts hung from hangers, most featuring bright colors and a whole lot of bling.

The floor was ankle-deep in shoes and soiled clothing. The latter filled the small space with a sweaty, syrupy scent.

A single shelf L'ed above both of the high bars, filled to capacity. Rolls of toilet tissue and paper towel. Shoe boxes. A printer. A blender. A fan. Plastic tubs whose contents I couldn't identify.

I spotted the duffel in the corner where the long stretch right-angled into the short. It was olive-green polyester with black handles and a front zipper pouch. Wading through the muddle of Walmart fire-hazard chic, I pushed a handful of hanging garments aside. A stepladder lay against the baseboard. As I grabbed it, my eye took in something on the wall, half concealed by a large suitcase. My pulse quickened.

Later.

After backing out of the dresses, I positioned the ladder. Then, with Ryan acting as my spotter, I scampered up the rungs.

Three tugs and the duffel came free. Its weight suggested there was little inside.

I lowered the duffel to Ryan, who handed it to Ollie. We retraced our steps to the living room. Running water behind the bathroom door suggested Devereaux was still engaged in her morning toilette.

Ollie gestured for me to do the honors. I spread the duffel's handles and yanked the zipper.

The bag held four objects. A pair of cheap plastic sunglasses with one cracked lens. A snow globe with a panda and butterflies inside. A rusty Bic razor. A tire-tread sandal probably dating to the Woodstock era.

"Our job is easy now."

Ryan and I looked at Ollie.

"No way she's not coming back for these jewels."

No one smiled at Ollie's joke.

"What about the front compartment?" Ryan suggested.

I checked. It was empty.

We were standing there, mute with disappointment, when the bathroom door opened. We all turned.

Devereaux's hair was combed and sprayed into a blond updo, and her face was a Gauguin palette of color. Green and lavender lids. Rose cheeks. Red lips. Had her situation not been so sad, I might have found it comical. Like *Toddlers & Tiaras*.

Ignoring us, Devereaux crossed the room, dropped to her knees, and yanked a suitcase from under the bed. With angry movements, she began tossing in clothing from the shelves and floor. No folding or layering. A wrinkle-free look was not a priority.

Lowering my voice, I told Ollie and Ryan what I'd seen behind the suitcase in the closet.

"The panel is removable?" Ryan asked.

"I think so."

"May provide access to the bathroom pipes," Ryan said.

"You're thinking another dead baby?" Ollie's expression was grim.

My gaze slid to Devereaux. She was emptying a dresser drawer, oblivious to our conversation.

I nodded.

Wordlessly, we returned to the closet. Ollie and I watched as Ryan dragged the suitcase from behind the clothes.

The panel was approximately twelve inches square, attached to the wall by nails at the corners.

My eyes did a three-sixty. Landed on a pair of orange stiletto pumps. I grabbed and handed one to Ryan.

Hooking the tip of the heel onto the edge of the panel, Ryan pulled with the body of the shoe. The nails slid free with little resistance.

It was Saint-Hyacinthe all over again. I held my breath as Ryan inserted his fingers, levered downward, and pulled the panel free. The opening gaped black and foreboding.

Ollie produced a penlight. Ryan thumbed it on and aimed the beam into the darkness. As expected, the tiny white oval landed on pipes. They were dark and wrapped with frayed insulation.

I watched the oval probe. It crawled up a vent stack. Over a flange. Left across a horizontal.

Banging down the hall told me Devereaux was checking the kitchen drawers and cabinets.

Banging in my ears told me my pulse had gone apeshit.

The oval doubled back, continued to the right, then started probing downward.

Seconds passed. Eons.

And there it was. Jammed in the hollow of a U-shaped trap.

I felt sick to my stomach.

The towel was blue with a small appliqué on one side. It was tightly rolled, with the thick end pointing our way.

"Call the ME?" Ryan asked.

Ollie shook his head. "Let's be sure. Don't want to bring a doc out here for nothing."

A voice in my head was rejecting the brutal reality of the visual input. *No, God, no!*

Ryan set the penlight on the floor and took a series of shots with his iPhone. Checked the results. "Got it."

As I kicked aside clothing to clear floor space, Ryan reached in and removed the bundle. Both men looked at me. I dropped to my knees and took a steadying breath.

The fabric was degraded and easily torn. The layers were tightly adhered, sealed by fluids that had long ago dried and congealed. My fingers trembled as I tried to gain entry without doing damage.

The world went deadly quiet, all sound obscured by emotions inside me.

Finally the terry cloth yielded. I rolled the bundle sideways.

The bones were small and brown and curled around a fragmented skull.

"Jesus Christ!"

I looked up.

Ollie's face was the color of oatmeal. I realized he hadn't seen the other dead infants.

Moving as gently as possible, I rewound the towel.

"That's four that we know of." Ryan was using the light to make one last round in the opening.

"This murdering bitch left a trail of dead babies from Quebec to Alberta! And we can't find her sorry ass?" Fired by loathing, Ollie's words came out way too loud.

Ryan got to his feet. "We'll find her."

I rose and placed a calming hand on Ollie's arm.

"Call the ME," I said.

15

By one-thirty Ryan and I were suited up and standing beside a stainless-steel table with Dr. Dirwe Okeke, one of the Alberta ME's newest hires. Okeke had done his prelims—photos, X-rays, measurements, descriptive observations. I'd done a little dry-brush cleaning and arranged the baby's bones in anatomical position.

Rather than a pathologist, Okeke looked like he played defensive tackle for Edmonton High, and parents of opposing teams wouldn't have demanded a birth certificate. He stood six-two, weighed 250. Had I seen him on the street, I'd have put his age at maybe eighteen.

When I'd phoned the ME office, a receptionist had listened to my story, then rolled my call to Okeke. He hadn't interrupted as I'd introduced myself and explained the dead babies in Quebec and the one at Susan Forex's house.

As expected, Okeke elected to visit the scene

personally. He arrived in an Escalade with a front seat specially outfitted to accommodate whales. Two techs followed in a van.

When she saw Okeke, Devereaux's attitude did a rapid 180 to meek. I couldn't blame her. The good doc looked like he was of another species, huge and dark to her small and pale. Without moving or speaking, Okeke seemed to fill her wee bedroom to overflowing.

Okeke had asked few questions, viewed the tiny bones in silence. Then he'd interviewed Devereaux, who swore she knew zip. She hadn't met Ruben, had never had reason to pry the panel from the wall.

Forex also knew nothing. Or so she claimed. Her shocked expression suggested she was probably being straight.

Ollie had waited for Devereaux to stuff her closet sparklies into the second suitcase, then he drove her to a women's shelter. I suspected the gesture came partly out of compassion but mostly out of a desire to avoid an up-close-and-personal with the bones of a newborn.

Ryan, Okeke, and I had watched the techs enlarge the opening with a handheld power saw, then search inside the wall. Other than a nest of startled roaches, their efforts produced zilch.

Leaving the techs to photograph and process the scene, Okeke transported the remains in the Escalade. Ryan and I rode with him to the ME office on 116th

Street. On the way, we learned that Okeke was from Kenya and that he studied medicine in the UK. That was it. The guy wasn't a talker.

And here we were.

As with the Saint-Hyacinthe attic baby, nothing was left of this infant but a skeleton and fragments of desiccated tissue. Lacking flesh to hold it together, the skull had fallen apart. The individual cranial bones lay spread like an illustration in an anatomy text.

"Please clarify." Okeke's voice was deep, with a Masai Mara lilt reshaped by years of British schooling.

"The baby was at least seven gestational months at the time of its death."

"Not full-term?"

"It may have been. If so, it was in a very low percentile for size. But the fetus was definitely viable."

As I explained my measurements and observations, Okeke jotted notes. The clipboard looked like a child's toy in his enormous hands. "Gender?"

"I can't determine that from the bones."

When Okeke nodded, the scalp above his neck rippled, then smoothed.

"Trauma?"

"None," I said. "No fractures or indications of physical abuse."

More jotting. "Cause of death?"

"The bones and X-rays show no evidence of malnutrition, disease, or deformation." I thought of the wadded tissue in the throat of the window-seat baby.

"No intrusions or foreign objects."

"What of ancestry?"

"The cheeks may have been quite wide, but it's hard to tell with nonarticulated bones. And I may have seen slight shoveling on an upper central incisor."

"Suggesting what was once called Mongoloid racial background."

"Yes." I told him about Simone's DNA finding for the bathroom-vanity baby.

"So this child may be of aboriginal heritage?"

"Assuming it is a sibling or half sibling of the baby that was tested."

"Is there any question the infants are of the same mother?"

I looked at Ryan. So did Okeke.

"We have no proof," Ryan said. "Yet. But we believe Annaliese Ruben gave birth to all four babies."

"Why would a mother kill her own children?"

Oh, yeah. Okeke was new at the game.

"It happens."

Okeke's dark eyes darkened. "Where is this woman now?"

"We're looking for her," Ryan said.

Okeke was about to ask another question when a phone shrilled loudly. "Excuse me."

Two steps brought Okeke to a desk beside a sink at the back of the autopsy room. For me, the trip would have required five.

Okeke stripped off a glove, punched a button, and

lifted the receiver. "Yes, Lorna." Pause. "I choose not to speak with anyone at this time."

Lorna said something. I assumed she was the receptionist who triaged my call.

"Who is this man?" There was another, longer pause. "Where did Mr. White obtain this information?"

As he took in Lorna's response, Okeke's eyes rolled to me. "Put him through."

Lorna did.

"Dr. Okeke."

White's voice had greater power than Lorna's. The buzzy whine carried past Okeke's ear.

"I can't release that information, sir."

The next whine ended on a high note, suggesting another question.

"I'm sorry, that's confidential."

Anxious to proceed with the analysis, I crossed to the counter to untangle the towel that had wrapped the baby. It was like the movie *Groundhog Day*, autopsy room four all over again. Same cautious twisting and pulling. Same fear of causing damage.

Oblivious to Okeke's end of the conversation, I focused on inserting my fingers, lifting, inserting deeper, lifting more. Millimeter by millimeter, the gunk yielded and the kinks came free.

I vaguely registered that, in the background, Okeke's answers were growing increasingly clipped. I kept teasing and tugging.

Eventually, the towel lay flat with only one corner

stuck. I pulled gently. With a Velcro-like *frip,* the fibers disengaged. I laid back the flap.

Yep. *Groundhog Day.* But this time my find wasn't a bag of sand and small green pebbles.

Pasted to the underside of the corner was a scrap of paper. I tried freeing an edge with the tip of one gloved finger. No go. The thing had become one with the terry cloth.

I adjusted the Luxo lamp and leaned close. There was lettering, uppercase, black, on a blue background. Above the lettering was what might have been a white border.

I rotated the towel to try to make sense of the message. LA MONFWI.

I was running possible meanings, adding letters on both ends, when Okeke's comment brought my head up sharply.

"I was told you were calling with information about Annaliese Ruben."

Ryan looked my way. His brows rose slightly. So did mine.

Okeke waited out a whine. "May I ask why you are interested, sir?"

The whine launched into a long explanation. Okeke did not let it finish. "Are you a reporter, Mr. White?"

Again the whine droned on. This time Okeke cut it off by slamming the receiver into its cradle.

Okeke attempted to make a note on his clipboard, shook his pen, then winged it onto the desk. It bounced to the floor. He made no move to retrieve it.

"That was a journalist?" I guessed.

"A Mr. White. If that is his real name."

"Who does he work for?"

"It does not matter." Okeke flapped his clipboard toward the sad little bones. "How did he learn of this baby? Of the others?"

"He knew about the Quebec cases?" I couldn't keep the shock from my voice.

"He did." Okeke's angry eyes drilled me with a look. It was an intimidating sight.

"He got nothing from me. Or Ryan." Curt. The implied accusation piqued me.

"Neither Dr. Brennan nor I speak to the press about ongoing investigations."

Okeke turned the angry eyes on Ryan. "Yet this man knew."

"Information about this baby had to come from Devereaux or Forex." Ryan spoke in a low and very even voice. "Or from one of your technicians, though that does not explain the Quebec angle."

Ollie knew all of it, I thought. Didn't say it.

"Why would a member of my staff do such a thing?"

Ryan rotated a thumb against his fingertips. "Someone rings White, claims to have insider information about a woman leaving a trail of dead babies across Canada. Says the scoop goes to the highest bidder. Thinking the story might have legs, White agrees to pay."

Okeke shook his head in disgust. "Such thirst for

the lurid and heinous. Like your famous Butterbox Babies. A book, even a movie. Why?"

Okeke referred to the case of the Ideal Maternity Home, a Nova Scotia facility for unwed pregnant mothers operated from 1928 until 1945 by William Peach Young, an unordained minister and chiropractor representing himself to be a Seventh-day Adventist, and his wife, Mercedes, a midwife. After years of delivering babies and placing them up for adoption, accumulated allegations of profiteering and of high infant mortality rates brought the home under scrutiny.

The investigation revealed that the Youngs had purposely killed "unmarketable" babies by feeding them only molasses and water. A deformity, serious illness, or "dark" coloration meant no placement potential, no revenue, and therefore, death through starvation.

Dead babies were buried on the property in small wooden grocery boxes typically used for dairy products: thus the term "Butterbox Babies." Others were tossed into the sea or burned in the Ideal Maternity's furnace. Estimates suggested between four and six hundred infant deaths at the home.

"I want to know who did this." Anger thumped a vein in Okeke's right temple.

"As do we," I said.

"You will inform the RCMP sergeant who was present at the scene?"

"Mmm."

A dripping faucet made soft *thups* in the stainless-steel sink. Finally, Okeke circled the desk to snatch up his pen.

"I found something in the towel," I said.

Both men followed me to the counter, leaned in, and studied the truncated message.

"The beginning of the first word and the end of last word are missing," I said.

"Not necessarily."

I was about to query Ryan's meaning when my iPhone offered another performance of the Irish National Anthem.

Ollie.

I pulled off a glove and clicked on. Ryan and Okeke continued staring at the scrap.

"Where are you?" Ollie asked me.

"Still with Okeke."

"Bones tell you anything?"

"Ruben found motherhood inconvenient. What's up?"

"After depositing Devereaux at WIN House, a delight I hope never to repeat, I dropped in at headquarters to see if anything had popped. Had a message from a Constable Flunky."

"Seriously?"

"You want to hear this?"

"I'm putting you on speaker. Ryan's with me." I hit the button and, stupidly, fixed my eyes on the phone.

"—big guy to miss anything. Anyway, I broadcast Ruben's pic, asked our officers to show it around on the street. Flunky actually did."

Reception was lousy, and Ollie kept growing loud then fading. I looked up to see if Ryan was paying attention. He was punching buttons on his own iPhone.

"An agent at the Greyhound station remembered a woman who looked like Ruben tried to buy a ride to Hay River."

"When?"

"Yesterday."

"Where's Hay River?"

"The south shore of Great Slave Lake."

"In the Northwest Territories."

"Gold star for geography."

"Was the agent sure it was Ruben?"

"No. But get this. At first he refused to sell her a ticket because of the pooch."

"The woman had a dog?" I felt my heart skip a beat.

"Yeah. Greyhound has a no-pet policy. The only exception is a service animal."

"So she didn't get on?"

"The guy finally took pity and let her ride."

I thought a minute. It made sense. The NWT has a large Dene population. I was about to say that when Ryan surprised me.

"I know where Ruben's gone."

16

Okeke and I both eyed Ryan skeptically.

"She's trying to get to Yellowknife."

"What's he saying?"

Ignoring Ollie, I gestured with my free hand for Ryan to explain.

"The last string of letters forms a complete word."

I reconsidered the scrap.

"Monfwi is an electoral district for the Legislative Assembly of the Northwest Territories."

"And you know this because?" Without looking up.

"Two years ago I busted a kid from Monfwi for dealing crack out of the Guy-Concordia metro station in Montreal. Turned out the little twerp had juice. Twenty minutes after I let him phone Daddy, I got a call from his MLA." Ryan used the abbreviation for Member of Legislative Assembly.

"What's he saying?"

Ignoring the sputtering coming from my mobile,

Ryan read from the screen of his iPhone. "'The Monfwi district consists of Behchoko, Gamèti, Wekwèeti, and Whatì.'"

"Dene communities."

"The Tlicho people, to be exact. There are five main Dene groups. The Chipewyan, living east of Great Slave Lake; the Yellowknives to the north; the Slavey along the Mackenzie River to the southwest; the Tlicho between Great Slave and Great Bear lakes; and the Sahtu living in the central part of the NWT."

"Gold star for ethnography." Stealing a line from Ollie.

"Google." Ryan waggled his phone. "Ya gotta love it."

I refocused on the scrap. "You're thinking LA is the end part of MLA?"

"The fragment probably got torn from a constituency newsletter. Politicians distribute them so voters will think they're earning their pay. The rags all look alike."

"The Monfwi district is near Yellowknife?"

Ryan nodded. "And the Legislative Assembly sits in Yellowknife."

"That doesn't mean Ruben went there."

"What the hell's he saying?" Ollie was growing more and more vociferous.

"I'll call you back." I clicked off.

"I checked the bus schedule." Ryan again waggled Mr. Phone. "To get to Yellowknife from Edmonton, you take a Greyhound to Hay River, then you transfer to a Frontier coach line."

"There's nothing direct?"

Ryan shook his head.

"Besides Yellowknife, where else can you go from Hay River?"

"Not many places."

I thought a moment. It all tracked. Ruben was, in all likelihood, at least part aboriginal. Ralph Trees said Roberts/Rogers/Rodriguez spoke accented English. Phoenix Miller thought Ruben came from someplace other than Edmonton. A woman resembling Ruben had tried to board a bus to Hay River. With a dog. Trees said Roberts/Rogers/Rodriguez had a dog. There was a pet bowl in the Saint-Hyacinthe flat. A scrap probably from a Monfwi district newsletter got wrapped in with the baby found at Susan Forex's house.

Besides, we had nothing else.

I called Ollie.

Yellowknife lies approximately fifteen hundred kilometers north of Edmonton. To go by car, one travels north to the 60th parallel to cross into the Northwest Territories near Enterprise, then west to Fort Providence to catch a ferry across the Mackenzie River. One then skirts a vast bison sanctuary, avoiding freedom-sniffing *Bovinae* wandering the pavement. At Behchoko one cuts back southeast to the north shore of Great Slave Lake.

The drive takes up to eighteen hours. Most travel

advisory sites recommend making it while the sun shines. And bringing a whole lot of bug spray.

Unless it's winter. Then you can brave the ice road.

Not a chance this kid was enduring that trip. Nope. Not me.

As with bus travel, airline options were limited.

Ollie booked us onto a Canadian North flight leaving at eight-thirty p.m. The bad news: we wouldn't land at YZF until after ten. The good news: sunset would occur many hours after our arrival.

Ollie spent the rest of the afternoon and early evening re-interviewing the Greyhound ticket agent and making calls to Hay River, Yellowknife, and other places I'd never heard of. Ronnie Scarborough, the pimp, had finally surfaced, and Ollie had invited him in for a chat. Ryan and I would join them at six p.m.

Using a list that Ollie provided, Ryan and I spent our time visiting bars and hotels favored by Edmonton's fair ladies. Some of the establishments made the Cowboy look downright chic.

We floated Ruben's picture, asked if anyone knew or had seen her. We also asked about the big spender Ruben was to have met the night she boogied to Quebec.

We learned two things. In the underbelly, three years is way past anyone's memory horizon. And we were as welcome in that world as a roach infestation.

Upon arriving at RCMP headquarters, we found that Ollie had learned about as much as we had. Which was zilch. Which made him surly as hell.

Ronnie "Scar" Scarborough was cooling his heels in an interview room. Which made him surly as hell.

Ollie suggested it would be best if he conducted the interrogation alone. We agreed, and he set us up for remote observation.

On-screen, we watched Ollie enter a small cubicle and take a chair opposite a guy who looked like he'd been sent from central casting to play a New Jersey wise guy. He was wiry in a ferret sort of way, with acne-pocked skin, deep-set eyes, and a hooked nose that overhung a scarred upper lip. Gold neck and wrist chains. Shiny gray jacket over a tight black tee that glorified chest hair. Pointy black shoes. The only thing off was the tattoo wrapping the back and sides of his neck. It looked like a stylized bird that had escaped a totem pole.

Scar was sitting with legs outthrust, ankles crossed, right arm draping his chair back.

"How's it hanging, Scar?"

Scar's eyes rolled toward Ollie.

"Nice tee. Glad to see you're secure in your own sexuality."

"Why the fuck am I here?"

"I thought we could discuss future career options."

"I wanna call my lawyer."

"You're not under arrest."

Scar drew in his feet and rose. "Then I'm outta here."

"Sit down."

Scar remained standing, contempt crimping his features.

Ollie slapped a photocopy of Annaliese Ruben's mug shot on the table, spun it to face Scar. The rodent glare remained fixed on Ollie.

"Look at it, asshole."

Scar's gaze flicked down, back up. He said nothing.

"Know who that is?"

"Tell your sister I ain't dating right now."

"Annaliese Ruben. My intel says you pimped for her."

"I make it a point to ignore unsubstantiated rumors."

"Project KARE has her on our list. We think maybe Ruben got herself killed." True enough. At least at one point.

"Life can be brutal."

"Here's the thing, Scar. Since we're uncertain if Ruben's alive or dead, we're thinking we should take a real close look at her last known associates."

Scar performed an impressive one-shoulder shrug.

"Starting with her pimp."

Scar shrugged again. Same shoulder.

"Starting with a warrant for his cell phone records."

"You can't do that."

"I can do that." Ollie augured a finger into the printout.

Blowing out a sigh, Scar dropped into his chair and glanced at the photo. "OK. Yeah. Maybe it's the fat kid used to hang around some."

"Amazing how the mind works."

"So I forgot. I been busy."

"Altar-boy duties."

"That's it."

"Or maybe you've been working the bus depots. Looking for young stuff, you know what I mean?"

This time the shoulder hitch seemed less cocksure.

"Maybe we should talk to your workforce. Check a few IDs. See how many candles these girls will be blowing out on their next cakes."

"This is harassment."

"How old was Ruben when you turned her out?"

Scar's mouth curled up in a smarmy half-smirk. "It wasn't like that."

"What was it like?"

"I tried to help her."

"Right. You were her mentor."

Scar wagged his head slowly. "You're so fucking dumb, you don't have a clue."

"You her baby daddy?"

"Ruben didn't have no baby."

"Yes. She did."

"News to me."

"You help her kill it?"

"You're fucking nuts."

The more I watched, the more repulsive I found the little weasel.

"Where is she?"

"I haven't seen the bitch in three years."

"That so?"

"Yeah."

"Why?"

"She moved on."

"With who?"

"Tom fucking Cruise. How should I know?"

"That make you angry? Ruben taking off like that?"

"It's a free country."

"Did Ruben mule for you, Scar? That it? She leave you with a gap in your distribution system?"

"The dumb cunt didn't have the brains to pick her own nose."

"Or was it the lost revenue? One less whore paying for the right to do back-alley blow jobs?"

"The kid was a whale. Not worth piss."

"Did you cap her? Use the hit to send a message?"

"You really are. You're fucking crazy."

Sensing fault lines in the tough-guy bravado, Ollie offered silence.

"Look, I hope nothing's happened to the kid. Honest. I wish I could help."

Ollie leaned back and folded his arms. "Tell me what you know about her."

Scar looked as though the request confused him.

"Is Ruben Francophone? Anglophone? Aboriginal?"

"She spoke English."

"Where's she from?"

When Scar wagged his head, I could see moisture glistening on his upper lip.

"Who'd she hang with?"

"I heard she lived with a chick named Foxy."

"If Ruben left Edmonton, where would she go?"

Scar raised his hands and eyes to the ceiling.

"How would she travel?"

"Jesus, man. I'm telling you. I don't know. I never get involved in the girls' personal lives."

That did it. My anger boiled over. "This runt-ass bastard hooks kids on drugs, makes them whore to feed their addictions, bullies them, exploits them financially, but he's not involved in their *personal* lives?"

Ryan clasped the upturned palm I'd thrust toward the screen. For a moment our eyes locked. He looked away first. I disengaged and dropped my arm to my side.

It went on like that, Ollie asking questions, Scar insisting he knew nothing, me fighting the urge to reach through the monitor and throttle the little turd.

At seven, Ollie gave Scar the old saw about not leaving town. Abruptly, he rose and left the room.

Scar flung curses at Ollie's retreating back. Before the monitor went dark, he shouted one last zinger at the door.

"You're so fucking clueless, you might as well be working right between your cheeks."

We spoke little during the drive to the airport, the check-in process, and the brief wait at the gate. By some fluke, our flight boarded on time. Thanks to a malicious god, I drew the seat next to Ollie.

We were buckling our belts and powering down our mobiles when the pilot's voice came over the speakers. I knew right away that he did not have good news.

Mechanical problem. Thirty-minute delay.

"Holy Mother of God. Do these airlines ever take off on time?"

Feeling a response would be pointless, I offered none.

"If it's not the weather, it's something wrong with the plane, or the crew's gone missing, or some other damn thing."

Making no attempt at subtlety, I opened my Ian Rankin novel and began to read. Sergeant Sensitive did not take the hint.

"Scar's a real piece of work, isn't he?"

My eyes remained glued to my book.

"We think he's trying to expand, run product north into the territories."

I turned a page. Damn, I was going to miss Rebus.

"The bastard's smarter than he looks. Keeps a layer between himself and the street. Impossible to pin shit to him."

Nope.

Ollie gave up talking to my right ear. Several minutes passed while he flipped through the flyer on safety instructions and the on-board magazine. Then, sighing theatrically, he returned both to their pouch.

"I think Scar knows more than he's saying about Ruben."

That got my attention. Closing my book, I turned sideways. "Why?"

"Remember how the creep got his name?"

"He burned a girl."

"Story goes, he tracked her all the way to Saskatoon. Wanted to send out a warning."

"To?"

"Anyone thinking of quitting his employ."

"Ruben left Edmonton three years ago. Why wait so long?"

"Montreal's big. And far away. Ruben changed her name and laid low, so she was able to fly under Scar's radar. Now she's back on his turf. And there's one other detail I haven't shared."

I waited.

"Scar's from Yellowknife."

"How do you know that?"

"We've been trying to nail the bastard for years. We know."

"You think he might go after Ruben?"

"Word is Scar's trying to move in on the action up there. To do that, he needs to show he plays hardball."

A cold hollowness filled my gut. I leaned into the seat back and closed my eyes. Why such apprehension? Fear for Ruben's safety? In all likelihood, the woman had killed her own babies. Abandoned their bodies without a backward glance.

Or had she? Had it been Ruben's choice? Had someone else done it or forced her hand? It could not have
been Scar in Montreal. Then who? Was that person
helping her now?

Nothing made sense.

Forex and Scar both said Ruben wasn't very smart.
Yet she'd gotten herself to Quebec and lived incognito
for three years. She'd concealed her pregnancies,
delivered and murdered at least four infants. She'd
eluded the Project KARE task force. She'd eluded and
continued to elude both the RCMP and the QPP.

How? A complex support network? A single partner? Street smarts? Blind luck?

I turned to Ollie. "Scar said you were clueless. What
did he mean by that?"

"Braggadocio."

"Good word."

"I downloaded an app that pops you a new one
every day."

"They ever send 'clueless'?" I hooked quote marks.
I wasn't amused.

"It's just trash talk. The last thing Scar wants is me
shining a light up his ass."

"He used the word twice."

"Maybe I'll send him a link for the app."

Our flight finally took off at ten-fifteen. We never
learned the nature of the plane's mysterious ailment.

All I remember about the Yellowknife airport is a
stuffed polar bear presiding over the baggage claim

area. And a whole lot of empty. Outside the terminal, a mix of rain and snow was blowing diagonally. And it was colder than crap.

A Sergeant Rainwater drove us the short distance into town. Ryan and I sat in back. From overheard snatches of the front-seat conversation, I gathered that Rainwater had been doing some investigative work for Ollie, the sort of thing we'd tried in Edmonton, showing the mug shot, asking about Ruben. With essentially the same result.

We hit the Explorer Hotel just past midnight. I noted a hilltop location, a long sweeping drive, and an eight-foot inuksuk guarding the main entrance.

Check-in was mercifully quick. Also mercifully, Ollie was uninterested in providing escort service.

My room was on the fourth floor. It had a king bed, a minibar with microwave, a flat-screen TV, and a view of some body of water the name of which I resolved to query in the morning.

I docked my iPhone in the clock-radio and dialed up the sound of crashing waves. Sleep took me down in under five minutes.

17

The baby reached out, fingers splayed, little limbs trembling, begging for help. My help.

I tried running, but my feet dug deeper and deeper into the sand.

The scene zoomed in.

The baby was sitting in the shallows on a long black beach. Behind it, over choppy waves, purple storm clouds darkened a menacing sky.

As I watched, the wispy nimbus haloing the baby's head thickened to form a crown of blond curls. The tiny features crystallized into a familiar pattern. The irises morphed from blue to green.

Katy!

I tried calling out. Again and again.

No sound left my throat.

Desperate, I strained to get to my daughter.

My legs were lead.

The water now covered Katy's belly.

The tide was rising!

Heart pounding, I pumped my legs harder.

The gap between us grew wider.

A figure materialized on the beach, indistinct. Face, even gender, unclear.

I struggled to call out.

The figure did not react.

I pulled with all my strength.

My efforts were futile.

The water now covered Katy's chest.

I shouted again, tears streaming my cheeks.

The scene shimmied like a desert mirage.

The water rose to Katy's chin.

I strained with every fiber in my body.

Screamed.

The scene popped. Evaporated like confetti in mist.

I blinked, confused.

I was sitting rigid in bed, heart pounding, skin slick with perspiration. My hands clutched the sheets in tight little balls.

The digits on the clock said 5:42. A predawn gray lit the windows I'd failed to curtain five hours earlier.

Outside, the snow shower had stopped, but the nameless oval of water looked dark and frigid. Inside, the air felt cold enough to make ice.

I relaxed my fingers, lay back, and drew the quilt to my chin.

Just a dream.

Just a dream.

Following the mantra, I tried my usual post-night-mare deconstruction. Which requires no sophisticated psychoanalytical skill. My subconscious isn't all that creative. The old id just spits out a remix of recent events.

Baby under threat. No Freudian mindbender there.

Katy. I hadn't talked to my daughter in a week.

The beach. My iPhone was still broadcasting soothing sea sounds.

The hazy figure. That one called for some digesting. Annaliese Ruben for murdering her children? Ronnie Scarborough for possibly threatening Ruben? Ryan for abandoning our relationship?

My mother for potty-training me too early?

Whatever.

Tossing back the covers, I tiptoe-ran to my suitcase, pulled on jeans, a long-sleeved tee, my gray lululemon hoodie, sneakers, and socks. In June. Welcome to the subarctic. Or the tundra. Or wherever the hell we were.

Water on the face. Quick brush of the teeth. Hair up in a pony.

The clock said six. Praying the hotel had a restaurant and that it was open, I headed downstairs.

Happy day! The Trader's Grill was serving up eggs. Or preparing to do so. A woman was positioning stain-less-steel servers on a stretch of skirted tables spanning one wall. On hearing my footsteps, she turned and gestured toward a two-top at the windows. Her name tag said Nellie.

Nellie's hair was black and braided down the center of her back. Her cotton blouse and long red skirt covered a body built along the lines of a Tonka truck.

I seated myself as directed and looked for a menu. Finding none, I settled back and scanned my surroundings.

Nellie and I weren't the only early risers. Two men occupied a table beside a circular copper-hooded fireplace, now cold. Both wore jeans, boots, and plaid shirts and had beards that badly needed trimming.

Nellie vanished and reappeared moments later bearing a steel coffeepot and a thick china mug. After topping off Paul Bunyan and his pal, she crossed to me.

"Sorry. The buffet doesn't open until seven." Nellie raised the pot in question. Her broad cheeks and copper skin suggested aboriginal ancestry.

"Yes, please."

Nellie filled and set the mug before me. "I can fix you some breakfast, long as it's simple."

"Eggs and toast would be great."

"Scrambled?"

"Sure."

Nellie chugged off.

I sipped my coffee. Which was strong enough to hold a spoon upright.

My eyes drifted to the window. Beyond the glass was a sort-of Zen scenario. Stacked boulders, scraggly plants sprouting amid haphazardly spread pebbles, rubber hoses snaking the ground. I couldn't tell whether the project was under construction or crumbling due to neglect.

At the edge of the rock garden, two enormous black birds circled low over a stand of surrealistically tall pines. As I watched their slow lazy loops, my mind drifted back to the dream.

Why hadn't Katy called?

I checked my iPhone for a signal. Four full bars. But no voice message or text from my daughter.

I scanned my e-mails. Twenty-four had landed since I'd left Edmonton. Most I ignored or deleted. Bill notifications. Ads for penis enhancers, pharmaceuticals, skin products, vacation villas. Offers of no-fail foreign-investment schemes.

Pete had fired off a short note stating that Birdie was well and bullying his chow, Boyd.

My sister, Harry, had written to say that she was dating a retired astronaut. His name was Orange Curtain. I hoped that was an auto-correct error.

Katy had linked me to an Evite for a friend's bridal shower. OK, she was fine. Just busy.

Ollie had sent an empty note containing an attachment. The subject line read: *Save on phone.* Curious, I downloaded and opened the document.

Annaliese Ruben's mug shot, scanned then enlarged. Though some detail had been lost, the face was still clear.

Good thinking, Sergeant Hasty. My copy of the printout had become quite tattered.

I studied the image. Dark hair. Round cheeks. Features you might see on any street in Dublin, Dresden, or Dallas.

"Hope you're not one of those vegetarian types." I'd been so focused on Ruben, I hadn't heard Nellie approach. "I tossed on some bacon."

"Bacon is good." I set down the phone and drew in my elbows.

Nellie parked the plate in front of me. In addition to eggs and bacon, it contained toast, hash browns, and a small brown object whose provenance was unclear.

"That it?" she asked.

I nodded.

Nellie pulled a check from the waistband of her skirt. "More coffee?"

"Please."

As she reached across the table, her gaze fell on my mobile. Ruben's face still filled the screen.

Nellie flinched as though zapped with live current. Coffee overshot the mug and splattered the tabletop. With a sharp intake of breath, she straightened and stepped back.

I looked up.

Nellie's lips were tight. Her eyes refused to meet mine.

Had Ruben's picture upset her? Or was I imagining it?

"Sorry." Mumbled. "I'll get a rag."

"Too much bother." I lifted the iPhone to mop up

the spill with my napkin. "You've no idea the abuse I heap on this thing."

Nellie's mouth remained clamped.

"You might find this interesting." I glanced at the image, casual as hell. "I believe this woman was born in Yellowknife." I raised the phone so Nellie could see the screen. She kept her eyes on her shoes. "Her name is Annaliese Ruben."

No response.

"Do you know her?"

Nothing.

"I think she may have returned to Yellowknife recently. From Edmonton."

"I have to get back to work."

"It's important that I find her."

"I've got to finish setting up the buffet before I can go."

"I may be able to help her with a problem."

Across the room, Paul Bunyan and company rose to leave. Nellie's eyes tracked their exit.

Seconds passed.

I was certain Nellie knew who Ruben was, perhaps where she was. I was about to give it one last shot when she asked, "What kind of problem?"

"I'm sorry. I wouldn't want to breach a confidence."

Nellie's eyes finally lifted to mine. I could feel her trying to read my thoughts. "This about Horace Tyne?"

"What do you know about Tyne?" Bluffing knowledge I didn't possess.

"What do *you* know about Tyne?" Sensing my con.

Easy, Brennan. Don't scare her.

"Listen, Nellie. I understand you've no reason to trust me. But I really am trying to help Ruben. I mean her no harm."

"You a cop?"

"No."

Like a window at a speakeasy, the face above me slammed shut.

Stupid. Small hotel. Big grapevine. Nellie had undoubtedly heard gossip about Ollie and Ryan.

"But I am traveling with two police officers." I tried to make up for my blunder. "They're unaware that I'm asking these questions."

"Why are they here?"

"We believe Ruben may have gotten herself into some difficulty."

"And the cops want to save her."

"Yes."

Without a word, Nellie spun on her heel and walked off.

While eating my eggs, now cold, I reviewed my accomplishments so far that morning. I'd spooked myself with a dream, then performed an amateur post-mortem on the content. I'd tipped my hand regarding Annaliese Ruben. And I'd alienated an informant who might know her whereabouts.

But I had scored a name. Horace Tyne.

Brilliant. Ryan would probably propose my name

for the detective's exam.

I poked at the brown thing. Which, at one point in its life, may have been vegetable.

A different waitress appeared and, with a lot of rattling and clanging, resumed preparation of the breakfast spread.

I lifted my mug to drain the last of my coffee. My arm stopped in midair.

Nellie had said it was her job to organize the buffet. Only then could she leave.

So where was she?

After jotting my name, room number, and signature on the check, I bolted for the lobby.

Nellie was hurrying through the front door.

Call Ryan? Ollie?

Nellie was fast disappearing down the circle drive.

I scurried after her.

18

Morning mist thick as Gran's fatback gravy swirled in the glow of the hotel sign. Though the sun had never totally yielded the night sky, it had yet to get organized for another dawn.

In other words, visibility sucked.

But the advantage in elevation worked in my favor. While Nellie's torso was shrouded in a puffy gray jacket that blended with the fog, her bright red skirt was easy to spot. As I left the cover of the portico, the scarlet beacon was disappearing around the curve of the drive.

I hurried down the walk. Though I doubted Nellie would notice a tail, I kept to the inside of the arc for cover. I'd descended halfway when my quarry vanished. I kicked up the pace. At the bottom of the hill, I looked left and then right. The red skirt was swishing along Veterans Memorial Drive, which, at this hour, was largely deserted.

I made the turn, already regretting my decision to

sally forth sans outerwear. Vapor puffed from my lips each time I exhaled.

Downtown Yellowknife has the look and feel of a movie set trucked in and assembled quickly. Think *Northern Exposure*, but ramp up the number of bars, eateries, shops, and nondescript office and government buildings.

I followed Nellie to Fiftieth Street, moving as fast as possible to generate body heat but slowly enough to keep some distance between us. Which wasn't hard. Despite her short legs and considerable bulk, the woman was booking.

Yellowknife is similar to Charlotte with regard to street names. Shortly, Fiftieth Street met Fiftieth Avenue. Very creative.

Nellie trundled through the intersection without waiting for a green. To avoid detection, I hung back a few moments, then crossed and ducked into a recess at the front of a souvenir shop.

A half block below Fiftieth Street, I could make out a long orange awning spanning the front of a three-story building that had seen better days. A lot of them. Lettering on the awning and the second-floor stucco identified the place as the Gold Range Hotel. Without hesitating, Nellie pulled open the front door and slipped inside.

I yanked my iPhone from my jeans and tapped Ryan's number. My hands shook so badly from the cold I missed and had to try again.

Voice mail.

I left a message. *Call me. Now.*

Eyes darting between the Gold Range and my cell, I tried Ollie. Same result. I left the same message. Both text and voice.

Were the dolts still sleeping? Had they turned off their ringers? Were they already up and gone? Unlikely after less than six hours sleep.

Arm-wrapping my torso for warmth, I studied the Gold Range. With the garish awning, carved shutters, faux Tudor trim on the upper floors, and dark wood paneling at street level, the place looked like a cross between a Swiss chalet and a Super 8.

Did Nellie live at the Gold Range? Did Ruben? Might she be there now?

I considered my options. Go inside and try to locate one or the other? Wait? For how long? Screw the whole caper and head back to the Explorer?

Under my hoodie and thin cotton tee, an army of goose bumps puckered my skin. I pistoned my palms up and down my arms. Hopped from foot to foot.

Where the hell were Ryan and Ollie?

I stole a quick glance at the shop behind me. Through the plate-glass window, I could see posters, plastic polar bears, and other tourist kitsch. And something else: sweatshirts and jackets saying *I Love Yellowknife*.

Business hours were posted on the door. Monday through Friday, nine a.m. to eight p.m. Industrious. But useless to me. Besides, I hadn't brought cash or a credit card with me to breakfast.

I glanced at my watch. Seven-ten.

I stared at the Gold Range. The hotel stared back, windows silent and dark in the predawn fog.

Seven-fourteen.

Shivering hard, I tried Ryan and Ollie again. Neither answered.

Decision. I'd wait until seven-thirty, then storm the hotel.

If I hadn't died of hypothermia.

I resumed hopping and arm-rubbing.

Gradually, the refrigerated mist changed hue. Uphill, behind the Explorer, pink and yellow backlit long pewter clouds paralleling the earth's rim.

Seven-seventeen.

All quiet at the Gold Range. In the growing light, I could see twisted fabric looping hammock-style behind one window. Nice touch.

After what seemed an hour, I checked my watch.

Seven-twenty.

A stakeout was definitely not the heart-racing excitement it was cracked up to be.

I was about to alter my plan and move on to phase two when the hotel's front door swung outward. Head down, Nellie stepped onto the walk and chugged straight toward me.

I admit: the old cardiac muscles did a bit of high-stepping at that.

Before reaching the corner, Nellie diagonaled across

Fiftieth Street and turned right onto Fiftieth Avenue.

Exhaling a cone of breathy relief, I hurried in her wake.

Yellowknife was now bustling with activity. Meaning I could see three people on the main drag.

At the A&W, two men stopped their conversation to track my movement, faces barely visible under raised parka hoods. At the Kentucky Fried, I passed a kid in a red tracksuit, black fleece vest, and orange tuque carrying a yellow skateboard under one arm. Both times I smiled and said good morning. Both times I got only unfriendly stares.

All righty, then.

Somewhere beyond Forty-fourth Street, Fiftieth Avenue became Franklin. Charlotte-style all the way. Hustling along, I memorized street names and the turns I was making.

Several blocks past School Draw Avenue, Nellie hooked a right onto Hamilton, then another onto an unpaved lane. A sign on a rock said *Ragged Ass Road.* That's one you'd never see on the Queen City map.

Nellie barreled up Ragged Ass, still oblivious to my presence. I held back at the turn, fearful that my footsteps on the gravel would give me away. Flicking glances left and right, I took in my surroundings. The sun was higher now, burning off the mist. Detail was clearer.

The neighborhood was residential, with browned-out grass hugging up to the road and utility wires hanging low overhead. I smelled fishy water and bracken mud and sensed a lake nearby.

The 'hood's architectural theme was northern hodgepodge. The newer homes looked like they'd been assembled from mail-order kits. Aluminum siding. Prefab windows. Faux-colonial shutters and doors.

The older homes resembled cottages at a hippie summer camp. Unstained frame exteriors painted with murals or images taken from nature. Metal downspouts and smokestacks. Whirligigs, plastic animals, and ceramic gnomes in the yards or topping the fences.

Every house had at least one outbuilding, a rusted tank, and a mound of firewood. And, I suspected, occupants hostile to uninvited strangers.

Dogs? I put that alarming image aside.

As roads go, Ragged Ass wasn't much. Just two blocks long. Never casting a backward glance, Nellie beelined toward the far end, up a dirt drive, and into a structure whose owners were firmly grounded in the summer-camp school.

Oblivious or indifferent to the early-morning intruder, Ragged Ass dozed on.

Skin tingling with cold and apprehension, I crept forward.

No Rottweiler barked. No pit bull lunged.

There you go. I was surveilling.

The house Nellie had entered was little more than a

shack, wood-frame, maybe nine hundred square feet of interior. Reflective numbers nailed to the street-facing wall said 7243.

A jerry-rigged plastic and wood greenhouse clung to one side of the house, and a tattered brown awning jutted from the other. Beneath the awning sat a vinyl table-and-chair set and a rusted charcoal grill.

No vehicle was parked in the short dirt drive or under the carport.

Now what?

So far, waiting had served me well. I decided to do it some more.

Using a small shed for cover, I watched from the opposite side of the road.

As on Fiftieth, time moved at the pace of a glacier.

I thumbed on my phone.

Seven-fifty. No voice mail or text.

I dialed Ryan and left an update on my whereabouts.

Thermally, the new location was a trade-off. Though sunrise had atomized the mist and kicked the temperature up a notch, a steady breeze pumped moisture off the unseen water.

I crossed my arms and tucked my hands under my pits. My breath was no longer forming cones, but it was close.

For an eon the only action on Ragged Ass involved ravens jockeying for position on the overhead wires. Then a door slammed and an engine fired to life.

My head whipped left. Thirty yards north, a red

pickup was backing down a drive. I watched the truck wheel out, stop, then head toward Hamilton.

By eight-fifteen my enthusiasm for surveillance had dropped lower than my core body temperature. A million arguments for leaving swirled in my brain.

This house might have nothing to do with Ruben. Maybe it was Nellie's home and she was inside, warm in her bed, with Ruben back at the Gold Range. Maybe Nellie had stopped by the hotel to tip Ruben about our presence in Yellowknife. Maybe Ruben had already gone underground and I'd blown it again.

What the hell? I knew the address. We could return later to see if Ruben was here.

Occasionally, I give myself good advice. In rare instances I take it. Unfortunately, this was not one of them.

Before bailing, I decided on one quick peek. No, that's not quite accurate. There was no conscious decision. My semi-numb feet just started moving toward the house.

Quick scan left and right, then I scuttled across Ragged Ass, up the drive, and around the awning side of the house. Circling the barbecue with what I hoped was stealth, I flattened my back to the wall beside a pair of sliding glass doors.

Breath frozen, I listened.

From inside came the muted cadence of a radio or television talk show. Outside, around me, nothing but stillness.

Ever so gently, I disengaged my right shoulder and rolled left.

Pointless. A set of thin metal blinds covered the inside of each glass door. Both sets were fully extended with the slats firmly shut.

I slid to my right and tried the same maneuver on a window whose sill was at shoulder height. More closed blinds.

I was about to give up when I heard what sounded like yapping coming through the wall. Ruben's dog?

Totally amped, I stole toward the rear of the house.

On the right of the backyard, a clothesline ran from the house's rear wall to a stunted birch maybe twenty feet back. Opposite the birch, across mostly dirt, was an aluminum storage shed. Beside the shed was a weathered wooden Dumpster with an angled flip lid.

A set of sagging wooden steps descended three treads from a door at the house's rear center. On their far side sat a cracked ceramic planter. Beyond the planter was a rickety wooden table. A stained surface and rusty gutting knife suggested it was used for cleaning fish.

Between the house's left corner where I stood and the steps was another, slightly higher window. Though I couldn't be certain from my angle, shadowing hinted that the blinds stopped six inches short of the sill.

Senses on high alert, I rounded the corner and began inching along the rear wall. A raven cawed and took flight from the birch.

I froze.

Nothing.

More inching.

Eight steps brought me to the window and the edge of a shallow pit centered in the ground below it. The pit appeared to have been dug by hand, then lined with black plastic and surrounded by stones. A garden hose snaked from the stones to a faucet on the house. Surrounded by muck and holding four inches of opaquely iridescent green water, the thing looked like the koi pond from hell.

I tried peering into the house from the far side of the pond. From that angle, I could see zilch through the gap below the blinds.

I gauged the distance between the pond's front edge and the house's rear wall. Two feet. Tricky but enough for footing.

Palm-bracing against the wood, I sidestepped slowly along the wall. The mud felt slick and gushy below the soles of my sneakers.

Two steps and I'd cleared the window frame. The sill jutted just above nose-level. Gripping it with icy fingers, I raised up on my toes.

Though the lights were off, some objects stood out in the house's dim interior. The top of a refrigerator. A wall clock shaped like a fish. A very successful strip of flypaper.

I was about to take one more step to my left when something hard cracked my shin. Fire shot up my leg. I smothered a cry.

Had I been bitten? Struck?

Before I could look down, tentacles wrapped my ankles. Squeezed.

My feet flew from under me.

Black and iridescent green raced up toward my face.

19

My feet winged out. I hit the ground on my elbows and chin.

The unseen tentacles yanked hard, dragging my body backward over mud then rock. My face plunged down.

Fetid water filled my eyes, my nose, my mouth. I couldn't breathe or see.

Terrified, I clawed for purchase. Found the border of the koi pond. Pulled with both hands.

My torso slithered across muck filled with things I didn't want to imagine. My head cleared the surface.

Gasping for air, still blind, I tried hauling myself onto the strip of lawn from which I'd been toppled. Felt resistance. Tightness around my ankles.

My mind was flailing for an explanation when my feet jerked skyward. My spine hyper-flexed, jamming my lumbar vertebrae and shooting arrows of pain straight into my brain.

My body lurched backward, away from the house. I lost my grip. My chin whacked the stones, then my head went underwater again. My arms followed, fingers trailing across the slime-coated plastic.

Like a fish on a line, I felt myself dragged feet-first from the pond and dumped onto the lawn.

Heart pounding, I raised up on my forearms, struggling for breath. And comprehension.

An upward wrenching of my feet flattened me again. I tried to roll over. A boot between my scapulae sent me back onto my belly. Pinned me to the cold, muddy grass.

"What do you think you're doing?" Though high, the voice was male and decidedly unfriendly.

"Looking for someone," I gasped.

"Who?"

"Annaliese Ruben."

No reply.

"I thought she might be in the house." Ragged. My pulse pounded, and my breathing was not quite under control.

Silence.

"I have important information."

In the corner of one eye, I could see a dark silhouette blocking the sky above me.

"I need to find her."

"That how you find folks? By spying in their windows?"

"I was trying to—"

"You a perv?"

"What?"

"Trying to ogle people bare-ass?"

"No. I was checking that I had the right address."

"Ever think of knocking on the door?"

He had me there.

"I meant no harm."

"How do I know you're not aiming to clean the place out?"

"Do I look like a burglar?"

"Close enough for my liking."

Though I couldn't see his face, I sensed the man glaring down at me.

"You're hurting my back."

A beat, then the pressure eased on my spine. I heard the swish of nylon, then the silhouette disappeared from my peripheral vision.

I rolled to my bum and, with trembling fingers, dragged slime-water hair from my eyes. Then I looked up.

My captor was of medium height, muscular under jeans and a dark blue windbreaker. His skin was butternut, his eyes the color of day-old coffee. His hair was gelled to form a shiny black helmet.

I noticed that his hands were chapped and leathery. In the left one he held a rope arrangement with a loop at one end and three long strands at the other. The strands led to slant-cut hunks of bone wrapping my ankles.

"Nice kipooyaq."

"So you speak a little Inuit. Very impressive."

"Easy one." Right. I'd had to dig way back to an undergrad course on circumpolar archaeology.

The coffee eyes roved my face, assessing my threat potential.

"May I?" Gesturing at my legs.

The man gave a tight nod.

With numb fingers, I began to untangle the bola.

"I asked what you're doing here."

"I told you. I'm looking for Annaliese Ruben. Do you know her?"

"You ever think of phoning?"

"I don't have a number."

The man said nothing.

"Maybe you could help me with that?"

"Try directory assistance."

"Could be unlisted. Makes it tough to call."

"People do that for a reason."

"Does Annaliese live here?"

"I'm thinking if the lady wanted you to have her address, she'd have shared it."

"Do you know Annaliese?"

"One thing I'm certain, I don't know you."

I loosened the final tangle and freed my feet. As I stood, the man gathered the cords around one hand in even-sized loops.

"ID."

"What?" *Shit*.

"Driver's license? Medicare card? Something with a photo."

"I have nothing with me."

"I get a complaint that someone's peeping windows on Ragged Ass Road. I come out and find you nose to the glass. Now you tell me you got no ID."

"I'm staying at the Explorer. I wasn't planning to leave the hotel."

"Yet here you are."

"My name is Temperance Brennan. I'm a forensic anthropologist." Teeth chattering. "I am in Yellow-knife on official police business."

"And that business would involve spying on unsuspecting citizens?"

Though I hadn't a clue who this guy was, I had no choice. And I was freezing. I gave a modified version. Ollie. Ryan. The possible threat to Annaliese Ruben from Ronnie Scarborough.

The man listened, expression neutral.

"I have my mobile. We can phone Detective Ryan or Sergeant Hasty. Or Sergeant Rainwater. He's with G Division. RCMP. Here. In Yellowknife."

Realizing I was babbling and seeing no objection, I dug my iPhone from my pocket and pushed the power button with a trembling thumb.

Nothing.

I tried again.

And again.

No amount of tapping or shaking brought the screen to life.

Shit. Shit.

I looked up. The man's face was still unreadable.

"It's dead."

No response.

"It must have gotten wet in the koi pond."

Eyes hard on me, the man pulled a cell from his belt and hit speed dial. "Zeb Chalker. Is Rainwater there?"

Pause.

"Living the life. You know a K Division guy name of Oliver Hasty?"

Pause.

"Why's he in town?"

Long pause.

"Hasty traveling alone?"

Pause.

"Marsí."

Chalker reclipped the cell to his belt, crossed his arms, and regarded me a very long time. Finally, "Here's the deal. You get yourself back to the Explorer. Going forward, you stick with your pals. Got it?"

Chalker's attitude irritated the hell out of me. Who was he to give orders? But I wanted nothing more than to return to my room and take a very hot shower. And I was in no position to object.

I nodded.

Without another word, Chalker strode off.

"Don't worry about me," I muttered to his retreating back. "I'll flag a taxi."

By the time I reached the street, Chalker was nowhere in sight. As I jogged up Ragged Ass, I wondered about the guy. Why had he bola'ed me? Was he a vigilant neighbor? A relative of the homeowner? Some sort of cop?

Chalker knew Rainwater. Seemed to have him on speed dial. But this was Yellowknife, population under twenty thousand. Wouldn't everyone know everyone?

Whatever. Chalker had revealed nothing.

It was definitely not my day. I was rounding the corner onto Hamilton, head down, legs pumping, when a bicycle blasted into my side.

I went flying. Wobbling wildly, the bike continued downhill.

I landed bum first, my wind knocked somewhere into tomorrow. For a moment I could focus only on taking in oxygen.

I was struggling to breathe when I heard gravel crunch, then a loud hoot. I looked over my shoulder.

Five yards downslope, the Kentucky Fried kid was straddling a clunky red Schwinn that looked like it had rolled off the line sometime in the fifties. His yellow skateboard jutted from a metal basket attached to the bike's rear fender.

"Hoo-hooh!" Laughing, the kid pointed a skinny finger my way. "You look like my grandma when she fell in with the pigs."

"And you look like you should have left the training wheels on."

The kid was tall, maybe up to my chin. Under

the oversize tracksuit, his body was scarecrow-thin. I guessed his weight, soaking wet, at maybe sixty pounds, his age at approximately twelve.

"Yeah? How old you think I am?"

My lungs remained too much in spasm to answer.

As I got to my feet, the kid moved closer. He had dark eyes set too far apart and dark hair curling from beneath the tuque. A scar on his upper lip suggested a surgically repaired cleft palate.

"Man, you look like shit."

The kid had a point. My chin was raw. My hair was wet. My clothes were soaked and covered with mud.

"Smell like shit, too."

"Won't your kindergarten be coming up short on the head count?" Childish. But the little twerp provoked it.

"If you're looking for the old folk's home, could be my grandma could help."

"Could be your grandma could coach you on manners."

"Wouldn't matter. You'd still be older than dirt."

I started jogging up Hamilton. The kid pedaled along at my side.

"I saw you this morning on Fiftieth."

"Brilliant. But I'm out of lollipops."

"You was following Ms. Snook."

Nellie Snook. I noted the surname.

"Whatcha doing down here in Old Town?"

"Looking for a friend."

"How come you're covered in pig slop?"

"I fell."

"Probably Alzheimer's."

"And you'll probably need a jock strap in ten or twelve years."

"Just about the time you'll be peeing your diaper."

Slowing to a walk, I glanced over at the kid. His expression was cocky but held no hint of malice.

"My friend's name is Annaliese Ruben."

"Why you looking for her?"

"I have something to deliver."

"Give it to me. I'll get it to her."

"You'll get it straight to a fence."

"Can't fault a man for trying." The kid grinned broadly, revealing gapped and crooked teeth.

"So you know Nellie Snook?"

"Never said that."

"Do you know Annaliese Ruben?"

"She an old crone like you?"

"What's your name?"

"Binny."

"Binny what?"

"Binny Mind-Your-Own-Business."

I was sure Binny would peel off when I turned onto Franklin. He didn't. We'd gone a half block when a thought struck me.

"Hey, shrimp."

"Yeah, Granny."

"You know a guy named Horace Tyne?"

"Everyone knows Horace."

"Why's that?"

"He's a environmentaler."

"Environmentalist?"

A flicker of embarrassment crossed his face.

"Lots of people are going green. Why's Horace so special?"

"Everyone talks a big game. Horace does stuff."

"Meaning what?"

"Meaning he tries to save the caribou and shit like that."

"How's he going to save the caribou?"

"By creating a preserve. No one can fuck with the herds if they're on a preserve."

"Does Grandma approve of your foul language?"

"Does anyone approve of your wrinkly old face?"

"Why aren't you in school?"

"I've got chicken pox."

Again I thought the kid would take off. Again I was wrong.

Walking along, I rewound my conversation with Nellie. Her question had implied a link between Ruben and Tyne. This kid knew Tyne.

"That KFC open when you were there this morning, shrimp?"

"No. Granny."

"They open now?"

"Doubt it."

"You old enough to eat pancakes?"

"You buying?"

"Can we talk about Horace Tyne?"

"Fire up your hearing aid."

20

Binny and I were approaching Forty-third Street when the sound of an engine caused us to glance over our shoulders.

Ryan was at the wheel of a white Toyota Camry. He'd come up from behind and was crawling the curb.

I stopped. Binny hesitated, looked to me, then dropped one sneaker to the sidewalk to brace himself.

Ryan drew up beside us. Through the windshield, I saw him shift into park. Not so gently.

I crossed to the Camry. Binny watched, one foot flexed on a pedal.

Smiling, I leaned down and tapped the passenger-side window. Instead of lowering the glass, Ryan yanked his door handle, launched himself out, and circled the trunk.

"Boy, am I glad to see you," I said. Still smiling.

"What the shit, Brennan?" Ryan's expression was a

wild mix of anger and relief.

"I'm freezing my ass off." The smile wavered but held.

"Where the hell have you been?"

Binny's elbows winged up, and his fingers tightened on the handlebar grips. Knowing the kid was about to bolt, I tried diffusing the tension with humor. "Detecting." Eyebrow wiggle.

"You think this is funny?"

I spread my arms to show the state of my person. "A little."

"Are you for real?"

"You didn't get my calls?"

"I got your calls! My finger is raw from hitting redial!"

"Easy, muchacho." I'd never seen Ryan so worked up.

"Why didn't you answer?"

"My phone took on a wee bit of water." Again I spread my arms.

For the first time, Ryan noticed my condition. Normally, he'd have gone all Don Rickles on my après-koi pond appearance. Instead, he thundered on. "This is amateur hour, Brennan."

Amateur? That did it. The smile crumbled. "Are you accusing me of being unprofessional?"

"Sloppy. Inconsiderate. Stupid. Irresponsible. Shall I continue?"

"I may have found Ruben."

Ryan was in full tirade and not hearing a word. "We didn't come here for a Boy Scout Jamboree. Scar and his pals play hard, and they play for keeps."

"Take a lap, Ryan."

"Did you just tell me to take a lap?"

"Ease back on the drama."

"Every cop in Yellowknife is looking for you. That drama enough?"

With that, Binny fired up the block, skinny legs pumping like mad. At the corner, he cut a right and disappeared from view.

"Now, *that* was unprofessional." I met Ryan's glare with my own.

"Get in the car." Ryan stepped around me and wrenched open the passenger-side door.

"That kid might have useful information."

"Get in."

I didn't move.

"Get in the goddamn car."

I threw myself into the passenger seat, slammed the door, buckled up, and chest-crossed my arms.

Ryan slid behind the wheel, drew in and released a ten-mile breath. His jaw clenched, unclenched, then he keyed a number into his mobile. "I have her." He waited out a response. "You've got that right. We're heading for the Explorer."

After repocketing the phone, Ryan secured his belt, started the engine, and joined the traffic on Fiftieth.

"Don't forget to cancel the choppers and dogs." Keeping my eyes straight ahead, my mouth hooked down at the corners.

Icy silence.

Fine. I was mad, too. But also humiliated. Rainwater had obviously talked to Ollie following his conversation with Chalker. Ollie had phoned Ryan. My cheeks burned at the thought of how many others had been put on alert.

Jesus.

Ryan finally spoke when we pulled up at the Explorer. "Ring when you're ready."

Back in my room, I took a very long, very hot shower. Screw Ryan. Let him wait.

After toweling off, I blow-dried my hair, all the while staring at my reflection in the mirror. Middling thick hair, not long or short, not blond or brown. A few tentative grays sending out feelers.

While applying mascara, I studied myself some more. Jawline still tight. Angry green eyes between upper and lower lids holding firm.

By the time I'd added lipstick and blush, my reflection appeared almost composed.

Except for my chin. Which had donated a lot of skin to the koi pond rocks.

I bundled my clothes, filled out the laundry request form, then dialed Ryan. He asked that I meet him in the restaurant.

When I arrived, Ryan was talking on his cell, seated

at the same table I'd occupied a few hours earlier. A mug and six empty sugar packets suggested he'd been there a while.

As I took the chair opposite, the buffet-replacement waitress appeared with a mug and coffeepot. At my nod, she set me up. I considered asking her about Nellie, decided against it.

Based on Ryan's comments, I guessed he was talking to Ollie.

After disconnecting, he stirred his coffee with a diligence that was truly impressive.

When the silence had gone on way too long, I asked, "That was Ollie?"

Ryan nodded, still working the spoon.

"Discussing Scar's entrepreneurial aspirations in Yellowknife?"

More nodding and swirling.

"And the local talent."

"And that."

Ryan studied the would-be Zen arrangement outside the window.

"You going to brief me?" I asked.

"The main players are Tom Unka and Arty Castain. Unka's got a jacket thick as a laptop. Castain's had better luck."

"They a tag team?"

"Yes."

"What do they run?"

"Mostly coke, grass, some speed."

"Unka and Castain are displeased with the prospect of competition?"

Ryan nodded. "And word on the street says both are stone-cold killers."

I waited.

"A couple years back an ounce-man from Jasper tried freelancing up here. First Unka and Castain sent a warning by killing the guy's collie. As an added touch, they mailed him the dog's ears. The guy kept dealing. A bush pilot spotted his body floating facedown in Back Bay three months later."

"Sans ears."

"You got it."

"If Scar wants to expand into Yellowknife, these are the guys he needs to intimidate." By harming Ruben. I didn't say it.

"And their clientele." Ryan sipped his coffee. "The story on Ruben went national."

The quick change left me in the dust. "What?"

"White," Ryan said by way of explanation.

My face must have telegraphed my confusion.

"The dick who dimed Okeke."

"The journalist who phoned the autopsy room?" I was horrified. "He wrote a piece about the Edmonton infant?"

"*National Post*. And not just Edmonton. All four. The story went viral. Got picked up all over Canada." Ryan raised his mug in sarcastic salute. "Nothing like dead babies to boost readership and ratings."

"Wait." This wasn't making sense. "How did White get access to confidential information?"

"From us."

"What?"

"Aurora Devereaux overheard us talking in her flat, sniffed an opportunity, jumped on it. As you suggested to Okeke, Devereaux probably sold her scoop to the highest bidder."

"Sonofabitch," I said.

"Yeah," Ryan agreed.

For a long moment we both stared at the garden.

"You want to explain your thinking this morning?" Cold.

"Don't take that tone with me, Ryan."

"Fine." Two butane flames drilled me with a look. "How was your morning, Dr. Brennan?"

I told him. Ruben's mug shot. Nellie. The Gold Range. The house on Ragged Ass. Chalker.

"The guy took you down with a bola?" The hint of a smile softened his expression.

"It's a formidable weapon. In prehistory it was used to hunt mammoth." I wasn't sure about that, but it sounded good.

"And dragged you through a koi pond?"

My look told him I was in no mood to be the butt of stand-up. "And where were you when I called, what, three times?"

Ignoring my question, or in answer to it, Ryan pulled out his spiral and flipped a few pages. "The house on

Ragged Ass is deeded to Josiah Stanley Snook."

"Nellie Snook. That's the name of the waitress I followed."

"Funny that the woman would go home after clocking out of work."

"I'm telling you, she tore out of here because I asked about Ruben. She was supposed to finish setting up the buffet."

"Uh-huh. You say Snook first stopped at the Gold Range. Ruben's probably gone to ground there. The place is hooker central and would be in her comfort zone."

"With a dog?"

"What's with you and the dog?"

"Ralph Trees said Ruben had a dog."

"Based on the woman's history, my guess is the pooch hit the curb long ago."

Ryan picked up and dialed his phone. Again I heard only one half of the conversation.

"Better. Except for the chin."

Great.

"Any luck at the Gold Range?"

I checked my own mobile. Still dead.

"Hasty still talking to Unka and Castain?"

Pause.

"Big surprise."

Pause.

"Is she credible?"

Pause.

"OK. Keep me in the loop." Ryan clicked off and signaled for the bill.

"Ollie has people checking the hotel?"

"Rainwater. Ollie's working Unka and Castain."

"What's he learned?"

"The homeboys are not real chatty."

"You asked about credibility. Whose?"

"A prossie claims she saw a guy fitting Scar's description at Bad Sam's around three this morning."

"Bad Sam's?"

"The tavern at the Gold Range. The locals call it the Strange Range."

"Those rascals. *Is* she believable?"

"When sober."

"Crap. Should we go over there?"

"Rainwater's on it. He'll call if Ruben's there."

"Now what?"

"Now we wait."

"But—"

"Brennan. I am visiting law enforcement. Do you know what that means? It means I have no jurisdiction here. As a visitor, I do as requested by my hosts."

"I heard a dog barking inside the Snook house."

"Jesus, there you go with the dog again."

"Suppose Ruben's not at the Gold Range? Suppose she's at Snook's house? If Scar really is in Yellowknife, how long do you think it will take him to find her?"

Ryan said nothing.

"We should do something."

"We are doing something. We're waiting for word from Rainwater. Remember, we don't have a Quebec warrant for Ruben. She is a suspect wanted for questioning. The only warrant is from Edmonton for skipping court."

"Why not ride out to Ragged Ass? We don't have to knock on the door or anything. We can observe from the car. In case anyone enters or leaves the house. What harm can it do?"

The waitress came, and Ryan signed the bill. Then he looked at me and came to a decision.

"Let's go."

21

We'd been parked on Ragged Ass for thirty minutes when Ryan got the call.

Rainwater had questioned the night and day clerks, checked the register, interviewed every lodger who would talk to him. Done what he could without a warrant. He was confident Ruben was not at the Gold Range, doubted she'd ever been there.

Shortly after Ryan disconnected, the Snooks' front door opened, and Nellie emerged. She was wearing the same gray jacket but had substituted jeans for the red skirt.

I turned to see if Ryan was on her. His aviator shades were pointed her way.

Oblivious to our presence, Nellie whistled and slapped one thigh. A small gray dog bounded through the door, leaped off the stoop, and like a tiny whirling dervish, began racing circles on the lawn.

"Yes!" I pumped one arm.

"Two out of three households in North America have a dog."

"You made that up."

"I'm sure the stat's close."

"Tank," Nellie called, "do pee-pee."

Tank? From where I sat, the mutt looked like a cross between a Yorkie and a gerbil.

Tank continued his mad looping.

"Tank, you do pee-pee now."

More frenzied circuits.

"I have treats." Nellie shook a small bag.

Tank stopped and looked at Nellie, ears up, head cocked. Satisfied that she had the goods, he sniffed several spots, then squatted and held position. For a remarkably long time.

Bladder empty, Tank trotted back to Nellie and got his reward. She then scooped the dog up and plopped him inside.

After closing and locking the door, Nellie disappeared under the awning, reappeared shortly, pulling a wheeled cart.

"Looks like she's going shopping," I said.

"Could be."

"While she's gone, we could snoop around. Maybe—"

"That approach didn't go well for you."

"Fine. You stay on the house and I'll talk to her."

"Nor did that."

Ryan's attitude was wearing on my nerves. As was

frustration born of inactivity. And I'd had a whole lot of coffee.

"You know what? I don't need a warrant to ask a few questions. And I don't need your permission."

With that, I popped from the car and hurried up the road. The sound of the cart bouncing over gravel masked my approach. Or Nellie was hard of hearing.

I spoke when I was six feet out. "Nellie."

She turned. Her expression moved through surprise, confusion, settled on alarm.

"Please." I raised both hands. "Can we talk?"

"You tried to break in to my house."

"No. Really."

"I saw you. I called my cousin. He came and found you in the yard."

"Housebreaking wasn't my intent."

"Why are you stalking me?"

"I told you at the restaurant. I'm worried about Annaliese Ruben."

"Why do you care about her?"

Zinger. Why did I? Ruben had probably killed four infants. Did I want to protect her? Or did I simply want to catch her to charge her with murder?

"I don't like to see people hurt," I said.

She seemed to relax a bit at that.

"Is Annaliese at your house?"

"I told you, I don't know her."

"Is she at the Gold Range?"

Her fingers tightened on the cart handle.

"Why did you stop at the hotel this morning?"

"My husband works there."

"Josiah."

Fear rekindled in her eyes. "Leave me alone."

"Can you tell me why you went to the Gold Range?"

"If I do, will you stop bothering me?"

"Yes."

She hesitated. Debating what to say? How best to escape? "I forgot my house key. My husband had one."

I was skeptical. That didn't explain her rushed departure from the Explorer. But I could think of no appropriate follow-up question.

Nellie's mention of Horace Tyne that morning had given me a small sense of victory. I felt I'd discovered a lead. A possible link to Annaliese Ruben. In fact, aside from a name—possibly of no significance—I'd learned nothing new. And that was maddening.

So I kept my word. I asked her nothing else. "My name is Temperance Brennan." Handing her a card. "Annaliese may be in danger. If you hear from her, please call me at the Explorer."

Back in the Camry, Ryan shot me a questioning look through the shades. I think. I shook my head.

"Ollie's got Rainwater coming out here."

I nodded.

We watched in silence another five minutes. Then, "Isn't that the boy who was walking with you earlier?" he asked.

I followed Ryan's sight line. Binny was sitting cross-legged on a boulder at the far end of Ragged Ass. His bike lay on the grass beside him. His eyes lay on us.

I lowered my window and waved. Binny did not wave back.

"His name's Binny."

"Weird-looking kid."

"I like him. He's spunky."

"Didn't look so spunky tear-ass pedaling up Fiftieth."

"Your meltdown scared the crap out of him." I waved again.

Binny hopped on his bike and rode off.

Maybe Ryan was right. My people skills really did seem wanting.

"What did you mean, the kid could be useful?"

"When I was asking Nellie about Ruben, she let slip a name. Horace Tyne. Binny claims to know the guy."

Ryan curled his fingers in a "go on" gesture.

"Binny told me Tyne is an environmental activist."

"What else?"

"Nothing else. Your tantrum freaked him out."

Ryan raised his shades to his forehead and dialed his cell. Disconnected. Dialed again. Disconnected. "OK. Let's try the easy way." Ryan worked some keys. A lot of keys. "Bingo." Eyes on the tiny screen.

"You found him on Google."

Ryan ignored me.

"Am I warm?"

"Sizzling. Horace Tyne runs an organization called Friends of the Tundra. According to the website, which is piss-poor, the organization seeks to preserve the native plants and animals of the tundra ecosystem of the Northwest Territories."

Ryan did some more reading and scrolling.

"Looks like Tyne is trying to establish some sort of wildlife preserve."

"Does the site provide contact information?"

"There's an address to which contributions can be sent."

"Here in Yellowknife?"

"Some place called Behchoko."

As Ryan was googling directions, an RCMP cruiser pulled up behind us. Rainwater was at the wheel. He flicked a wave.

Ryan returned it, then dropped the aviators to his nose.

And we were rolling.

Behchoko was a Dene community of about two thousand souls called Rae-Enzo until 2005. Not sure why the name changed. No idea about Rae. But according to a rental company map I dug from the glove compartment, Enzo was a chief at one time.

We didn't need GPS to find our way. The Yellowknife Highway was the only option.

Ryan won the argument on who would drive. His rental, he would captain the ship. Once again I would just sit. At least Ollie wouldn't be firing zingers from the backseat. He was still squeezing Unka and Castain.

Our destination lay about fifty miles northwest of Yellowknife. I also learned from the map that after Behchoko, the paved road crossed Dehk'è, the Frank Channel, continued roughly forty miles, then fed into the seasonal ice roads used by commercial trucking for mine supply. I assumed that meant gold.

I shared this knowledge with Ryan. Normally, he'd have busted into a few bars of "Livin' on the Edge." Today no Aerosmith.

The drive took roughly an hour. We saw no other cars, just many, many trees.

Behchoko consisted of a cluster of buildings hugging a scraggy shoreline dotted with boulders that, according to the map, was the northern tip of Great Slave Lake.

As Ryan navigated the town's main road, I noted a school with a timber-frame swing set in the yard. A windowless outhouse with an ATM sign. Frame homes featuring weathered variations of redwood, brown, gray, and blue. Dozens of power-line poles leaning at odd angles.

The vegetation consisted of patchy grass and the occasional stand of trees. There wasn't a single paved street.

Ryan parked in front of a small log cabin displaying an RCMP sign in French and English. We both got out.

The office held a desk and chair, a few file cabinets, and little else. The desk was occupied by a corporal whose name tag said Schultz.

Schultz looked up when we entered but said nothing. He was in his late twenties, short and stocky, with chipmunk cheeks that made him look soft.

Since Schultz was locked on Ryan and ignoring me, I let the captain do the talking.

"Good afternoon, Corporal." Removing his sunglasses.

"Good afternoon." If Schultz was surprised to see us, he didn't let on.

"We're looking for Friends of the Tundra."

Schultz tipped his head and scratched the back of his neck.

"Horace Tyne?"

"Right. Brain freeze." Schultz pointed four fingers toward the door at our backs. "Go to the end of the main road. Turn left at the blue house with the green shed. Four doors down is a red number with a white door and a fence. That's the one."

"You acquainted with Tyne?'

"I see him around."

We waited, but Schultz offered nothing further. We turned to leave.

"You up from Yellowknife?"

"Yes."

"Family?" I recognized the "casual cop" tone.

"Nope."

"You Greenpeacers?"

"You know anything about Tyne's organization?"

"Not really. Guess it keeps him busy."

"Meaning?"

"The guy's been underemployed since the gold mines shut down."

"When was that?" I asked.

"Early nineties. Before my time."

"He seem pretty solid?"

Schultz shrugged one shoulder. "Doesn't get drunk and start throwing punches."

"What more could you ask?" Ryan slipped on his shades. "Thanks for your help."

The corporal's directions were good. We found the house without difficulty. It was small, with cranberry siding and a pair of metal pipes jutting from the roof. The fence was made of unfinished boards nailed vertically with two-inch gaps in between. A scraggly birch threw fingers of shadow across the dirt yard. A gray pickup sat in the drive.

"Not quite the panache of Trump Tower." Ryan was eyeballing the property.

"Maybe all Tyne needs is a computer."

"Keeps the overhead low."

"Leaving more for the caribou."

Ryan pulled open the gate. We crossed to the stoop, and he knocked on the door.

Nothing.

He knocked again. Harder.

A voice barked, then the door swung in.

I searched my memory archives.

Nope. It was a first.

22

Tyne was wearing a leopard-skin loincloth, beads, and an elastic hair binder. That's it.

His bald pate gleamed like copper. His ponytail, which contained perhaps twelve hairs, was long and black and started from fringe wrapping the south end of his head. Both fringe and pony glistened with either grease or moisture. I wasn't sure whether the guy was honoring the ancestors or just out of the shower.

"How are you, Mr. Tyne?" Ryan extended a hand. "I hope we aren't intruding."

"I never buy nothing I don't go looking for. If you're not looking, you probably don't need it."

"We're not salesmen."

"Church?"

"No, sir."

Tyne shook Ryan's hand, mine, then slapped a palm to his bare chest. "I was about to do my sweating. Helps the circulation."

Ryan launched in, using a tactic that implied more familiarity than we actually possessed. "I'm Andy. This is Tempe. We got your name from Nellie Snook. We're associates of Annaliese Ruben."

For several beats Tyne said nothing. I thought he was about to tell us to hit the road when he grinned ever so slightly.

"Annaliese. OK. We'll go with that."

"Sorry?"

"Nice girls, those two. Known them all their lives. And their kin. Used to get themselves into some mischief. Annaliese left here some years back. Wouldn't mind hearing how she's doing."

"We think she's returned to Yellowknife."

"Seriously?"

Did I imagine it, or did Tyne's eyes narrow ever so slightly?

"Annaliese was living in Edmonton. We've come from there. We know her former landlady. When Ms. Forex heard we were headed to Yellowknife, she gave us some belongings Annaliese left behind. We'd like to find her before we leave town."

Each sentence, taken by itself, was absolutely true.

"Come on in." Tyne stepped back. "You tell me what you know, and I'll tell you what I know."

We trailed Tyne through a dimly lit foyer to a living room furnished in standard-issue Sears. The flooring was linoleum trying to be brick. The air smelled of onions and bacon.

Tyne gestured to the couch. Ryan and I sat. He offered coffee. We declined.

When Tyne dropped into an armchair opposite us his bony knees V'ed out, providing an all-too-clear view of Mr. Happy and the Bong Bongs.

I was glad I had not eaten lunch.

"Please feel free to put on warmer clothing." Ryan smiled. "We don't mind waiting."

"Don't want the lady distracted by my squeeters." Tyne winked.

Ryan smiled.

I smiled.

Tyne left, returned moments later in a sweatshirt and jeans. "So. Let's put our heads together."

That image was almost as revolting as the prospect of the squeeters.

"First off, thanks for talking with us," Ryan began. "We won't take up a lot of your time."

"One thing I've got, it's time."

"That's a luxury."

"Not when the bills roll in."

"You're unemployed, sir?"

"Worked fifteen years at Giant. One day they up and shut her down. 'Sorry, buddy. You're shitcanned.' Did some staking for a while. Some trucking. Not a lot of opportunities around here."

"Giant is a gold mine?" I asked.

"Was. For decades gold was the lifeblood of this region."

"I didn't know that."

"'Course you didn't. Everyone's heard of the Klondike gold rush. Well, Yellowknife had her own day in the sun."

"Is that so?" Ryan had no interest in gold. I knew he was trying to loosen Tyne up.

"Eighteen ninety-eight. A prospector on his way to the Yukon got lucky. Overnight this place was a boomtown." Tyne laughed. It sounded like a hiccup. "Meaning the population soared to a whole one thousand. Wasn't until this century that mining had any real economic impact."

"How many mines operated here?"

"Con opened in '36, shut down in 2003. Giant opened in '48, shut down in 2004. Depleted reserves, high production costs. Same old corporate bullshit. 'Profits are down, so, chump, you're out of a job.'"

"I'm sorry," Ryan said.

"Me, too." Tyne wagged his head. "Con was really something. Her workings go down a hundred and sixty meters and extend under most of Yellowknife and Yellowknife Bay, almost to Dettah. And Giant wasn't no slouch. In 1986 she was one of only a handful of mines churned out ten thousand gold bricks. I'm talking worldwide."

I recalled another of the Giant mine's claims to fame. In 1992 a disgruntled miner murdered nine men, six of them scabs who'd crossed the picket line. His bomb demolished their cart while two hundred meters underground. The crime was the worst in Canadian labor history.

"We understand you're involved in environmental conservation," I said.

"Someone's got to take a stand."

"For the caribou."

"The caribou. The lakes. The fish. Diamond mining is going to destroy the whole damn ecosystem."

That threw me. "Diamonds?"

"Treasure under the tundra?" Tyne's voice dripped disdain. "Death to the tundra is more like it."

Ryan slipped me a look. Enough circling. "You say you know Annaliese Ruben's family," he said, wishing to get to the point.

"Knew her father pretty well. Farley McLeod was quite a character."

"Was?"

"Dead. He and I worked for Fipke."

"Fipke?"

"Seriously?" Tyne looked at me as though I'd asked him to explain soap.

"Seriously."

"Chuck Fipke is credited with discovering diamonds in the Arctic. Which he did with a guy named Stu Blusson. Everyone thought the two of them were crazy. Turned out they weren't. Now, thanks to them, the caribou are taking it in the pants."

"Diamonds have replaced gold in the territory?" I asked.

"Seriously?"

Tyne loved the word. This time I didn't play parrot. "How many mines?"

"Ekati opened in '98, Diavak in 2003, Snap Lake in 2008. She's the only one underground."

"Where are they?"

"Couple hundred kilometers north. Snap Lake is De Beers's first mine outside of Africa. Now they're trying to bring another one online. Gahcho Kué. Won't be a caribou left when these bastards get through."

My knowledge of the diamond industry was limited. No. That's being too generous. I knew that Cecil Rhodes founded De Beers in the late eighteen hundreds, that the group was based in Johannesburg and London, and that it was responsible for 75 percent of the world's diamond production. I knew that Angola, Australia, Botswana, Congo, Namibia, Russia, and South Africa were diamond-rich. I had no idea Canada was a player.

"You said you did some staking. What's a staker?" I asked.

"A guy drives in stakes."

"To register a claim."

"You're quick, little lady."

"Seriously quick."

Tyne pointed two fingers at me. "Once Fipke found his pipe, all hell broke loose. Made the Klondike rush look like a garden party." Tyne hiccup-laughed again. "'Course, that's ancient history. Today there's not a square inch of tundra hasn't been staked by some bonehead hoping to strike it rich. And the big boys have sucked up every claim worth a spit. Rio Tinto. BHP Billiton. De Beers."

"What's a pipe?" I asked.

Tyne's eyes went flat. "Thought your interest was in Annaliese Ruben."

"It is," Ryan said. "Did Annaliese live with Farley?"

"Farley wasn't the parenting type. Spawned 'em and left 'em, kinda like carp."

"Annaliese lived with her mother?"

"Micah Ruben. Then she changed it to Micah Lee. Don't think she ever married. Those two just liked changing up names."

"Oh?"

"Micah named the kid Alice. At one point she was Alexandra. Then Anastasia. Thought they sounded fancier."

"What happened to Micah?"

"She was a drinker. Five, seven years back a neighbor found her lying in the snow, a human Popsicle."

I remembered the DNA. "Was Micah aboriginal?"

"Dene."

"Farley?"

"Plain old white bread. Farley passed not long after Micah. Two thousand seven, I think."

"How old was Annaliese?"

Tyne appeared to give that some thought. "I think she'd just started at the high school. What would that make her? Fourteen? Fifteen? 'Course, Annaliese wasn't the sharpest stick in the bag. She could have been older."

"How did Farley die?"

"Crashed his Cessna into Lac La Martre. Hunter saw it go down. Searchers found debris, not Farley." Tyne paused. "I think Annaliese may have been living with her daddy then. Because of Micah being gone."

"Where was that?" I felt a tickle of excitement.

"Little shithole in Yellowknife." Tyne wagged his head. "Farley lived month to month. When the deposit was gone, orphan or not, the kid got the boot. Her siblings didn't reach out, so I let her crash with me for a while. I was living in town then."

"And?"

"And then she left."

"To do what?"

Tyne shrugged. "Girl had to survive."

"Meaning prostitution," Ryan said.

"I'm only guessing. Based on her ma."

"Did you try to intervene?" The tickle of excitement was morphing to disgust. "Urge her to stay in school?"

"I'm not kin. I had no say."

"She was—"

Sensing my hostility, Ryan cut me off. "You say she had siblings."

"All's I know about are a half brother and a half sister." Again the hitchy laugh. "Probably a whole platoon out there. Farley had a way with the ladies."

Dazzled with the squeeters. I didn't say it.

"Who was the half brother?"

"A guy named Daryl Beck. Different mother. Beck was a bit older than Al—Annaliese."

Ryan noted the verb tense. "Beck is dead, too?"

"One too many lines of blow, I guess. House burned to the ground. Heard they hardly found enough to ID."

"Beck was a crackhead?"

"I only know what I hear."

"When was this?

"Three, four years back."

"Was there an investigation?"

"Cops tried."

"Meaning?"

"Folks keep to themselves up here."

"Was Annaliese close to her brother?" I asked.

"Damned if I know."

"Did Beck have other family?"

"Same answer."

"While she was staying at your place, did Beck ever visit? Call?"

"No."

"Anyone else?"

Tyne just looked at me.

"Where did Annaliese live after she moved out?"

"The kid left no forwarding address."

Again the tickle. "Did you ask around?"

Tyne's eyes roved my face. I could feel him trying to read my thoughts.

"Did you and Annaliese part on bad terms?" Pointed.

"I don't like what that implies. You ask a lot of questions for people trying to deliver a package."

Tyne pushed to his feet. The interview was over.

"We appreciate you talking to us." Ryan placed his aviator shades on the bridge of his nose.

At the door, I squeezed in a few last questions.

"Do you know why Annaliese left Yellowknife?"

"It was none of my business."

"If she has come back, do you know where she'd go? Who she'd contact?"

"Maybe the half sister."

"What's her name?"

Seriously?

23

Nellie Snook.

Neither Ollie nor anyone at G Division had uncovered the link.

The whole way back to Yellowknife, I'd been trying to wrap my mind about that. "Snook's name never popped when they ran checks on Ruben?"

"No reason it would."

"Fewer than twenty thousand people live in this town." I wasn't believing this. "Wouldn't it be common knowledge that Snook and Ruben are half sisters?"

"Apparently not."

Ryan parked in a strip of dirt fronting a bright blue shack. We got out of the Camry and crossed to it.

"And not one single person they questioned had a clue?"

"Tyne told you. Folks keep to themselves up here."

Antlers, snowshoes, and an oddly shaped paddle

hung above the shack's door. A sign had been nailed to the siding beside it. *No Sniveling*.

Ryan pointed to the sign and raised his brows.

"I'm not sniveling." I wasn't. I was venting.

Ryan pointed to another sign. *Hot Beer. Lousy Food. Bad Service. Welcome. Have a nice day*. Then he opened the door. Bells jangled us in.

To our left was a stuffed moose head doing duty as a hat and coat rack. Opposite Bullwinkle was a combo bar, fry kitchen, cashier's station. A woman in a black Mao cap, plaid shirt, and jeans was scraping the griddle with a spatula. The rest of *le bistro* was taken up by wooden tables and high-back chairs, some plain, others carved.

On hearing the bells, Mao turned. "Got reservations?" Her vocal chords had seen a whole lot of smoke.

Ryan and I looked at each other, surprised. It was three in the afternoon. The place was empty.

"Gotcha!" Mao laughed, showing gaps once occupied by molars. Then she swung the spatula to indicate we could sit wherever.

We chose a graffiti-scarred table next to a window shaded by venetian blinds. Through the slats, I could see trees and blue picnic tables. The adjacent wall was layered with photos and business cards, many faded to illegibility.

"Good thing I'm not the 'I told you so' type." I continued pressing my point. "Because I'd be saying it."

"We'll see."

When Mao appeared at our table, Ryan and I both ordered fish and chips. Rainwater had sent us to Bullock's saying everything on the menu came straight from the lake.

"Let's hope we're not too late." When Mao was back at the griddle, I rolled on. "Again."

"Rainwater said no one's entered or left the house since Snook got back from the store."

"Ollie asked him to talk to her?"

"About ten minutes ago. But if she refuses, he can't go inside."

Mao brought our drinks. Diet Coke for me. Moosehead for Ryan. I hoped his choice didn't offend our buddy on the wall.

Ollie arrived as Mao was delivering our food. His face was tense, his cheeks flushed with asymmetrical raspberry splotches. I knew the look. The hunt was on, and he was loving it.

Turned out Ollie and Mao knew each other. Her name was Mary.

"What you cooking today, sweetheart?" He gave her his trademark jaw-hitch maneuver.

"Cod, trout, and pike."

"What's good?"

"Everything."

"Pike."

"Excellent choice."

Ollie waited until Mary was out of earshot, then

spoke to me. "Nice. Very few have the poise to carry off the hamburger-chin look."

"I used to model for Chanel."

"Really?"

"No. Who's Zeb Chalker?"

Big grin. "Bola'ed you over, I hear."

My look suggested I wasn't amused.

"Chalker's MED."

I tipped both palms in question.

"Municipal Enforcement Division. They've got maybe six constables, a couple of supervisors, some patrol cars and snowmobiles. Do mostly traffic, animal, and crowd control. And, of course, koi ponds."

"Hilarious. What about Scarborough?"

"He's in town, all right. Staying with one of his greaseball pals."

"Unka and Castain know he's here?"

Ollie's eyes rolled to Ryan. "Both claimed to be unacquainted with the gentleman."

"They denied Scar was trying to cut in to their action?" I asked.

"They didn't admit to having any action. Hadn't a clue the meaning of my questions. They're honest citizens trying to make a buck leading outdoor adventures for tourists. Castain offered to take me bird-watching."

Mary arrived with Ollie's root beer. Left.

"So you got nothing," Ryan summed up.

"I learned that neither Unka nor Castain cares for me."

"Indeed."

"Both called me unpleasant names. Unka was more creative."

"You had to kick them?"

"We know where to find them."

"Someone's working a tail?"

"Hadn't thought of that."

"Scarborough, too?"

"Hadn't thought—"

"For God's sake." Already it had been a very long day. I was not up to their testosterone wrangling. "Knock it off."

Ryan and I cleaned our plates. Then we sat in awkward silence until Mary delivered Ollie's pike. While he ate, I provided further details of our visit with Horace Tyne.

"We ran the half sister," he said when I'd finished. "Snook's her married name. She was born Nellie France in Fort Resolution."

"Where's that?"

"The south shore of Great Slave Lake. Where the pavement ends."

"Literally?"

"Yes."

"So people in Yellowknife might actually be unaware of Snook's connection to Ruben."

"It's possible, though Chalker should know." Ollie dipped a french fry in mayo and ate it.

"Rainwater's with Snook now?"

241

"He'll try making nice. If that fails, he'll ask for a warrant. What's your take on Tyne?"

"The guy's a sleaze. But an environmentally conscious sleaze."

"Friends of the Tundra." Ollie dipped and popped another fry. "Never heard of it."

"I was surprised to learn that diamond mining is big business here."

"You haven't noticed the banners on every lamp-post?" Ollie made a marquis gesture with one hand. "Yellowknife, Diamond Capital of North America. There's a big-ass rock on the official city logo."

"You ever hear of this guy Fipke?"

"You're kidding." Ollie regarded me with the same incredulity Tyne had displayed. "Chuck Fipke's a legend."

"Fine. I'll get a book."

"Copies in every souvenir shop in town. Or google Fipke."

"Is Tyne right about the caribou herds?"

"Some locals, mostly aboriginals, claim that diamond mining is disrupting the migration routes. It's a hot issue up here. When De Beers proposed opening Snap Lake, some of the chiefs banded together. Set the project back years. Environmental-impact studies and all. Now De Beers wants to bring another operation online. I forget the name."

"Gahcho Kué."

"That's it." Ollie bunched and tossed his napkin.

"You should talk to Rainwater. He knows more about the mining controversy than I do."

I was draining my Diet Coke when Ollie's phone rang. The conversation lasted under a minute. I got little from his end. Except that he was irked.

"Snook stonewalled." Jamming the cell back onto his belt. "Rainwater's going to ask a judge to cut paper."

"Now what?"

"Now we wait for someone to screw up."

Three hours in my room produced an unplanned nap, a message from Katy saying she had news too important for e-mail, and voluminous information on Chuck Fipke and geological exploration.

Before booting my laptop, I knew that diamonds are carbon transformed by extreme heat and pressure into the hardest, clearest mineral on earth. That because of their rigid tetrahedral molecular structure—a triangular pyramid with four faces—a diamond can be cut only by another diamond or a laser.

I knew that the sparkly little rocks are pricey as hell. And that they create an eyeful of bling.

That was about it.

Every thirty minutes I'd interrupt my research to phone Katy. Each time her phone would roll to voice mail. Uneasy, I'd dive back onto the Internet.

In between dialing, I learned the following.

It takes forty-four to fifty kilobars of pressure at a

minimum of a thousand degrees Celsius to change carbon into diamond. I understood the temperature but wasn't sure the exact nature of a kilobar.

The appropriate combo of heating and crushing existed a few billion years ago at depths of eighty to a hundred and twenty-five miles in rock formations called cratons, dense old slabs of continental plate.

Later, underground volcanoes sent magma—or molten rock—minerals, rock fragments, and occasionally diamonds bubbling up through the cratons. The mixture expanded and cooled along the way to form either carrot-shaped pipes to the surface, or wide flat underground structures called dikes. It then solidified into rock called kimberlite.

Most diamondiferous kimberlites are associated with cratons from the Archean era, an early part of the Precambrian, when the earth was much hotter than today. *Much* hotter. Many kimberlite pipes lie underneath shallow lakes formed in inactive volcanic craters called calderas.

So. To score diamonds, you locate a pipe rising from a really old craton. Piece of cake, right? Wrong. The buggers are incredibly hard to find.

That's where Chuck Fipke and Stu Blusson came in. Both knew that the Slave craton, which underlies the Northwest Territories from Great Slave Lake in the south to Coronation Gulf on the Arctic Ocean, is one of the oldest rock formations on earth. And they developed an effective technique to explore it.

Fipke understood the significance of indicator minerals, the traveling companions of diamonds. Those in kimberlite include calcium carbonate, olivine, garnet, phlogopite, pyroxene, serpentine, upper mantle rock, and a variety of trace minerals. Fipke focused on the trifecta of chromite, ilmenite, and high-chrome, low-calcium G10 garnets.

Blusson understood the significance of glacial movement during the last ice age. He reasoned that, after eroding a kimberlite pipe, a retreating glacier would leave a debris path containing diamond indicator minerals. Track the path to its source, he argued, and you'll find the pipe.

Fipke and Blusson spent a decade scouring the tundra, mapping, surveying, coring, and collecting when temperatures were bearable, analyzing samples in their lab when the weather was too harsh. Everyone in the mining world thought they were nuts.

One day, on his own with a bush pilot, Fipke flew over Lac de Gras, source of the Coppermine River. Spotting an esker, a winding ridge of gravel and sand left by meltwater from a retreating glacier, he ordered the pilot to land on a peninsula called Pointe de Misère.

The esker protected a small lake with a sandy shore containing a dark striation. There he collected sample bag G71, the last in his mammoth, decade-long exploration.

Pointe de Misère was at the Glacial Divide. From where Fipke stood, ice had flowed east to Hudson

Bay, north to the northern islands, south into central Canada, and west into the Mackenzie River and Blackwater Lake. He'd sampled the entire expanse stretching west, over two hundred thousand square miles.

Back in the lab, Fipke tried to make sense of the pattern that his samples were producing. Sample by sample, using large, detailed maps, he plotted the results. With scanning electron microscopy, he examined bag after bag.

His conclusion: the indicator trail began at Blackwater Lake, spread east, and two hundred miles northeast of Yellowknife, stopped near Lac de Gras.

He checked the contents of sample bag G71. It contained over 1,500 chrome diopsides and 6,000 pyrope garnets.

Fipke had found his pipe. Or pipes.

He began staking like mad.

More sampling. More analysis. Confirmation.

Fipke named the site Point Lake, partly for geography, partly to confuse the competition. There was another Point Lake northwest of his find.

Next step was to pinpoint the exact location of the diamonds. And that cost money.

With the existence of kimberlite pipes confirmed, Fipke and Blusson were at last able to obtain big-money backers. In 1990 Dia Met, a company founded by Fipke in 1984, and BHP, an Australian mining conglomerate, signed a joint-venture agreement for the Northwest Territories Diamond Project. For 51 percent ownership, BHP would finance exploration in exchange for shares in any future property. Dia Met would hold 29 percent. Fipke and Blusson would retain 10 percent each.

In 1991 Dia Met and BHP announced the discovery of diamonds at Fipke's Point Lake site. The news sparked the NWT diamond rush, the biggest staking frenzy since Klondike.

Lac de Gras in French. Ekati in the language of the local Dene people. Fat Lake in both.

In 1998 Ekati became Canada's first diamond mine. The following year she produced one million carats. Today she does $400 million annually and coughs up 4 percent of the world's rocks.

Fat Lake, indeed.

In 2003 the Diavik mine, owned by a joint-venture partnership between Harry Winston Diamond Corporation and Diavik Diamond Mines, Inc., a subsidiary of the Rio Tinto Group, began operation. The mine, Canada's second largest, lies 186 miles north of Yellowknife. It consists of three kimberlite pipes on 7.7 square miles on a tiny chunk of real estate in Lac de Gras, locally called East Island. Diavik is a major supplier of the "Jeweler to the Stars."

In 1997 kimberlite was discovered at Snap Lake, 137 miles northeast of Yellowknife. De Beers Canada bought the mining rights in the fall of 2000. In 2004 permits for construction and operation were granted.

Unlike most diamond-bearing kimberlite deposits that are pipes, the Snap Lake ore body is a two-and-a-half-meter-thick dyke that dips from the northwest shore down under the lake. Thus, Snap Lake is Canada's first completely underground diamond mine.

Snap Lake mine officially opened in 2008. According to De Beers's website, by the end of 2010, $1.5 billion had been spent on construction and operation. Of that total, $1.077 billion had gone to NWT-based contractors and suppliers, including $676 million with aboriginal businesses or joint ventures.

The article on Snap Lake concluded with a statement emphasizing De Beers's commitment to sustainable development in local communities, and pointing out that the Snap Lake mine had signed impact-benefit agreements with the Yellowknives Dene First Nation, the Tlicho Government, the North Slave Métis Alliance, and the Lutsel K'e and Kache Dene First Nation.

Between the lines, I got a whiff of the aboriginal-versus-mining hostility to which Ollie had alluded.

I was trying Katy for the gazillionth time, now genuinely concerned about Birdie, when a loud knock rattled my door. I crossed to it and squinted through the peephole.

Ryan.

Something was wrong.

24

"Castain's dead."

Ryan strode past me and began pacing my room.

"What?"

"Someone shot him."

"When?"

"About an hour ago."

"Where?"

"Three rounds to the chest. Christ. Does it matter?"

"No." Having to track a moving target wasn't helping my comprehension. "I meant where was Castain when it happened?"

"Banging his girlfriend."

"Stop pacing."

Ryan never slowed.

"Do they have the shooter?"

"No."

"But he was under surveillance."

Ryan snorted loudly. "Rainwater's idea of a tail

was to ping-pong a car between Snook, Unka, and Castain."

"Jesus."

"Claims he doesn't have enough manpower to maintain surveillance in three locations."

"That may be legit."

"Why the fuck didn't he say so? You and I could have taken Snook. Or Sergeant Shithead could have sat on her."

I ignored that. "So no one's watching the house on Ragged Ass?"

"You know the annual homicide count in Yellowknife?"

I didn't.

"Every chump with a badge will want a piece of this one."

"Is Unka a suspect?" I asked.

"One among many."

"Where is he?"

"In the wind."

"What about Scar?"

"Ditto."

"Shit."

"Exactly. I'm heading to the scene."

I grabbed my jacket, and we raced to the Camry.

Ryan smoked. Didn't ask if I minded. Just lit up.

"Castain's girlfriend was a stripper named Merilee Twiller. Mercifully, she lived not far from the Explorer.

Ollie's directions took us to Sunnyvale Court, a horseshoe of tiny bungalows on tiny lots. While a few were reasonably well maintained, most were in disrepair, and several were boarded up and abandoned. I guessed it had been a while since the court had lived up to its name.

Twiller's address was at the far end, on the north side of the curve. The place needed paint, new screens, and a bucket of weed killer. Maybe a bulldozer. Twiller's next-door neighbor had two garbage pails on his stoop and a car on cinder blocks in the drive.

We arrived to the usual hubbub of activity. The front door of Twiller's house was open, and every indoor and outdoor bulb was blazing. Blue and yellow Evi Lites dotted the lawn, marking the locations of trace evidence, perhaps bits of Castain.

A sheet-covered body lay on a walk leading to a porch enclosed by a rusty iron railing. Crime scene tape triangled between the railing and two stunted pines in the yard. Portable halogens were focused on it.

More tape paralleled the curb on the opposite side of the cul-de-sac, a restraint for gawkers out for a glimpse of someone else's misery. Possibly members of the media.

Ryan was right. It seemed every conceivable member of law enforcement had turned out. I saw cruisers from the RCMP and MED, a hearse, a panel van, and at least a dozen unmarked cars and pickups.

Most had flashing lights on their roofs or dashboards. Radios added staticky sputter to the tumult of voices calling back and forth.

Ollie was off to one side, talking to a woman whose dress was too short and too tight for her heavy thighs and the rolls of fat outlining her bra. I assumed this was Merilee Twiller.

Ryan pulled to the end of the line of parked vehicles. An RCMP corporal approached his door. Ryan badged us in. We got out and walked toward Ollie.

As we drew close, I could see that Twiller was in her forties, trying hard not to look it. Despite an overload of makeup, I noted puffy lower lids, networks of deep lines, and starbursts of capillaries on either side of her nose.

Ollie didn't explain us to Twiller. "You take a look at him?"

Ryan answered for both of us. "Not yet. What have you got so far?"

"Around seven Castain dropped in for a little poontang with the love of his life here." Ollie flicked a thumb at Twiller.

"You're a real dick," she said.

"Castain left around eight. Never made it to the property line."

"Any witnesses?" Ryan asked.

"The grieving girlfriend says she heard shots, then squealing tires. Didn't get a look at the shooter or the car."

"That's how it went down." Defensive.

"Where was lover boy going from here?"

"We've been over this." Twiller kept her angry rainbow eyes on Ollie.

"I'm slow. Explain it again."

"Arty didn't tell me shit."

"And you didn't ask."

"No."

"I'm guessing he was heading out to deliver more product. That's why he came here, right? You're on the spike, aren't you, princess?"

"Screw you and the questions you galloped in on."

"How about I give you a ride to the cage?"

"Because my boyfriend got shot?"

"What do you suppose we'll find in the house?"

"A shitpot of cat hair."

Anger bunched the muscles below Ollie's temples. He knew Twiller was right. She'd have flushed any drugs before calling the cops.

Ollie's brusqueness was getting us nowhere. I caught Ryan's eye and tipped my head toward the house. He dipped his chin in understanding.

"How about you show me the vic?" Ryan suggested.

Ollie nodded. Told Twiller to stay put.

I watched them weave through the melee of cops and technicians swarming the cul-de-sac.

"My condolences for your loss," I said to Twiller.

For the first time, she glanced my way. In the pulsing red light, her mouth looked taut, her cheeks stretched and hollow. "Right" was all she said.

"Can you think of anyone who might want to hurt Arty?" I asked.

Twiller drew her right arm across her belly, rested her left elbow on it, and began chewing a thumb cuticle that already looked raw.

Behind us, I saw Ollie and Ryan join a woman standing over Castain. Under the bright spots, the logo on her jacket was easily recognizable.

In the Northwest Territories, all sudden deaths are investigated by the Coroners Service, a division of the Department of Justice. The service has its main office in Yellowknife and roughly forty coroners throughout the territory. The NWT has no staffed facility for performing postmortems.

I knew that the deputy chief coroner was a woman named Maureen King. I guessed I was looking at her. And that she would order Castain's body transported to the office of Alberta's chief medical examiner in Edmonton for autopsy.

"Had Arty argued with anyone?" I asked Twiller. "Made anyone mad?"

Twiller shook her head.

"Received any strange phone calls or visitors?"

"I already told the other cop. We didn't hang out that much."

"Was Arty seeing other women?"

"We weren't going steady, if that's what you mean." Twiller swiped both palms down her cheeks. "He didn't deserve this."

"I know."

"Do you? What the hell do you know?"

"I'm sorry."

Ten yards beyond us, King lifted a corner of the sheet. Ryan dropped to a crouch for a closer look at Castain.

"It's that bastard Unka." She said it so softly I almost didn't hear.

"Excuse me?"

"Unka thought Arty was skimming."

"Arty told you that?"

"I overheard a conversation. When he's pissed, he gets ugly."

"Unka."

She nodded.

"Ugly enough to kill?"

"He'd gut-stab his mother, then order up pizza."

It was past ten when the hearse finally rolled. Ollie stayed to help canvass the neighbors. The hit wasn't his problem, but he hoped to pry something loose on Scar.

Ryan and I rode to the Explorer in silence. I looked out my window at the bare trees straining to bud, the patches of last night's snow struggling to hang on. Felt the frustration they depicted.

Ryan spoke first. "Your friend has the interrogation skills of a slug."

"He's not my friend."

"He was."

"What's your point?"

"He was incompetent." Ryan patted his jacket pocket.

"Don't smoke," I said.

Ryan shot me a look but stopped searching for a cigarette.

"You've both been acting like jerks," I said.

"I'd never be that callous."

"He felt she was holding back."

"Was she?"

"Yes."

As we ascended the circle drive, I told him what Twiller had said about Unka.

"You just proved my point," he said.

We got out of the car and crossed to the hotel.

"It gets to him," I said, not sure why I was defending Ollie.

Ryan cocked a skeptical brow.

"He gets tired of the violence. Of constantly dealing with skanks who make you want to scrub your whole body with Lysol."

"You speaking for shithead or yourself?"

Damn good point. I didn't concede it.

"We both know Castain just bounced Ruben to the back burner, perhaps kicked her from the stage altogether."

Normally, I'd have made fun of Ryan's mixed metaphor. Not then.

"This whole thing is just too freaking frustrating." I started for the elevator.

"We'll find her."

I turned.

"But now we'll have to rely on ourselves," he said.

"And shithead."

"And shithead."

A truce. Of sorts.

Back in my room, I tried my iPhone. To my surprise, it gave a listless flicker. Hopeful that the working bits just needed to dry out, I plugged it in to charge.

Using the landline, I phoned my elusive daughter. She remained elusive. I left another message.

Exhausted, I did a quick toilette, then dropped into bed. But my mind refused to disengage. I wondered about Arty Castain. Who had killed him? Why? Was it really Unka, or was it a major move by Scarborough? Had Castain's death been the first in a bloodbath about to commence? What secrets had Castain taken to the grave?

Where was Tom Unka? Ronnie Scarborough?

What had Scarborough meant when he said Ollie was clueless about Annaliese Ruben? Had Scar been more than her pimp? Did he know things we hadn't even thought about?

Ryan was right. The locals would focus on the Castain homicide, on the erupting feud over control of the drug trade. But I couldn't give up my obsession with Ruben. The woman had murdered four babies.

People had described Ruben as not very bright. Scarborough. Forex. Tyne. How had she eluded capture this long? Gotten from Saint-Hyacinthe to Edmonton to Yellowknife? Did she even know the law was in pursuit? Surely she did. But was she more worried about Scar?

Had Scar helped Ruben? Had Nellie Snook? Was Ruben hiding in the house on Ragged Ass? Or had she gone elsewhere? A half sibling of whom we knew nothing? A local officer who was perhaps a cousin or other relative?

Ruben's father was Farley McLeod. Her mother was Micah Lee. Micah was Dene. Did Ruben's familial network extend to places closed to outsiders?

And what about Horace Tyne? Tyne had worked with Ruben's father, was at least thirty years her senior. Had his relationship with Ruben been strictly paternal?

Round and round it went. Images. Speculation. Questions. Mostly questions.

I'd just drifted off when the landline rang. Thinking it was Katy, I snatched up the receiver. My eye caught the digits on the bedside clock. Eleven-fifty-five.

"Is this Temperance Brennan?" Soft. Childlike.

"Yes."

"I need to see you." Slight accent. It didn't sound like Binny.

"Who is this?"

The answer sent my heart rate into the stratosphere.

25

"I'm in the woods."

"What woods?"

"Behind the hotel."

"OK."

"Come alone."

"But I—"

"If someone is with you, I'll go away."

"I'll be there in ten minutes."

"Five."

Click.

I shot out of bed. Yanked on the clothes I'd tossed to a chair. Grabbed my jacket. Shoved a flashlight, my room key, and by habit, my cell phone into one pocket. Flew out the door.

Buzzing with adrenaline, I bypassed the elevator, pounded down the stairs, and raced across the lobby. The hotel had to have rear exits; not sure where, I played it safe and slammed out the front door.

The night was cold but not enough for snow. A light rain was slicking the grass underfoot.

As I ran around the building, I considered possibilities. Had Ruben tired of running? Did she want to turn herself in? Or was this a setup to throw me off?

To take me out?

That thought brought me up short.

Was Ruben dangerous? She'd killed her offspring, but could she pose a threat to me? What would that gain her?

I pulled out my iPhone. The thing responded with a bit more enthusiasm but still lacked the juice to allow normal function.

It didn't matter. I had to get to Ruben.

I stopped again at the garden. Zen and the art of murdering babies. Odd. But that's what my gray cells sent up.

The moon was a fuzzy sliver, casting soft copies of stacked boulders and dead plants on the wet pebbles below.

I peered into the eerie dusklike dimness ahead. Saw only dark shapes I knew to be pines.

I took out and thumbed on my flash. Partly to light my way. Partly to let Ruben know I was coming.

Barely breathing, I hurried on.

I was almost at the tree line when a solitary figure took shape in the shadows. Indistinct. Smudged by the drizzle.

The figure remained motionless, the face a pale oval pointed my way.

I deliberated tactics. Cajole? Persuade? Coerce?

Come quietly. Let me help you. Or do I call the guys with badges and guns? What's it going to be, Annaliese?

I continued walking, the light from my flash fizzing in the rain.

Please, God. Don't let her be packing.

I entered the woods.

As though reading my mind, Ruben raised both arms and stepped into my beam.

She was short and probably classified as obese by medical standards. Her hair was long and dark, her face pretty in a pudgy-toddler sort of way.

Tank sat at her feet.

Ruben's message was clear. She wasn't carrying a weapon and meant me no harm.

Two pairs of eyes watched me close in.

Before I could speak, Ruben rotated slowly, arms straight out at her sides. Tank looped at her feet as though showing that he, too, posed no threat.

Ruben came full circle and faced me. Tank went bipedal and placed his forepaws on her knee. She did not reach down to pet him.

"We've been looking for you, Annaliese."

"People told me."

"We need to talk."

"You're scaring my sister."

"I'm sorry about that."

"I want you to stop."

"I will if you agree to meet with the police."

"No."

"Why not?"

"They'll say I did bad things."

"Did you?"

"I don't do that anymore."

"You can lower your hands."

She did. Tank jumped into her arms.

"Tell me about your babies."

"Babies?" Her confusion sounded genuine.

"They're why we've been looking for you."

Lines creased her forehead. She looked down at the dog. He looked up at her. She scratched his ear. "I figured it was the men."

"What men?"

"The men who gave me money."

She thought we wanted to bust her for turning tricks.

"The police want to know what happened to your babies."

She said nothing.

"Did you kill them?"

The rain had separated the fur on Tank's head into spiky wet tufts. Ruben began plucking at them with quick nervous gestures.

"Did you hurt the babies?"

Her fingers grew more agitated.

"We found four, Annaliese. Three in Saint-Hyacinthe and one in Edmonton."

"You found the babies." Flat.

"Yes."

"They died."

"How?"

"They had to."

"Why?"

"They couldn't live."

"Why not?"

"I gave them something bad."

"Annaliese." Sharp.

Ruben stopped pulling Tank's fur and pressed him to her chest.

"Look at me."

Her head came up slowly, but her eyes stayed down.

"I wrapped them in towels," she said.

"What do you mean, you gave the babies something bad?"

"Something inside."

I didn't follow but let it go. Time for that later. "Do you know who the fathers are?" I asked.

Annaliese kept her gaze pointed at Tank. "Please don't tell Nellie."

"You have to explain the babies to the police," I said.

"I don't want to."

"You have no choice."

"You can't make me."

"Yes. I can."

"I'm not a bad person."

Standing there in the moonlight and rain, I realized

a sad truth: Annaliese Ruben wasn't a monster. She was simpleminded.

"I know," I said softly.

I was reaching out when something over her right shoulder caught my eye. The needles on one pine seemed wrong, their edges too light amid the surrounding darkness.

I stepped to my left to see around Annaliese.

A beat, then a flicker, as though a torch had been lighted then quickly extinguished.

"Annaliese," I whispered. "Did you come alone?"

I would never get an answer to my question.

A muffled crack broke the stillness. I saw a flash.

Annaliese's mouth opened. A glob flew from her forehead, and a black hole appeared above her right brow.

With a terrified yelp, Tank pushed from his mistress's chest and darted into the woods.

I hit the ground.

Another crack rocked the night.

Annaliese's body bucked and rotated toward me. Then she dropped.

Belly to the earth, I scrabbled to her, pulling with my elbows and pushing with my feet.

Annaliese lay with her eyes wide open, as though startled by what had taken place. A black river ran from the exit hole, across her face, and into her hairline.

I pressed trembling fingers to her throat. Felt no pulse.

No! No!

I probed the soft flesh, desperate for vital signs. Nothing.

Heart pounding, I tried to think. How many were out there? Had Annaliese been the target or had I?

Think!

What did the shooter expect?

That I'd run. Or stay to give first aid.

Do neither!

Keeping low, I crawled back to where I'd been when the shot rang out. Contact with the ground made me aware of a hard object in my pocket.

I held for a moment, straining my senses. Saw no light. Heard no movement.

I groped for my flashlight among the pine needles blanketing the ground. Finally, my fingers closed around it. Covering the glass with one palm, I shook the batteries to life. Then I arced the thing toward Annaliese's body, keeping the bulb pointed away from the shooter. The flashlight landed with a soft tick, its beam barely visible above the groundcover.

I froze.

No gunfire.

No sound but drops hitting the boughs overhead.

I rolled to my side, dug the phone from my pocket, and held it close to my belly. Hoping against hope, I thumbed the indentation on the bottom front.

The screen flickered, went black.

I tried again, maintaining the pressure with my thumb.

For seconds.

Hours.

I was about to give up when the icons burst forth in glorious color.

Almost crying with relief, I tapped the little green phone symbol, then a number on my speed-dial list.

"Ryan." Groggy but trying to sound alert.

"I'm in the pines behind the hotel," I whispered.

"I can't . . . you."

"The woods behind the hotel."

". . . peat . . . you said."

"Ruben's been shot," I hissed.

". . . breaking up."

"Come to the woods behind the Zen garden," I hiss-whispered as loud as I dared.

"Hang up . . . back . . . else . . . the landline."

"I'm not in my room. I need you to come—"

The connection went dead. I tried texting. No go.

I was on my own.

I shoved the phone back in my pocket.

Listened.

The woods were absolutely still.

Sudden thought.

Tank.

The little dog was on his own, too. Coyote bait. Or wolf. Or whatever the hell else was on the prowl.

Call out to him?

I couldn't risk it. The shooter could be out there.

A soft yellow glow marked the spot where

Annaliese lay. She was past help. But I felt driven to get responders to the scene. To get her body out of the rain.

To get my ass out of danger.

Would Ryan make sense of my garbled message?

How long to wait?

I gave it ten minutes.

Checked for landmarks.

Ruben was lying below a large pine with a gnarly growth five feet up its trunk. To its left was a smaller, asymmetrical pine on which every other branch looked dead.

Satisfied I could relocate the spot, I bolted.

26

Ryan opened his door wearing jeans. Just jeans. His hair was tousled, but he looked fully awake.

"No need to pound." Ryan took in my wet hair and the pine needles clinging to my clothes. His grin vanished. "What the hell—"

"Ruben's dead." I was breathless from running. Shaking. Fighting back tears.

"What?"

"She's not a monster, Ryan. She's retarded. Oh, God. We're not supposed to say 'retarded.' What? What do we say now? 'Challenged'? What word do we use?"

The shock at finally coming face-to-face with Ruben. The terror at seeing her shot. The relief at being back in the hotel. I was babbling, couldn't help myself.

"She probably never knew she was pregnant. Probably had no *concept* of pregnant. No concept of *concept*."

Tears were running full-out. I made no effort to brush them away.

"I didn't get a look at the shooter."

"Slow down." Ryan was not understanding. Or not hearing my words through the blubbering.

"Two shots. The one to the head probably killed her." Loud. Too loud.

Ryan pulled me into his room. Closed the door. Dug a tiny bottle of Johnnie Walker from his minibar and handed it to me. "Drink this."

"I can't. You know I can't."

He unscrewed the cap and thrust the Scotch at me. "Drink it."

I drank.

The familiar fire roared down my throat. I closed my eyes. The heat spread from my belly to my chest, my brain. The trembling lessened.

I raised my lids. Ryan was studying my face. "Better?"

"Yes." Dear God. It was.

"Now," Ryan said. "Start over."

"Ruben's dead. Her body is in the woods behind the hotel."

"Tabarnac!"

"The dog ran off."

"The dog?"

"Tank. The little—"

"Forget the dog. Tell me what happened."

"Ruben phoned me right around midnight. Said she wanted to meet."

"How'd she get your number?"

"Probably from Snook."

Ryan's hand shot his hair. That meant he wasn't happy.

"Ruben told me to come alone."

"Jesus Christ, Brennan. If she'd told you to slice off a tit, would you have done that, too?"

"It was *moi* solo or no meet." I was still wired, and Ryan's reaction was pissing me off.

Ryan just stared at me.

"I phoned you. It's not my fault the signal sucked."

"You met her in the woods in the middle of the night."

"Yes."

"You had no business going off by yourself." The Viking-blue eyes simmered with anger.

"I'm a big girl," I snapped.

"You could have been killed!"

"I wasn't!"

"But Ruben was!"

Ryan's words felt like a slap.

I looked away. To hide the hurt. Mostly to hide the guilt. Because deep down, I knew he was right.

"I didn't mean that." Ryan's voice was softer.

"Call it in," I said curtly.

Ryan crossed to the bedside table, picked up and dialed his cell. He spoke with his back turned to me. When finished, he dug a sweatshirt from his carry-on and pulled it over his head. The static did not improve his hair situation.

"And?" I asked.

"They're sending a unit."

"We should tell Ollie."

Ryan dialed again, spoke, disconnected. "He's still at the Castain scene."

"What did he say?"

"You don't want to know."

Ryan drew in a deep breath. Let it out. Then he made a comment that melted my resentment.

"I'm sorry. I shouldn't have said that. But at times you go with your heart, not your head. I worry that one day you will pay a price. I couldn't stand it if something happened to you."

I kept my face empty.

"It wasn't your fault, Tempe."

Yes, I thought. *It was*.

The unit was driven by Zeb Chalker. No crime scene truck. No hearse. Just Chalker. Apparently, the death of a hooker didn't merit pulling personnel from a really cool murder.

Ryan and I met Chalker in the lobby. He did not look pleased to be there.

I described where I thought the shooter had been standing. Chalker called for another unit to check that sector of the woods and to drive the stretch of road closest to it.

"When we get there, I'll go in first. Not a chance the doer hung around, but until I know what we're dealing with, I prefer to play it safe."

Ryan and I nodded.

Chalker led us out the front door, dug Maglites and slickers from the trunk of his patrol car, and handed them to us.

Single-file, we circled the building, crossed the garden, and squished toward the pines, our soles leaving shallow depressions in the mud and soggy needles.

At a point along the tree line, I indicated the position of Ruben's body. "She's about ten feet straight ahead."

Chalker continued alone. In under a minute, we heard him call out. "Clear."

Feet spread, flashlight pointed at the ground, Chalker watched us approach.

I joined my beam to his.

And caught my breath in surprise.

Ruben's body was gone.

"This is the spot." Pointlessly, I shone my light on the pine with the tumor.

Chalker said nothing.

"She was here." Working my beam back and forth at the base of my marker trees.

"It's pretty dark, miss. Maybe—"

"I'm not an idiot," I snapped, still riding my adrenaline-fed high. Or the Johnnie Walker.

"You sure she was dead?" Ryan asked.

"She had an exit hole in her forehead the size of my fist!"

"Maybe animals dragged her off."

"Maybe." I didn't think so.

I expanded my search, slowly moving farther and farther out. Ryan and Chalker did the same.

Ten minutes later, we reconvened at the original location. My hands were shaking, and blood was fizzing in my chest.

Both men regarded me. Dubious.

"I swear. She was lying right here." Dropping to my knees, I worked a close-up grid with my beam.

The needles appeared uniformly damp. None looked recently broken, displaced, or overturned. I spotted no blood, hair, tissue, or bone fragment.

There wasn't a shred of evidence to indicate a person had been killed.

In shock, I stood and aimed my light in the direction from which the shots had come. "We need to check that area for casings."

"I think we're done here."

"Hardly."

Chalker exhaled up toward his eyes, the personification of patience. "Now, miss—"

I lost it. "Don't you dare go all Trooper Murray on me. Someone fucking killed a woman out here! I saw her fucking brains blasted into tomorrow!"

"You need to calm down."

"Calm down? *Calm down?*" I lunged forward and thrust my face into Chalker's. "You think I'm some premenopausal dingbat looking for drama?"

Chalker took a step back. I felt a hand on my shoulder. No matter. I was in full rant.

"Let me tell you something, *Constable* Chalker. I was working crime scenes when you were still hoping for your big-boy shorts. The combined fucking genius of the RCMP and the SQ couldn't find Annaliese Ruben. But I did." I jammed a trembling thumb to my chest. "Ruben reached out to *me*. And some motherfucker put a slug through her skull!"

"We're done here."

Chalker brushed past me and strode out of the woods, his boots softly rustling the tangle of wet needles.

I turned to Ryan. "That guy has it in for me."

"Let's go," he said gently.

"I'm not crazy."

"I believe you."

Back at the hotel, I stripped off my wet clothes, showered, and pulled on sweats. It was going on two, but my brain was wired on adrenaline and booze.

I was booting my laptop when I heard a knock.

As before, I hit the peephole.

Ryan was still wearing the jeans and sweatshirt. He held a flat square box in front of his chest. I opened the door. "Pizza?" he asked.

"With anchovies?"

"You're finicky now?" Ryan's brows floated up.

"A girl can't be too picky."

"No anchovies."

"I accept."

As we ate, I briefed Ryan on every detail I could

remember, from Ruben's call to my showing up at his room.

"How could someone launder a scene that effectively?" I was incredulous.

"The rain helped."

"They moved fast."

"Very."

"Do you think Scar's the doer?"

"I'm looking forward to asking him that."

We each helped ourself to a second slice.

"You'll make them put full effort into investigating Ruben's murder?"

"I will."

"Thank you."

"Under one condition."

I cocked a brow.

"You clear something up."

I nodded.

"Who the hell is Trooper Murray?"

"What?" The question was not what I'd expected.

"You threw the name at Chalker."

"I did?"

Ryan nodded.

"Trooper Stephen Murray of Lincoln, Maine. You've never seen the video of his traffic stop?"

Ryan shook his head.

"It's been on Court TV, YouTube. The thing went viral. Murray's been dubbed the most patient cop in America."

Ryan reached for more pizza. Said nothing.

"Come on. Chalker's long-suffering forbearance act didn't make you want to puke?"

"The guy was doing his job."

"The guy was acting like a supercilious ass," I said.

"I doubt you'll be topping his hit parade, either."

We ate in silence awhile. It felt easy. Like old times.

Then I thought of something. "If Scar wanted to send a message saying he's a badass, why take Ruben's body? Why not leave her where she'll be found?"

"Remember the gatecrasher from Jasper?"

"The guy with the collie?"

"Someone whacked him and his dog and hacked off their ears."

I pictured Ruben's face in the moonlight.

Something cold crawled my spine.

27

The phone woke me from a jumble of disconnected dream fragments. Ryan and I eating pasta. Ruben waving from a bus. Ollie shouting words I couldn't understand. Tank snapping at a raven dive-bombing his head.

"Brennan."

"Hi, Mom."

I was thrilled to hear Katy's voice. My happiness lasted about thirty seconds.

"How are you, sweetheart?"

"You sound sleepy. Oh my God. I forgot. It's only seven out there."

"I was just getting up. Have you talked to your dad? Is Birdie OK?"

"He's great."

Though sun filled the room, frost bordered the edges of the window glass. I closed my eyes and lay back.

"Are you sitting down?"

"Mmm."

"I joined the army."

"You won't believe what I thought you just said." Yawning.

"You heard right. I enlisted."

My lids flew open. I sat straight up. "You what?"

"I report to Fort Jackson on July fifteenth."

I was speechless. Katy was the little girl who liked pink and wore tutus to the dentist.

"Are you there?"

"I'm here."

"Surprised?"

"Stunned. When did you sign up?"

"Last week."

"Do the recruiters allow a grace period? Time to reconsider?"

"Like buyer's remorse?"

"Yes."

"I'm going through with this, Mom. I've thought about it a lot."

"Are you doing this for Coop?"

Webster Aaron Cooperton was Katy's boyfriend. The previous spring he'd been killed while serving as an aid worker in Afghanistan.

"Not *for* him. He's dead."

"Because of him?"

"In part. Coop lived to help people. I don't do shit."

"And the other part?"

"I hate my job. The army will allow me to make new friends. To travel."

To places where people get blown up and shot. I swallowed.

"Coop wasn't in the military," I said.

"But I will be." Resolute.

"Oh, Katy."

"Please don't fight me on this."

"Of course I won't."

"It will be an adventure."

"Just tell me you won't do anything crazy, like volunteering for combat."

"Women can't go into combat."

True. Officially. But I could think of too many ways that women ended up on the front lines. Fighter pilots. MPs. The Marine Corps Lioness program.

"You know what I mean," I said.

"I love you, Mom."

"Katy?"

"Gotta go."

"I love you, sweetheart."

I sat with the phone pressed to my chest, a million images swirling in my head. Katy at her singalong birthday party when she turned two. At a dance recital dressed as an elf. Going to prom in a wrist corsage twice the size of her arm.

I felt—what? Dubious that she'd survive boot camp? Fit in to military life? Anxious that she would? Betrayed that she hadn't discussed her decision with me? Terrified that she'd be sent to a war zone?

All of that. But more.

I felt guilty over my reaction to Katy's news. The military performed an invaluable service. Provided vital defense for the country. Every branch needed capable volunteers. The sons and daughters of others were enlisting. Why not mine?

Because Katy was still my little girl.

The Irish anthem vibrated into my sternum.

I raised the phone to my ear. "Brennan."

"I heard about your little adventure last night."

In no mood for censure from Ollie, I said nothing.

"You're not winning any points with the locals."

"Is that what you called to tell me?"

"I called to tell you I need information. And I need it now. What I don't need is a lot of crap."

I waited, too irritated to speak.

"Describe what went down with Ruben."

I did.

There was a long silence. I guessed Ollie was taking notes.

"I've got to ask you something, Tempe."

His tone put me on alert.

"Did you knock a few back last night?"

"What?"

"You heard me."

"Why in God's name would you ask me that?"

"Chalker says he smelled booze on your breath."

I felt a flash of heat in my cheeks. The minibar Scotch.

"Chalker's a jackass," I said.

"You and I both know you've had your moments."

"Which is why I don't drink."

"Just had to ask."

"Has CSU finished at Sunnyvale?" I changed the subject.

"Two hours ago."

"Have you bagged Scarborough or Unka?"

"We've got Unka. The locals are sweating him. Ryan and I are doubling down on Scar."

Really? Détente?

"Do you think Scar shot Ruben?"

"He's capable of anything." A beat. Then, "A guy from headquarters will come to the hotel around nine. I want you to take him through your version of events."

My version of events?

"Then I want you to return to your room and sit on your pretty little ass. Got it?"

"Gee, Sergeant Hasty, can I go buy that book about diamonds, pretty please?"

"Yeah. You can do that."

I got dressed and grabbed a quick breakfast of French toast and bacon. Nellie Snook was not in the restaurant.

Constable Lake called up from the lobby at nine-fifteen. He was blond and freckled and obviously worked out. He walked with me across the garden and through the woods to the spot where Ruben died.

Even in daylight, I could see no trace of blood. No boot or shoe mark. Not a scrap of physical evidence. Pine needles are resilient. There were no footprints from me or Ryan or Chalker.

"Nothing but needles," Lake said after looking around.

"That's the point. The shooter took the body and cleaned up the scene. Why bother to do that? Why not simply haul ass?"

"Where did the shots come from?"

"Over there." I pointed.

Lake followed me. We did another visual scan.

"No brass," he said.

"Of course not. If he'd take the body, he'd take his casings."

Lake nodded. "Let's check by the road."

Any tire tracks or footprints had long since been obliterated by rain.

Lake looked at me a very long time. Then, "Come in to headquarters and we'll write it up."

Message clear: further analysis of the scene would not take place.

"I'll do that."

Lake shrugged. "These things happen."

Before I could ask his meaning, Lake turned and trudged off toward the hotel.

What things happen? People getting shot? Bodies disappearing?

Drunks taking cops on wild goose chases?

Face flaming, I watched Lake disappear from the trees. He didn't question my hesitation. Didn't look back.

A raven cawed overhead.

Triggered a synapse.

"Tank," I shouted.

Waited.

"Here, Tank."

I retraced my steps, calling the name.

Several squirrels skittered out of my path.

But no dog.

Back in my room, I turned on the television and booted my laptop.

Twenty minutes later, I was unaware of what was on the computer screen. Of what was being broadcast on TV.

Guilt over Ruben. Worry over Katy. Apprehension over the meaning of Lake's odd comment. Jesus. How many people thought I'd been on a bender and imagined the shooting?

And the goddamn dog.

While I was sitting on my pretty little ass, Ollie and Ryan were running down Scar.

Screw that.

I transferred a folder to my purse, threw on a jacket, and descended to the lobby.

Through the front door, I could see the Camry parked in the lot across the driveway. Knowing Ryan's habits, I crossed to the desk. Working it was a woman whose name tag said Nora.

"Excuse me, Nora. Detective Ryan called and asked that I deliver a file ASAP. I know it's unusual, but I wonder if I could have a key to two-oh-seven?"

"I'm sorry, Miss Brennan. We must have explicit permission to let a guest into another guest's room."

"That's just it." I leaned in, an informant with top-secret information. "Detective Ryan is at a crime scene and can't be disturbed."

As I suspected, word of Castain's murder had already fired through the Yellowknife grapevine. With a conspiratorial nod, Nora swiped and handed me a key card.

"Thanks," I whispered.

"I hope it helps," Nora whispered back.

We acknowledged the gravity of her act by locking eyes for a long solemn moment.

"By the way," I said, "is Nellie Snook working today?"

Nora shook her head. "She's off weekends."

The keys were lying on Ryan's bedside table.

I hurried to the Camry, fired up the engine, and swooped down the drive. Game on. It felt damn good.

When I parked on Ragged Ass, Nellie Snook was in her carport changing the litter in a cat pan. She wore a baggy black turtleneck and the same faded jeans she'd worn the day before. I got out and crossed to her.

On seeing me, Snook dropped the bag, bolted through the side door of the house, and tried to slam it. I darted forward and checked the move with one hand.

"Go away," she shouted through the gap.

"Annaliese Ruben is dead."

"I'll call the police."

"Someone shot her."

"You're lying."

"I was there."

The only response was increased pressure on the far side of the door.

"Did Annaliese come back last night?" I asked.

The silence told me my question had hit home.

"I haven't been honest with you, Nellie. It's time I tell you why I've been searching for your sister."

One-handed, I worked the folder from my purse and slipped it through the crack. I heard it hit the floor.

"I'll take my hand away now. Just please, look at what's in that file." I stepped back.

The impact of the door rattled the jamb.

A lock snicked into place.

While waiting, I finished filling the cat pan. Then I secured and set the litter bag by the wall.

Finally, the lock snicked again.

Slowly, the door swung inward.

28

Snook's eyes were pooled in shadow. "Why are you doing this to us?"

"May I come in?"

"What is this?" She raised the manila folder containing pictures of Ruben's dead babies.

"Can we talk about it?"

Vertical lines puckered the skin between her brows. Her gaze drifted past me to the cat pan, then returned to my face. "Did you take these?"

"They're official crime scene photos."

"That wasn't my question."

"I'm not a police officer."

Her chin cocked up.

"I didn't take the pictures. But I was there when they were taken."

I expected to be sent packing. Instead, she stepped back.

I entered a dim little room with an ancient washer/

dryer combo and plastic bins lining one wall. The air smelled of chimney smoke, detergent, and household cleansers.

Snook closed and locked the door and led me into a sun-bright kitchen. Placing the folder on a counter, she offered tea. I accepted.

As Snook filled a kettle from the tap and draped bags into mugs, I looked around.

The kitchen was rimmed by knotty pine cabinets fitted with wrought-iron hardware. Affixed to each door were pictures of animals carefully cut from calendars or magazines. A hawk, an owl, a caribou, a rhino. A World Wildlife Fund calendar hung from a thumbtack on one wall. Canadian Wildlife Federation, Alberta Wilderness Association, Sierra Club, and Federation of Alberta Naturalists stickers covered the refrigerator.

A fishbowl sat on a small gate-leg table below a gingham-curtained window. An enormous tricolor cat dozed on a lattice-back chair beside it.

"I see you're interested in conservation," I said.

"Someone's gotta be."

"Yes."

"Between farming, forestry, mining, and good old-fashioned greed, over half the species in this province are in trouble. Twenty are endangered, two are already gone."

"I'm sorry if I damaged your koi pond."

"That's for frogs. They breed in the spring. I try to help them out."

"Beautiful cat," I said. He wasn't. "What's his name?"

"Murray."

The house was silent. I wondered if Mr. Snook was in another room, straining to hear our conversation.

"I apologize for disturbing you and your husband."

"Don't have a husband."

The kettle whistled.

"You said your husband gave you a key at the Gold Range yesterday."

"I lied."

"Why?"

"My doings are none of your business."

Okey-dokey.

Snook poured boiling water into the mugs. "Six years ago Josiah went out to buy beer and never came back."

"I'm sorry."

"I'm not."

Snook handed me my tea, and we took chairs at a dinette set generations younger than everything else in the room. Laminated wooden seats and tabletop, white arms and legs.

As Snook added sugar to her mug, I studied her face, trying to figure which way to go. She beat me to the punch.

"Is my sister really dead?"

"I'm so sorry."

"Someone shot her?"

"Yes."

"Who?"

"I don't know."

"Why?"

"I don't know."

"Why are you showing that to me?" Tipping her head toward the counter.

I got up and brought the folder to the table. "These are police and coroner's photos."

I flipped opened the cover. A five-by-seven glossy of the bathroom-vanity baby lay exposed. The print caught light from the window as I rotated it to face Snook.

"For the past three years, your sister lived near Montreal in a town called Saint-Hyacinthe. Six days ago she went to a hospital emergency room. Based on her symptoms, the attending physician thought she might have given birth. Since Annaliese denied having a baby or being pregnant, he reported his suspicion to the police. The next morning this newborn was found under the sink in Annaliese's bathroom."

Snook's eyes stayed on her tea.

"Look at it, Nellie."

Snook set her spoon on the table and did as I asked. She took in the sightless eyes, the maggot-filled mouth, the tiny bloated belly. Her shoulders slumped, but she made no comment.

I placed a second five-by-seven on top of the first. "This baby was found in a window seat."

A third. "This one was in an attic."

A fourth. "This one was hidden behind a wall in Annaliese's apartment in Edmonton."

I allowed Snook time to absorb the horrific reality I was dispensing. Finally, she looked at me, her face impassive.

"She doesn't know any better." Flat. "Didn't."

"I understand that now." Gently.

Her eyes settled on a spot halfway to her spoon. Halfway to another place or time, I suspected.

Behind Snook, Murray stretched and mewed softly.

"Do you have any idea who the father or fathers might be?"

"We tried to look out for her. My brother and me. Alice was slow." She gave a soft, mirthless snort. "Annaliese. She liked trying on new names. The doctors had a name for what was wrong with her. I couldn't pronounce it. But she was legally adult. And she hated being told what to do."

"Her death is not your fault," I said.

"Never is."

I thought it an odd comment but said nothing.

"Do the police have any leads?"

"They're questioning one suspect, looking for another. Do you know anything that might help?"

Snook wagged her head slowly.

"Why did Annaliese leave Yellowknife?"

"She was seventeen. There was nothing for her here."

"Was Annaliese into drugs?"

The dark eyes jumped up to mine, burning with resentment. "That's gotta be it, right? The kid was Indian, so naturally, she was a drunk or a junkie. It's what they said about our brother. It's what they'll say about me. Things never change."

"Are you referring to Daryl Beck?"

"You are thorough. I'll give you that."

"You're saying Beck wasn't a user?"

"There was a time Daryl hit the booze and drugs pretty hard. He got off to a rough start. His mother left when he was twelve. Our father didn't give a rat's ass."

"Farley McLeod."

"Only thing Farley gave his kids was a quick shot of sperm and a worthless piece of dirt in the middle of nowhere. His way of dealing with a guilty conscience, I guess."

"You're saying your brother had quit drinking and doing drugs?"

"Daryl was dry the last nine months of his life. He was working on his GED." Again the mirthless snort. "Wanted to make something of himself."

This didn't track. "Horace Tyne said Daryl was a doper."

Snook's brow puckered deeper, but she said nothing.

"I spoke to Tyne briefly after you mentioned his name," I added.

She shook her head at the irony. "So I'm the one set you on Annaliese's trail."

"Actually, I've been on Annaliese's trail since before I met you. You were simply a lead. Tyne said Annaliese lived in his house after Farley died."

"I wasn't in Yellowknife then."

"Tyne's quite a bit older than your sister."

"He is."

"You have any thoughts on that?"

"Besides my brother and me, Horace Tyne's the only person in this town gives a hoot about other creatures. He's a fine man and a hard worker. When he can *find* work."

"Did Annaliese like him?"

"No. But she could be like that."

"Like what?"

Snook hitched one shoulder. "Stubborn. The doctors said her thinking never made it past the fourth grade."

The cat sat up, shot a leg, and began grooming its belly. Which had very little fur.

"Do you know why Annaliese came back to Yellowknife?"

"I think something scared her."

"What?"

"I don't know. She was so tired, mostly she slept. I didn't press, figured we'd have plenty of time to talk." Snook lifted her mug. Blew on it, though the tea was now cold. "Pressing didn't work with my sister."

"Do you know a woman named Susan Forex? Or did Annaliese ever mention her?"

"No."

"Phoenix Miller?"

"No."

"We believe Annaliese went from Edmonton to Montreal with a man named Smith. Signed a lease for an apartment with him."

"Know about two dozen of those."

Good point.

"What about Ralph Trees? Goes by Rocky."

"No."

"Ronnie Scarborough?"

"Why are you asking about these people?"

"They're known associates of your sister." I said the next as gently as possible. "Ronnie Scarborough was her pimp."

Snook set her mug on the table. Held it tight.

"Scarborough is a prime suspect in Annaliese's murder," I added.

"You said you're not a cop. But you talk like one."

"I'm a forensic anthropologist."

"What's that mean?"

"I examine remains that are . . . damaged."

A new pucker suggested she didn't quite get it.

"I help coroners and medical examiners identify the deceased who are no longer recognizable. And I help figure out what happened to them."

She appeared to give that some thought. "The coroner gonna do an autopsy on my sister?"

I leaned in and placed a hand on hers. "Whoever shot Annaliese took her body away."

Her jaw went slack.

"We'll find your sister, Nellie. And the bastards who killed her."

Murray switched legs. His collar bell tinkled softly.

"What happened to Tank?" Snook asked.

"I don't know."

"You said you was there."

"He ran into the woods."

Snook's chin dropped to her chest.

I stared at the top of her head, feeling like a voyeur, wondering if I could be so stoic in the face of such grief.

My gaze drifted to Murray, then to the mismatched fish swimming in the bowl at his side. One was off-white, the other gold. Sunlight sparked the sand and rocks lining the bottom of their world.

A long, silent moment passed.

Then Snook said something that kicked my view of Annaliese's murder on its ass.

29

"Ronnie didn't kill Alice. Annaliese."

"How can you know that?"

"When I said my brother watched out for her, I didn't mean Daryl."

"I don't follow."

"I was talking about Ronnie."

"Wait. What? Scar is your brother?"

"Don't call him that. But yes. I was three when John Scarborough married my mother, five when he adopted me. Ronnie was ten."

Jesus. Was everyone related to everyone in this town?

"Scar *is* a dealer and a pimp," I said.

"I don't ask about his business."

"Uh-huh."

"Ronnie tried to keep my sister clear of all that. Gave her money and a place to live."

"But witnesses say Annaliese worked the streets." I gestured at the folder. "And she did become pregnant."

"My sister was impressionable. And she wanted . . . things."

"Meaning?"

"She saw Ronnie's life and thought it was glamorous. Every time he let down his guard, off she went."

"To turn tricks."

"She was trusting and sweet and craved attention."

"From what I understand, your brother practically rules the underbelly in Edmonton. Why not put it out that Annaliese is off-limits?"

"You think Ronnie can control every lowlife with a dollar and a dick? Excuse my French."

"Where is Scar now?"

"I honestly don't know."

"He was at the Gold Range yesterday. That's why you went there."

She nodded. "But I'm certain Ronnie would never hurt Annaliese."

"Why is your brother in Yellowknife?"

"I called to tell him Annaliese was at my house. He was furious, said she wasn't safe here."

"Why not?"

"I think it had something to do with his business. But like I said—"

"I know. You don't ask."

Back in the Camry, I sat staring at nothing, my emotions a jumble of guilt, confusion, annoyance, and frustration.

Snook's father had abandoned her, then perished in a plane crash. Her brother had died in a fire, her sister in a shooting. All in a short five years. Had showing her pictures of her dead nieces and nephews been too cruel?

Was Snook being honest about Scar? Daryl Beck? Her version was at odds with that of Horace Tyne. Tyne said Beck was a junkie. Was he mistaken? Or was Snook bending the truth, trying to paint both brothers in the best light possible?

I believed Snook knew nothing of Ruben's pregnancies. Her shock at seeing the pictures had been real. As had her pain at hearing of Ruben's murder. I doubted she'd protect her sister's killer.

Even if the gunman was her brother?

Whatever. For me, the hunt was over. I'd come to Yellowknife at the request of the RCMP. At Ollie's insistence. Ruben had been our quarry; now she was dead. At best, I would return to testify one day at the trial of her killer.

Would that ever happen? Would Ruben's murder be given the attention it deserved? Did the cops even believe she was dead? Did they think she'd eventually reappear? If not, that she was just another hooker who'd decided to move on?

I met my own eyes in the rearview mirror. They looked tormented. I'd been obsessed with finding a woman who slaughtered babies. Now I knew that woman was a victim herself. A child victim. Had my obsession refocused on finding her killer?

If Snook was right about Scarborough, then who shot Ruben? Unka? One of his henchmen? Would Ruben's body turn up mutilated in some horrible way? What motive would Unka have? To get at Scar? Did Unka know Ruben was related to Scar?

Was Scar bent on a massacre that would accomplish two things—avenge Ruben's death and wrest control of the local drug trade from Unka?

Every loop circled to the same mortifying point. My past had followed me to Yellowknife. The cops thought I'd been drunk and imagined a bogeyman scene in the woods. I was closed out of the investigation.

Had Ollie sabotaged my reputation? Surely not Ryan.

I remembered Ollie's cocky smirk as he pressed me to his chest in the Edmonton Burger Express. His frown as I slammed my hotel room door in his face.

I also recalled Ollie's voice as he talked of his work with Project KARE. His compassion for the women being slaughtered in Alberta.

Ruben had been on the Project KARE list.

No matter how much he resented me, Ollie would care about a child-woman gunned down in cold blood.

I threw the car into gear. The tires spit gravel as I roared up Ragged Ass.

And practically T-boned an RCMP unit.

I braked so fast my newly scabbed chin hit the wheel.

Ollie flew out of the driver's side of the cruiser. A

figure I assumed to be Ryan stayed in the passenger seat.

Static spit from the unit's radio as Ollie pounded my way.

I got out of my car.

"I told you to stay the fuck in your room." A vein pumped in Ollie's forehead. His cheeks flamed red.

"That shade of angry goes well with your hair."

"We've been looking for your ass all over town."

"You found it."

"You never think rules apply to you, do you, Tempe?"

"I don't cheat at Scrabble."

Ollie hip-planted both hands. "What is it with you people? You got to always be riding some kind of high? That what keeps you off the bottle? Taking risks?"

When irritated, I fire back clever retorts. When angry, truly white-hot furious, I go glacially calm. "You had no right to discuss my past." Cold.

"Is it?"

"Is it what?"

"Past?"

"Ask Ryan what happened."

"He told me about the Scotch."

"So we're clear on that."

"We're not clear on why you're out here when I ordered you to stay in your room."

"Ordered me?" Through gritted molars.

"Last I checked, you don't carry a badge."

I took a breath. Listened to it move in and out of my nose. "I just informed Nellie Snook that her sister is dead."

"You had no authority to do that."

He had me on that.

"I saw it, Ollie. Saw her brains fly out and her body go down."

His glare held.

"You believe me, right?"

He studied my face for so long I thought he wasn't going to answer. Then, "I believe you."

"You will investigate, right? Ruben was on the KARE list."

"Erroneously."

"Regardless, she's now one of your stats."

Ollie spread his feet and hooked his thumbs in his belt.

"The locals are totally focused on Castain," I said. "I don't want Ruben to fall through the cracks."

"It's all related."

"I'm not so sure."

Ollie gave me a what-else-could-it-be blink.

"Snook thought Ruben was running away from something in Edmonton," I said.

"What?"

"She didn't know."

"Uh-huh."

"Snook confirmed that Ruben was mentally challenged," I said.

"How come no one mentioned her being retarded?"

"People just thought she was slow."

"And her being knocked up at least four times: no one noticed that?"

"Ruben was obese and wore baggy clothes. It happens all the time."

"And she was clueless when kids just popped into her toilet?"

"Same answer."

"Why'd she go to the ER?"

"I'm guessing the blood scared her."

"She lied to the doctor."

"*He* probably scared her." Flashbulb image. "In the woods, Ruben said the babies died because she put something bad inside them."

"You found tissue shoved down one kid's throat."

"Maybe that was it."

"Why would she do that?"

"If she did it."

More static burst from the unit's radio.

"Snook swears Scar didn't kill Ruben."

"The scumbag's got no problem setting the kid up as one of his pavement princesses, but he draws the line at shooting her ass?"

"Scar is Snook's adoptive brother."

Ollie's brows shot up in surprise. "Snook is Ruben's half sister. What the fuck does that make Scar to Ruben?"

"I don't know. But Snook swears Scar was trying to keep her out of the life."

Ryan's door opened.

"So Scar learns Ruben's in Yellowknife and comes north to protect her," Ollie said.

"That's Snook's story."

Ryan climbed out and strode toward us.

"So it's not a wasted trip, Scar kills Castain to facilitate his move into slinging dope up here. In revenge, Unka caps Ruben."

It was a scenario I'd considered.

"What else did Snook say?" Ollie asked.

I told him about Daryl Beck.

"What the hell's that got to do with anything?"

"Probably nothing. But I don't like inconsistencies. Would there be a police report on Beck's death?"

"House fire with a fatality? Maybe. More likely, the case rolled straight to the coroner."

Ryan joined us, his face as tense as I'd ever seen it. "They've got Scarborough."

"Where?" Ollie asked.

"Stanton Territorial Health Authority. DOA with two slugs in his brain."

30

Ollie went really fast, using his siren. Ryan and I drove at a more sedate speed in the Camry.

We agreed there was little point in going to Stanton. But it wasn't far. And we had nothing else to do.

On the way, I told Ryan about Katy.

"That's terrific," he said.

"She could be deployed to a war zone," I said.

"She'll be fine," he said.

I updated him on everything I'd learned from Snook. Then we rode in silence. I was getting used to it.

We were right about the uselessness of our going to the hospital.

Entering the ER, we passed Rainwater on his way out. He told us that Scar's body was already en route to Edmonton and that Ollie had left for the scene. As he filled us in on details, I kept thinking he might as well be describing the Castain hit.

Scar was nailed while leaving the apartment of a woman named Dorothea Slider. She saw zip. The neighbors saw zip. The only difference was the level of boldness. Scar's drive-by took place in broad daylight.

Pointedly ignoring me, Rainwater asked Ryan if he wanted to help run down a tip on Unka. Ryan gave me the courtesy of a raised-eyebrow query.

I held out my hand.

Ryan dropped the keys onto my palm. Behind him, across a tiled lobby, I noticed Maureen King from the Coroners Service talking on a cell phone. She was smaller than my perception of her standing over Castain, maybe five-two, 110 pounds.

She had her back to us. She wore black jeans, a white turtleneck, and the same windbreaker as the night before.

King switched ears and hiked a large black purse onto her other shoulder. As her body turned, she noticed me. Face registering surprise, she gestured me over. I crossed to her.

King kept talking but raised one finger in a "hold on" gesture. A few more words, then she disconnected and dropped the phone into her purse.

I held out a hand. "Temperance Brennan."

"I know who you are." Maybe smiling.

We shook.

King was also older than I'd thought, probably late forties. Her hair was muddy blond and started too far back on her head. She tried to hide her expansive brow with long bangs, a mistake given their limpness and paucity.

"You're the anthropologist."

"You're the coroner."

"Deputy chief."

"Forensic."

We exchanged a grin. Then King's face went serious. "You fall off, you get back on."

"Excuse me?" I had no idea her meaning.

"You feel the need, I could find us a meeting."

Heat geysered up the front of my throat and spread across my cheeks. "I don't know what rumors you've heard, Ms. King, but—"

"Maureen. And don't bullshit me. I'm the empress of bullshit. Can spot it coming from three miles out."

I said nothing.

"I'm eight years dry. But still I have those days when I want to drive to another town, find a dark little bar where no one knows me, and erase the whole freakazoid world for a while."

Her words hit me like a Zamboni. Not because they weren't true. They were. I knew exactly what she meant. But this time I wasn't guilty. I hadn't sought escape, had downed the Scotch only at Ryan's insistence.

"Does the whole freakazoid world think I was drunk?"

"Some do."

"I saw Annaliese Ruben murdered. She was

standing six feet from me. Afterward I took a shot of Scotch to calm myself."

"That's another reason we do it."

"Yes."

We locked eyes. Hers were as green as mine.

"Do you believe me?" I asked.

"Sergeant Hasty says you're solid."

Does he?

"I understand you know Nellie Snook," she said. "Lives on Ragged Ass."

"She tells an interesting tale."

King gave a go-ahead gesture with one hand.

I explained the dead babies, the relationship between Snook and Ruben, Scarborough and Snook. I relayed what Snook had said about Scarborough protecting Ruben. She listened without interrupting.

"Now Ruben and Scarborough are both dead," I concluded.

"Runs in the family, I'm afraid."

"That's cold." I remembered Snook's comment about anglophone attitudes toward aboriginals.

"Don't mean it to be. I'm just stating a fact. Snook's other half brother also died violently."

"Daryl Beck."

"Yes."

"Was Beck drinking or doping at the time of his death?"

"Daryl had his problems."

"You knew him?"

"I might have seen him now and again."

Her eyes held steady on mine. I knew what she was saying. By not saying. She and Beck had attended the same meetings. She was respecting the A.A. bond of privacy.

"Did the Coroners Service investigate Beck's death?" I asked.

"We did. You've got to understand, Beck spent a lot of years waking up in his own vomit or sleeping off benders in the tank. Everyone assumed he got wasted that night and passed out while smoking."

"The chief coroner ruled his death accidental," I guessed.

"He did." Something in King's voice suggested I'd struck a chord.

"Do you disagree?"

King smiled in a way that imparted no humor. "There wasn't much of Daryl left to examine, and we're not exactly flush with anthropologist help up here. Besides, who'd want to kill the town drunk?"

"Snook says Beck was working toward a high school GED."

"I could verify that." She hesitated. Decided. "That call I just finished was Nellie Snook. Seems you made quite an impression."

"That's news to me."

"Yeah. I heard about the frog pond."

You gotta love small towns.

"Why did Snook phone you?"

"She wants me to dig her brother up."

"What?" I was stunned. "Why? Does she suspect murder? Arson?"

"Snook's always questioned the coroner's finding of accidental death. She knows you're here, and she understands what you do."

"You have the authority to order an exhumation?"

"At the request of the family."

This was insane. I'd gone from dead babies to a murdered hooker to a possible drug war. Now I was being asked to examine a corpse four years in the ground.

What the hell? It was better than sitting on my thumbs. I could be useful and keep the heat on the Ruben investigation at the same time.

And prove my sobriety.

"Can you provide a facility?" I asked.

"What do you need?"

"What will I be looking at?"

"The remains fit into one plastic tub."

"That doesn't sound promising."

"No. What do you need?"

"I can only do a preliminary evaluation. Any microscopy or specialty analysis will have to be done at my lab."

"Understood."

"Not much," I said. "A worktable. Gloves, masks, aprons. A means of magnification. Calipers. X-ray capability."

She pulled out a small spiral and began a list. "I'll need to obtain forms signed by the next of kin. Contact the cemetery for burial location. Round up a crew." She scribbled as she spoke. "Arrange transport for the coffin." She looked around. "We can do the analysis here. It'll take some time." She jammed the tablet in her purse and pulled out her phone.

I handed her one of my cards. "My mobile number."

"Snook can't afford your fee. And our budget doesn't allow for external consults."

"This one's on me."

"Let's dig him up," she said.

"Let's dig him up," I said.

Normally, the justice system moves at the pace of continental drift. By "time," I assumed King meant a couple of days.

I underestimated the sheer doggedness of Yellowknife's deputy chief coroner.

I was downing lo mein at the Red Apple on Franklin when my iPhone rang.

"Can you be at Lakeview Cemetery at six o'clock?"

"Give me directions."

"Take Old Airport Road north out of town for about a mile. Hang a right toward Jackfish Lake. You can't miss it."

"I'll be there."

I looked at my watch: three-twenty. King and I had parted only forty minutes earlier.

Pure pit bull.

I loved this woman.

I called Ryan to tell him what I was doing. He sounded surprised but rendered no opinion. Mostly, he sounded frustrated. "The tip on Unka was a bust. The asshole's still in the wind."

"I don't suppose Ruben's body has turned up."

"No."

"Is anyone looking for it?"

"I'll keep you in the loop."

At the Book Cellar, I bought a volume on the search for diamonds in the Arctic. Another on Canadian diamond mining. Then I returned to the Explorer.

Before going upstairs, I went into the woods for another go at Tank. Though I called and called, the dog made no appearance.

I stood a moment, breathing the odor of the dark, sticky pitch running through the trees. Who was I kidding? The dog was dead.

Feeling a deep ache, I returned to my room.

Four p.m.

I dug out my warmest clothes and set them on a chair.

Four-ten.

To kill time, I propped myself in bed and flipped open the book on mining. Though pumped about the exhumation, I could feel the effect of my recent lack of sleep. As a safeguard, I set my phone alarm to wake me at five-twenty.

On the book's inside back cover was a map of Nunavut and the Northwest Territories.

All my life, I've been fascinated by atlases and globes. As a kid, I'd close my eyes and arrow into a random spot with one finger. Then I'd read the place-name and imagine the exotic people who lived in that town or island or desert.

I was hooked.

And shocked.

I thought Yellowknife sat at the top of the planet. Not even close. There was a whole lot of geography north of the 60th parallel.

Umingmaktok. Kugluktuk. Resolute. Fort Good Hope. The names were a tip-off to the clash of cultures that had taken place in the region. And we all know the final score on that one.

Again I thought of Snook's bitterness over lingering prejudice toward aboriginal peoples. Wondered if she was right.

My room had two options for temperature control, neither dictated by the broken switch on the plastic thermostat half attached to the wall. The system's current choice was Tropic of Cancer.

My lids grew heavy. My head dropped, snapping me awake.

I refocused on the map. I found the Ekati and Diavik diamond mines, practically hugging the border between Nunavat and NWT. To the southeast was Snap Lake and south of that, Gahcho Kué.

My thoughts drifted.

Gahcho Kué. Formerly Kennady Lake. The new mine proposed by De Beers.

My lids again sought each other.

An image of Horace Tyne floated up from somewhere.

Horace Tyne opposed the Gahcho Kué project. Claimed its existence would threaten the caribou.

I saw a herd.

A sign saying *Wildlife Preserve.*

A sticker from the Alberta Wilderness Association.

A pair of fish, one off-white, one gold.

Gold.

Horace Tyne. The Giant gold mine.

Church bells bonged.

My eyes flew open.

Five-twenty.

I threw on my sweatshirt and jacket, laced on my boots, and dropped my iPhone into my backpack.

Time to unearth Daryl Beck.

31

One advantage of summer in the far north: twenty-plus hours of daylight. The sky was noon-bright as I drove the squiggle of road out to Lakeview.

Several cars and pickups were already parked in the lot. A kid sat behind the wheel of a hearse, playing a game on a handheld device. He did not look up as I pulled in beside him.

One disadvantage of summer in the far north: man-eater insects. Mosquitoes struck the instant I left the Camry, whining around me to telegraph the happy news of another food source.

Lakeview Cemetery had old-style markers, not just ground-level slabs for the convenience of mowers. Some were homemade: a wooden chair, a pair of carved elk or caribou horns, an engraved paddle. Others were more traditional headstones, featuring crosses or angels holding flowers or harps.

I spotted King to the right of a grave surrounded

by a white picket fence. At her side was a man in a tweed jacket several sizes too large for his frame. An idle backhoe sat ten feet beyond them, bucket in the upright and locked position.

I started toward King and her companion, slapping away predators the size of pelicans. Though damp, the evening was reasonably warm. The air smelled of dead grass, moldy wood, and freshly turned earth. *Eau de exhumation.*

King's crew consisted of six men, all native. They'd removed the topsoil and gone down three feet with the backhoe, then jumped in with spades. They stood shoulder-deep in the hole, shoveling dirt from around Beck's coffin and tossing it onto the ground above.

King introduced the tweed guy as Francis Bullion and explained that he was with the Department of Community Services. Bullion had confirmed the location of Beck's grave. We shook hands. He had gray hair, rimless glasses, and a very small head.

"Everyone was here, so I figured we might as well start," King said.

"I'm good with that."

"This is so extraordinary." Bullion sounded like a bird. A very excited one.

I smiled at Bullion, then refocused on King. "You move fast."

"People need work. Snook was eager."

"As was I." Bullion, chirpy. "I don't mind that today is Saturday. Not at all."

"Thank you, sir," I said.

"I saw this on television. It was just like this."

"I'm sure you did."

The crew was equally eager. And efficient. They had the coffin out by seven-forty. Loaded into the hearse by eight. Bullion offered to hang with the team. King thanked him and sent him on his way.

King and I followed the hearse to Stanton. A nurse and two male orderlies met us at a loading dock in back. They, King, the kid driver, and I wrestled the coffin onto a hospital gurney. Then it was just us girls.

The nurse's name was Courtney. She had long blond hair, hazel eyes, and looked about twenty. She addressed King by first name, so I assumed they were acquainted. Or related.

Courtney led us to a large room entered through swinging double doors. It had a green tile floor, buzzing fluorescents overhead, a wall clock with a second hand that moved in noisy little hops, and a stainless-steel tub and counter.

A second gurney had been centered on the tile. The items I'd requested lay on a tray on the counter.

We positioned the casket along one wall. It was an inexpensive model, probably eighteen-gauge steel. The exterior was pink, the hardware embellished with orchids. It was in good shape, given its four years underground.

Already the room had taken on the odor of the coffin and its contents. Rusting metal. Rotting fabric.

Moist earth. I noted none of the sickly organic smell associated with most disturbed burials.

King and I removed our outerwear. She set up a case file card and shot pictures. Then we all gloved and tied aprons behind our waists and necks.

I held out a hand. King handed me a metal implement. I stepped to the coffin and opened the locking mechanism. The upper portion of the lid lifted easily.

The plastic tub was snugged between mildewed and badly stained pink velvet cushions once marketed as an "eternal-rest adjustable bed."

King shot more photos.

I transferred the tub to the second gurney.

Courtney watched with very large eyes. She'd yet to say one word to me.

I lifted the lower portion of the casket lid. King offered a flashlight. I checked the coffin's interior, removing padding and fabric, probing creases and recesses with my fingers.

Found nothing.

I looked at King.

"Let's pop her," she said.

I pried off the lid of the tub.

King wasn't kidding. The fire had left little of Daryl Beck. More likely, those who'd processed the scene hadn't possessed the skill to recognize or the patience to recover badly burned bone.

The tub held only the thicker, more robust parts

of the skeleton. Or those portions protected by large muscle masses. I saw no vertebrae or ribs. No scapula, clavicle, or sternum. Nothing from the face, hands, or feet.

Every element had suffered extensive heat damage. The skull had exploded, then the individual fragments had burned. Only two small bits of mandible remained, each from the area near the angle of the jaw. The ends were missing from the six long bones that had survived. The pelvis consisted of two charred masses, once the hip sockets, and a hunk of sacrum.

I began arranging the bones in anatomical order. Cranium. Right arm. Left arm. Right leg. Left leg. Straightforward. Until I came to the pelvis.

Then I stopped.

Stunned.

Grabbing the lens from the counter, I reexamined each carbonized ilia under magnification.

No way.

I held them side by side. Reoriented them. Did it again. Again.

No freakin' way!

"What?" King picked up on my agitation.

I'd left the jaw fragments for last. Ignoring her question, I studied first one, then the other. The gonial angle. The foramen. The mylohyoid groove. The truncated bits of ascending ramus and dental arcade.

No freakinsonofabitching way!

But there was no question.

Palms sweaty inside my latex gloves, I set one pelvic fragment and one jaw fragment off to the side, then added their counterparts to my reconstruction.

"What does that mean?" King asked.

I pointed to the isolated fragments. "These are portions of jaw and pelvis. Both come from the right side of the body." I pointed to the corresponding fragments in the partial skeleton I'd created. "These fragments are from identical locations. They also come from the right side of the body."

"Meaning?" Her expression said she already knew the answer.

"There are two people here."

"You're shitting me."

"How was Daryl identified?"

"Mostly context. It was his house. His bike was there. A neighbor heard him pull in that night, never heard him leave. Said he would have heard, since the bike was noisy as hell."

"That was it? No dental records?"

"Daryl wasn't big on oral hygiene. Couldn't have afforded a dentist if he'd wanted one."

The lights hummed. The clock ticked.

"So which one is Daryl?" King was staring at the gurney.

"Both are male," I said.

"How do you know?"

"There's enough detail." I lifted the two hunks of ilia. "Both sciatic notches are deep and narrow." I pointed to a slice of crescent that had survived on each fragment. "These rough areas are the points where these ilia articulated with their respective sacra. Neither surface is elevated; both are flush with the surrounding bone. And neither has a groove along its edge."

"Male traits."

"Yes."

I noticed that Courtney had edged closer. "Would you like to see?" I asked her. She nodded. I showed her the features I'd described.

"There's a little of the acetabulum left on each fragment. The hip socket. Eyeballing the partial diameters, I can say that one man was larger than the other."

I got the calipers from the counter. The others watched as I took measurements to confirm my suspicion.

"Can you say anything about age?" King asked.

"A little." I held a fragment in each hand. "Notice that the larger man's articular surface is billowy and that the bone looks granular. That of the smaller man appears smoother and denser." Oversimplified but close enough.

I looked up. King and Courtney were clearly baffled.

I set the fragments on the table, got the flashlight, and killed the overheads. "Watch this."

I directed the beam horizontally across each surface. The subtle indentations appeared as transverse shadows on that of the larger man.

Courtney spotted the difference first. "The bigger guy has furrows. The smaller guy has none."

Maybe King saw it, maybe not. "What does it mean?" she asked.

"The bigger man was younger, probably in his twenties. The smaller man was more likely in his forties. These are very rough estimates. This aging technique only allows for broad ranges, and only a portion of each surface is observable."

"Daryl was twenty-four," King said. "A six-footer."

The hopping hand ticked off seconds.

"So who's the other guy?" King spoke aloud, more to herself than to us.

I raised both palms in a "who knows" gesture.

"Can you determine race?" King asked.

"Very unlikely. When exposed to extreme heat, fluids in the brain expand, causing the skull to explode. Then the fragments burn. That's what happened here."

"Did anyone go missing at the time of the fire?"

Good question, Nurse Courtney.

"You two good here if I leave to check on that?" King asked.

Courtney and I nodded.

"It's all so black and gray and crumbly." Courtney was staring at the partial skeleton. "How can you be sure the bones are sorted right?"

Nurse Courtney nails another one. Because of a preconceived mind-set, I'd made the amateur mistake of assuming the remains represented a single individual.

I turned on the lights and studied one jaw fragment under magnification. It was toast. I studied the other.

And felt a little flip in my gut.

"Hot diggety."

"Zippy whiz bang?"

I looked up. We both smiled.

"This fragment retains about two centimeters of the posterior end of the dental arcade, including two molar sockets. I may see root fragments down in them."

"Shazam!"

"Nurse Courtney, you're on for X-ray."

She did everything but snap a salute.

I got the tray, transferred the jaw fragments, and instructed her on the angles I needed. "While you do that, I'll reexamine every bone. Then you can shoot films of both individuals."

The skull fragments were mostly parietal and occipital. All edges and surfaces were fried. Not a single ectocranial or endocranial detail remained. Only DNA would sort them out. I doubted any had survived the fire.

Based on size, I was able to separate what remained of the midshaft portions of the long bones. A femur, tibia, and ulna stayed with Daryl. A femur and tibia transferred to the smaller man. A humerus went with the unassigned cranial fragments.

I was recording observations in my notebook when Courtney returned, pushing a portable light box. The jaw fragments sat atop small brown envelopes on the lower shelf.

"I think you were right." Electric with excitement. "And I think the older guy had dental work."

I slid the films free, clamped the first onto the box, and thumbed the switch. The fragments lit up in shades of gray. The one on the right showed nothing but amorphous trabecular bone. Courtney pointed to it. "That's Daryl. The younger guy."

The older man's fragment had more of the dental arch, including the sockets I'd spotted. They appeared as dark indentations in the spongy gray. Deep in each was a tiny white cone, a root fragment. Running vertically up the center of each cone was a brilliant white filament.

"Those are root canals, right? That could get him identified?"

She was correct. On both points.

That wasn't what stopped the breath in my throat.

32

The fragment looked like it was experiencing a blizzard. A cloud of white dots stippled the lower mandibular border. Outliers spread across the angle and up the ascending ramus.

"What is it?" Courtney asked.

"I want you to x-ray every bone." I kept my voice calm. "First Beck." I pointed to the partial skeleton. "Then the other man." I pointed to the pile containing the chunk of ilia, the femur, and the tibia. "Then those." I pointed to the cranial fragments and the unassigned humerus. "Do them separately. Do not mix them up. Got it?"

"Got it."

"Start with Beck." I removed Beck's jaw fragment and placed his other bones on the tray.

When Courtney had gone, I phoned King. She picked up right away.

"The older vic was shot," I said.

"No way."

"There was lead snowstorm on the X-ray of his jaw."

Silence.

"Very fine particles dispersed as a result of a high-velocity rifle round passing through the body," I explained.

"Like a hunting rifle?"

"That's my thinking," I said.

"Got a few thousand of those babies around here. What about Beck?"

"We're doing a full-body series. I'm also checking the bones I shifted to the older vic. You finding anything?"

"I pulled Beck's death certificate. DOD is March fourth, 2008. I checked MP reports for that entire year, moving forward from that date. No one fits your profile."

"The older guy had root canals on a couple of his lower molars, probably the second and third. We should run the film past a forensic odontologist, get it right before coding the dentals into CPIC."

"You got one on your speed dial?"

"I do. But he's in Montreal, and it's the middle of the night there." And flexibility was not one of Marc Bergeron's attributes. I didn't say it.

"Beck's been dead a while," King said. "He can wait a while longer."

Using my iPhone, I took photos of the older man's dental work, then e-mailed them to Bergeron. He'd have them when I called in the morning.

I looked at my watch. Twelve-ten. It *was* morning.

Figuring Ollie was tied up with Scar's murder investigation, I called Ryan. He and Rainwater were at a bar on Highway 4, following another lead on Unka. I could hear music in the background, the noise of a lot of people in a small space.

"Rainwater thinks we're being played." Ryan sounded as tired as I felt. "He's ordered a sweep, plans to sweat whoever gets caught in the net."

I told Ryan about the commingled remains and the lead scatter.

"Both were capped?"

"I'll know soon. The older vic had a couple of root canals."

"You plan to call Bergeron?"

"Tomorrow. I've sent him pics."

"Good thinking."

"Keep me in the loop," I said.

"Ditto."

Courtney returned as I was disconnecting. While she x-rayed the rest of the older man, I viewed Beck's postcranial films.

His femur and pelvic fragment were blizzard all the way. That answered one question. But generated more.

Had Beck and the older man both been murdered? If so, why?

Had one shot the other, then turned the gun on himself? If so, why? And which way around?

Had Beck and his companion fought following a night of drugs, alcohol, or both? Was Snook wrong about her half brother's new commitment to sobriety?

The murder-suicide scenario wasn't persuasive. Face-to-face shootings rarely involve a rifle. I made a note to ask if remnants of a weapon had been found at the scene.

Had Beck or the older man torched the house? Had someone else? Was the fire accidental?

Who *was* the older guy? Why had no one reported him missing? Was he not local?

I flipped to a blank page in my notebook and began a time line.

Farley McLeod died in 2007, Daryl Beck in 2008, Annaliese Ruben and Ronnie Scarborough yesterday. All were connected by kinship. Were their deaths connected? How?

Castain was also murdered yesterday. He wasn't a relative. Where did he fit in?

Castain and Scarborough were taken out in drivebys. Ruben was shot by a man on foot, almost certainly with a rifle. Beck and his buddy were killed with a hunting rifle.

Had the same weapon been used in all five shootings? Had the drive-bys been by pistol?

McLeod went down in a Cessna. His body was never recovered. Ruben's body was also missing. Was this coincidental? Significant?

I felt agitated. Too many questions and too few

answers. So complicated.

Too complicated.

And such a high body count. Even excluding the babies.

Courtney returned with the cranial fragments and X-rays.

Snowing on some, not on others. I saw no feature to allow assignment as Beck or non-Beck.

Courtney looked at me, eager for the inside poop.

"Thank you so much for your help." I smiled an ultra-sincere smile. "I couldn't have done this without you."

She opened her mouth to speak.

"Do you have something I can use to keep the bones separated?"

She hurried off, hurt darkening her hazel eyes.

I was placing Beck's bones in the tub when she returned with two cotton towels. I wrapped the cranial fragments in one, the older man's remains in the other, tucked the bundles next to Beck, and pressed the lid into place.

"And the casket?" A wee bit petulant.

"Call," I said. "The funeral home will collect it. And again: thank you so much. Maureen will be very pleased."

Courtney nodded, trying but failing to hide her disappointment.

"I'm sorry. You know I can't share details of an investigation."

"I know."

"Please keep everything you've seen here confidential."

"Of course."

"You'd make an excellent forensic nurse, Courtney."

"Honestly?"

"If you'd like, I'll send information."

"Yes, please. And . . . anytime."

"First I'll explain what I see. Then you'll explain why I'm looking at it on a beautiful Sunday morning."

Marc Bergeron hadn't given me the same time-zone consideration I'd given him. His call blasted me awake at six-forty-five.

"Do you have the images?" Booting my laptop.

"I've transferred them to my computer."

I pictured Bergeron squinting through grimy lenses, dandelion hair backlit by the screen.

"Are they clear enough to determine which teeth have the root canals?" I asked.

"They will do. I assume the issue is identity."

"The fragment was recovered from a house fire. It's from the right posterior, near the mandibular angle."

"I see that."

I'd also downloaded the images to my Mac. During the pause that ensued, I opened the file so we were looking at the same thing.

"I also see evidence of a gunshot wound," Bergeron said.

"Yes."

I waited quite a long time.

"From the positioning of the sockets relative to the ramus, their sizes, and the recurve and compression of the roots themselves, I'd say the mesial tooth is forty-seven and the distal tooth is forty-eight."

I'd been expecting him to say thirty-one and thirty-two. Then I remembered. CPIC uses the FDI dental scoring system, NCIC the universal system.

"The right second molar and wisdom tooth," I said.

"Though small, as is common, the third molar is well formed and fully erupted. Whatever necessitated the root canal came later. It's quite unusual to see one in a third molar."

"Terrific. Thanks. Listen, the coroner is striking out with MP reports here in Yellowknife. Can you get this into CPIC for me?"

"Is this a lab case?" Bergeron was a stickler for rules.

"Yes." In the very broadest sense, true. Three of Ruben's babies were found in Quebec. My involvement had started there.

I could practically hear Bergeron frown.

"I'd have Ryan do it, but I'm afraid he'd screw up the coding," I said.

"Does Dr. LaManche know of this case?"

"He does." I made a note to e-mail the chief immediately.

"Please give me the details."

"All we know is that the victim was male, in his forties, and not overly large. He died in March 2008."

"That's not much."

"It's not."

"If the system finds a match, we must request original records."

"Of course."

After shooting a note to LaManche, I grabbed my new books and headed downstairs.

Another dawn in the Trader's Grill. My fellow diners were an elderly couple all atwitter about wildflowers.

I didn't expect to see Snook and didn't. I ordered eggs and toast, then checked e-mail. Mostly out of boredom. It was too soon to hear from Bergeron, and I doubted King had learned much since midnight.

I was opening the book on Fipke and his pals when Ryan appeared. He looked like hell. Baggy eyes. Tension in his jaw that made him look gaunt. He spotted me and crossed to my table.

"Company?"

"Sure."

Ryan dropped into the other chair and looked around. "Glad I found an empty seat."

"Apparently, it will be hopping later."

Ryan cocked a brow.

"The place is famous for Sunday brunch."

"Don't they do brunch every day?"

"I'm just reporting what I read."

The waitress brought my eggs and poured Ryan coffee. He ordered what I was eating, and she left.

"Haven't seen much of you," he said.

"Things aren't going as we'd hoped." *And the locals think I'm hitting the sauce.* I didn't say it.

"You show me yours, I'll show you mine."

I smiled. It was our code for sharing info on cases. In the good days.

I briefed him on the exhumation and outlined my conversation with Bergeron.

He told me Rainwater had some of Unka's thugs cooling their heels at G Division. He and Ollie were heading over there shortly.

Updates exchanged, we sat, avoiding each other's eyes.

Ryan's breakfast came. He ate it.

Across the restaurant, the two gray-hairs pored over their book of flora. My gaze drifted to them. I thought, *How happy they look. How perfectly matched.*

I felt Ryan's fingers graze the back of my hand. They ran to my wrist, rested at my watch. My skin tingled in their wake. Startled, I looked over at him.

His eyes were on my face. I met them.

So impossibly blue. And tormented, like my own staring back from the rearview mirror.

"Lily's in jail," he said softly.

"She's using again?" I was shocked. "She was doing so well."

"The kid's a born actress."

"Oh, Ryan. I'm so sorry. How . . . ?" I let the question hang.

"She reconnected with the creep she was seeing last

year. He provided a few freebies, then she was on her own. Security nailed her boosting a smartphone at the Carrefour Angrignon."

"The mall out in LaSalle?"

"Yeah. This time there was nothing I could do."

Ryan looked so dejected, I wanted to wrap him in my arms and hold him close. To feel the scratch of his stubble against my cheek. To breathe the scent of his cologne.

Instead I sat, picturing in my mind the mixed blessing that was Lily. Recalling Ryan's account of her entrance into his life.

Lily's mother, Lutetia, was an Abaco Islander living in Nova Scotia during Ryan's disastrous undergrad days. The two weren't exactly lovers, but they were very, very compatible.

After getting knifed in a bar fight, Ryan changed allegiance from the dark side and joined the SQ. He and Lutetia went their separate ways but hooked up years later for a bonus round of enchantment.

Enter Lily.

Wanting to return to her Caribbean home and fearing Ryan might try to stop her, Lutetia didn't share the fact of her pregnancy. Though mother and daughter returned to Canada twelve years later, Mama opted not to correct that omission.

Fast-forward to the inevitable.

A few years back, Lily showed up at Daddy's door. She was seventeen, resentful, and angry as hell. And, it turned out, addicted to heroin.

Again and again Ryan got Lily into rehab. Again and again she went back on the junk.

Like every father, Ryan wanted to shield his child from pain, to protect her from every evil in the world. Lily made that impossible, and the toll on Ryan was heavy. One casualty was our relationship.

No matter. Ryan loved his little girl with every fiber of his being.

Dear God. I was worried about Katy joining the army, and Ryan's daughter had resumed shooting poison into her veins. I was mortified.

"Is there anything I can do?" I asked.

"Listen?"

"Of course I will. You know I'm always here."

"Where?" A ghost of the old Ryan grin.

"What?"

"Yellowknife? The Explorer? Trader's Grill?"

Eye roll. "You know what I mean."

"I do." Ryan stroked my hand, then gestured at the books. "Planning to invest in a diamond mine?"

"I'm trying to educate myself on the history of the place."

"What have you learned?" Ryan signaled for a refill.

"I've learned why bling is so bloody expensive. First you have to find the diamonds. Then you have to do a feasibility study to determine how much the mine will cost and how to build it. Then there's the red tape: environmental agreements, land-use permits, water licenses, impact-benefit agreements, socioeconomic agreements. Approval involves dealing with federal, territorial, and aboriginal governments, regulatory agencies, landowners—everyone from the local farmer right up to the pope."

The waitress poured Ryan's coffee.

"Then you have to build the mine, which, in this climate, is a nightmare. The sites are so isolated that all personnel and supplies have to be flown in or transported over winter roads."

"Ice road truckers!"

"Do you know what it costs to operate an ice road?"

"I do not."

I flipped to a page in my book. "Lupin runs for almost six hundred kilometers, from Tibbitt Lake, east of Yellowknife, to the Lupin mine site in Nunavut. Construction and maintenance cost roughly six-point-five million dollars annually." I looked at Ryan. "And the ice roads are only open maybe ten weeks a year."

"Big bucks."

"That's just one budget item. Landing strips, power stations, machine shops, sewage and waste disposal, water treatment plants, telephone networks, storage buildings, offices, processing plants. And the workers can't exactly drive home each night. The mines have to provide housing, food, recreational facilities. A lot of the miners work two-week rotations. That's a long time to have nothing to do. Listen to this."

I gave him no opening to opt out.

"Ekati construction cost nine hundred million dollars. Diavik cost one-point-three billion—that's *billion*—dollars. They drained a whole damn lake!"

"Isn't that the kind of thing that infuriates Mr. Squeeters? By the way, I saw him yesterday. When Rainwater and I drove past, Tyne was pulling out of the Giant gold mine."

"I thought it was closed."

"It is. But there are arsenic issues."

"Arsenic?'

"A by-product of gold production. When the mine shut down, the owners walked, leaving a few zillion tons of the stuff."

"Don't mining companies have to fork over millions up front to cover the cost of cleanup before they're granted permits to operate?"

"Ah, the good old days." Ryan knocked back the last of his coffee. "Listen, if you're really interested in this stuff, Rainwater says his great-uncle works at the mining recorder's office, knows everything there is to know on the subject."

"Sure, I'll pop right in on a Sunday."

"Rainwater says the old coot practically lives there. He's a retired geology prof, and the government cooked up some sort of make-work position for him after he retired. Or something like that."

"You and Rainwater going to be pen pals when this is over?"

Ryan raised palms and brows. "What? We've been

thrown together a lot. Gassing passes the time." He stood. "Can't let the grass grow. Keep me in the—"

"Got it. Loop."

So. Lily had blown rehab. Was that the reason Ryan had been so aloof with me? So snarky with Ollie? Not petty jealousy but anguish over his daughter?

My phone cut me off in midponder. Bergeron. I clicked on.

"I have a name for you."

33

"The descriptors generated only one match. Probably because a root canal in a third molar is extremely uncommon. Eric Skipper, white male, forty-four, residing in Brampton, Ontario at the time of his disappearance."

"When did Skipper go into the system?"

"March eighteenth, 2008. Descriptors were provided by Dr. Herbert Mandel of Brampton."

"Did you contact him?"

"I did. Dr. Mandel informed me that Mr. Skipper had a great deal of dental work, including extractions, restorations, and other root canals. He is sending the record by FedEx."

"Who filed the MP report?"

I heard paper rustle. "Mr. Skipper's wife, Michelle. Dr. Mandel says she remains a patient."

"Did you get her number?"

Bergeron read it to me, and I jotted it down.

"Anything else?"

"I'm an odontologist, Dr. Brennan. Not a detective. From you, I will need the actual X-rays."

"Coming your way."

"I will call when the ID is confirmed."

"Thank you, Dr. Bergeron. I owe you one."

"You do, indeed."

I called Maureen King. Voice mail.

It was a nice day. Nothing but sun and temperatures projected to soar into the upper fifties. I decided to visit the coroner's office.

"Hey, old lady."

I was on the walk leading to the Searle Building. I stopped and turned.

Binny was across Forty-ninth Street, straddling his bike on the courthouse lawn. The tuque had been replaced by a baseball cap sitting low on his brows. Same sweats. Same sneakers.

"Hey, bozo," I said.

"Bozo? That the best you can do?" Underlying the bravado was a tension I hadn't sensed in our previous encounter.

"Good morning, Mr. Binny Mind-Your-Own-Business."

"You remember good, for a granny."

"I'm pretty busy right now."

"At least you ain't covered in doodah."

"Nice turn of phrase."

Below the bill's shadow, I saw Binny chew his lip.

"Do you have something to tell me?"

"I never got no pancakes." Eyes skittish.

I reached into my purse and waggled the muffin I'd pilfered from the breakfast buffet. I know. But meals had been patchy. I wanted backup.

Binny crossed to me and took my offering. His fingers looked small and brown, digging the cake from its little paper cup. There was a crescent of dirt under each of his nails. When finished with the muffin, he wadded the wrapper and cocked his arm.

"Whoa, there, twiglet. Thought it was cool to respect the environment."

He looked confused. Then, "You talking about the crazy old geezer and his caribou?"

I raised both brows.

"Pffff."

"So I should lay off the caribou, but it's cool if I dump my trash in your bed?"

I held out a palm. Binny rolled his whole head but dropped the wrapper in it.

Two women passed us on their way into the building. One was young, pushing a stroller. The other had curly white hair and clutched her purse as if bandits hid behind every bush.

"You need to watch your back, old lady." Binny spoke quietly, face angled away from mine.

"What do you mean?"

"You got a knack for making people mad."

"What people?"

He shrugged a bony shoulder. "I'm just sayin'."

"Saying what? You have to make yourself clear."

"I don't have to make myself nothing no old hag says."

"Are you talking about Tom Unka and his goons?"

"I ain't saying who."

"You know things, don't you, Binny?"

"The street is my school. I stay low. I keep cool." He made a downward sweeping gesture with one hand. Laughed.

'Ow do you do? My name's Gavroche.

"You know anything about the Castain and Scarborough hits?"

"Assholes also made people mad."

"Why?"

"A patch gotta have one boss."

"And that's Unka now."

Binny looked at me from under his ridiculously large bill.

"Did Unka also kill Annaliese Ruben?"

The bill tilted downward. "Word is, that was outside."

"Who, outside?"

Binny lifted one sneaker to the pedal of his bike.

"Annaliese was my friend, Binny."

"Gotta bounce."

And he was gone.

King was at her desk, talking on a phone that looked like it dated to the Vietnam era. She did the finger-in-the-air thing, then pointed to a chair.

I sat.

"Right. Thanks." She cradled the receiver.

To me. "That was the ME in Edmonton. Castain and Scarborough were taken out with nine-millimeters."

"Handguns firing jacketed bullets."

She nodded. "Whether one or two weapons, neither was the one that killed Beck and his amigo."

"The second vic was a guy named Eric Skipper."

"What's his story?"

I told her what I knew. White, male, Brampton, lots of dental work. "I need to get the X-rays to my odont ASAP."

"No problemo. My assistant will scan and transmit them."

"She's working on a Sunday?"

"Let's just say she's keen."

I gave her the envelope and Bergeron's address at the LSJML. "Any word on Ruben?"

King shook her head.

"Did you talk to Snook?"

She was about to respond when the phone shrilled. She put the receiver to her ear. Listened. "What's his name?" Cupping the mouthpiece, she spoke to me. "You know a Mr. Mind-Your-Own-Business?"

"It's a kid named Binny."

"Binny Twiller?"

"The young man did not share his full biographical profile."

"Twiller's outside and wants to talk to you."

"Weird. I ran into him on the way in. Why does the name Twiller ring a bell for me?"

"Merilee Twiller."

No cerebral "aha!"

"Castain's girlfriend?"

Of course. Now it made sense.

"The kid claims word on the street puts Ruben outside the punch-up."

"What is he, twelve?"

"Binny keeps his ear to the ground."

"What's he say about Castain and Scarborough?"

"Nothing."

"Not surprising. Anyway, he won't come in."

"How about this? You deal with the X-rays, then phone Michelle Skipper. I'll see what the kid has on his mind."

Binny was doing his usual bike-straddle below a tamarack tree actually showing some green.

I walked over to him. Under the hat brim, his eyes were skittery. They landed on me a second, then moved on.

"Tell your cop friends to try Unka's house."

"They did. He's not there."

"Dig deeper."

"Thank you, Binny."

"You say you got anything from me, I'll say you're a pedophile."

As before, he rocketed up the block, twig legs

pumping the pedals like pistons.

I returned to King's office. My envelope was gone from her desk. A few of her questions told me she was still talking to Michelle Skipper.

I dialed my iPhone.

"Ryan."

"This may sound nuts. But remember the kid I was with on Friday?"

"Rosemary's Baby?"

"He has access to inside information."

"Meaning?"

"He's Merilee Twiller's son. And he listens. He just tipped me that Unka has gone to ground at his mother's house."

"Why take the risk of telling you that?"

"I'm charismatic."

"Must be it."

"And I gave him a muffin."

"We checked Mama's crib."

"Binny said dig deeper."

"Those were his words?"

"Yes."

"Thanks."

I debated mentioning Binny's warning that I watch my back. Decided to wait.

"Are you still at headquarters?" I asked.

"Yeah. One of Unka's goons is going canary."

"Why's he talking?"

"The cops found a Sig Sauer tucked in his shorts.

That violates his parole. Which means losing eight years of the beautiful life."

"What's he trading?"

"He says Scar owned Castain and Unka owned Scar."

"Merilee Twiller thought Unka killed Castain for skimming."

"Looks like she got it wrong."

"Is your guy going to testify?"

"We're discussing the benefits of his doing that."

"What's he say about Ruben?"

"Denies knowing anything about her."

I told Ryan about Eric Skipper and about the ballistics evidence suggesting a different weapon for him and Beck versus the ones used in the Scarborough and Castain hits.

"Most gang bangers own arsenals," Ryan said.

I noticed King hanging up, so I did the same.

She looked at her notes. "Skipper was a sessional instructor at a small university in Brampton. Had a master's in environmental ecology or something like that. Applied all over the country but never got an offer for a full-time university position. The wife blames it on arrests dating to Skipper's student years."

"Arrests for what?"

"Protests. Sit-ins. Rallies. Marches. The guy was a rabid tree hugger. According to the wife, the lack of employment left him with way too much time on his hands."

I saw where she was going. "He kept going to protests."

"Yep."

"One of which was here."

"Yep. You want the full story?"

"Yep."

"Ever hear of the Gahcho Kué project?"

34

"How much do you know about Gahcho Kué?" she asked.

"It's the new diamond mine De Beers Canada plans to open."

"Actually, it's a joint venture with Mountain Province Diamonds, but close enough."

"The project has caused some controversy, right?"

"Gahcho Kué is the aboriginal name for the Kennady Lake region. I think in some Dene dialect it means Place of the Big Rabbit. The area is lousy with barren-ground caribou and has traditionally been used by the Dene from Lutselk'e and the Métis from Fort Resolution. Back in the day, the Tlicho—or Dogrib Dene—also swung that way."

"So objections have mostly come from First Nations groups?"

She waggled a hand. Maybe yes, maybe no. "But they've had a big impact on the process. You want the full-blown?"

"Hit me."

"In 2005 the Mackenzie Valley Environmental Impact Review Board ruled that De Beers's applications for a land-use permit and water license would require a full environmental-impact study, an EIS. De Beers appealed the decision to the NWT Supreme Court but lost in April 2007.

"Long story short, in December 2010 De Beers finally submitted its EIS. Last July the review panel ruled that the EIS is in conformity."

"Meaning?"

"Meaning now the panel will read the monster, all eleven thousand pages of it. The review process is expected to be completed by 2013. De Beers hopes to begin production in 2014."

"How big is Gahcho Kué?"

"The proposed mine calls for recovery of four and a half million carats annually. They'll be working three pipes, 5034, Hearne, and Tuzo, using the open-pit method."

"For how long?"

"I think they put mine life at eleven years."

I did some quick math. Given the cost of development, construction, and maintenance, and a very limited life span, the profit in diamond mining had to be monstrous.

"Where is Kennady Lake?" I asked.

"Roughly three hundred kilometers north of here. Ninety kilometers southeast of De Beers's Snap Lake mine."

"What does this have to do with Eric Skipper?"

"Throughout the review process, the panel holds open sessions at the local level, so anyone interested can express his or her opinion."

I saw where she was going. "Skipper came to Yellowknife for one of these town meetings."

"And ended up dead."

"What did he plan to say?"

"Don't fuck with the caribou."

"How long was he here?"

"He left Brampton on March first. By bus."

"Allowing for travel time, that means he was in Yellowknife a few days before he died. Did he get into any trouble while he was here?"

"Let's find out." She dialed, then leaned back. The chair made a sound like an air compressor gasping its last.

"Hey, Frank. Maureen King."

A tinny voice said something I couldn't make out.

"I'm good."

More tin.

"Tell her to keep applying heat. She'll be fine. Listen, do you remember a guy named Eric Skipper? Came from Ontario to speak his piece at a review panel session in March 2008."

Tin laughter.

"Didn't think so. Do me a favor, run the name? See if anything pops?"

Tin.

"No, I'll wait."

She laid the receiver on the blotter.

To me, "This shouldn't take long."

It took ten minutes. As Frank spoke, King took notes. "Thanks. Have a good one."

She said to me, "Skipper made it into the books, all right. On March seventh, 2008, G Division got a call about two guys having a throw-down in a parking lot on Forty-seventh. The responding officers defused the situation and made no arrests. One combatant was Horace Tyne. The other was Eric Skipper."

That was a shocker.

"What were they fighting about?"

"The incident report consists of two lines."

"That doesn't make sense. Tyne sees himself as the savior of the tundra. He and Skipper should have been comrades."

Our eyes met. We were on the same page.

"A little face time with Captain Caribou?"

"Oh, yeah," I said.

Ryan called as we were pulling into Behchoko. For the first time in days, he sounded energized.

"We got him."

"Unka?"

"Yes."

"Where was he?"

I looked at King. She gave a thumbs-up.

"Some kind of root cellar under a barn behind

his mother's house. Looked like goddamn Saddam Hussein crawling out of his spider hole."

"You didn't notice it when you first tossed the place?"

"He'd parked an old truck over the pull-up panels, then crawled under and down. Bastard had the place tricked out with camping gear and a battery-operated TV. I guess Mama delivered meals."

"Where is he now?"

"Sitting in an interview room, trying to look tough."

"Will he be charged with Scar's murder?"

"Rainwater's talking with the crown prosecutor."

"Where's Ollie?"

"Catching heat from K Division."

"Why?"

"Not heat. They just want him to wrap it up. Guess he'll be booking a flight out tonight."

"Really?"

"Though Scar's from Edmonton, he bought it on G Division turf. So did Castain and Ruben. Shithead's boss is calling him home."

"Ollie's good with that?"

"He and I just don't talk like we used to."

I waited.

"He looks livid."

"What about us?" I asked.

"We could try counseling."

"Are we heading out?"

"Ruben killed babies on my patch. That's a

felony." All levity gone. "Someone helped her flee the jurisdiction. That person is an accessory."

"Meaning you plan to continue the case."

"I do. Where are you?"

I told him about Skipper and Tyne. "Ryan, I think there could be more than one thing operating here."

"Enlighten me."

"The locals, Ollie, you—everyone thinks these murders stem from Scar's attempt to usurp Unka's control of the drug trade up here. Maybe that thinking is overly simplistic."

"What are you suggesting?"

What *was* I suggesting? "Maybe there's no one single motive. One single set of killers."

"Go on."

"There's so much disconnect. Your informant fingering Scar and Unka but denying knowledge of Ruben. This guy wants to stay out of jail. Why hold back? The more he knows, the better his bargaining position. Why not offer everything he's got?"

I heard Ryan exhale through his nose.

"Binny says word on the street is Ruben is different. Why make that up?"

"The kid likes pastry."

Despite the sarcasm, I knew Ryan was listening. So was King.

"The ballistics. Ruben and Beck were shot with a hunting rifle, Scar and Castain with nine-millimeter handguns."

"Maybe relevant, maybe not."

"Daryl Beck was killed in 2008. There's no indication he was involved in the drug trade."

Ryan started to speak. I cut him off.

"A drug war can take a high toll. I get that. But maybe everyone's making the mistake of trying to fit the evidence into a preconceived model. A model that's wrong. That's all I'm saying."

"Piece of advice while you're with Tyne?"

"What?" Wary.

"Eyes off the squeeters."

"Aargh!" I jammed the phone into my purse.

"What?" King asked.

"Ryan thinks he's George freakin' Carlin."

"Most men do."

Tyne took his time answering the door. Today he was wearing a poncho with some sort of logo and jeans. And a look that said he was not thrilled to see us.

"You remember me, Mr. Tyne? We spoke on Friday about Annaliese Ruben," I said.

"I've got to get to work."

"I'm happy you found employment."

"Weekend security. Pay's shit."

"This is Maureen King. The deputy chief coroner."

Tyne's eyes went empty as glass. "Someone croak?"

"Annaliese Ruben."

Tyne slipped two fingers below the collar of his poncho and massaged his chest.

"Someone shot her," King said.

"Seems to be a lot of that going around."

"You know anything about that, sir?"

"Annaliese was a nice little girl, despite her troubles."

"That wasn't my question." King smiled benignly.

"No, ma'am, I don't. But I do know the whole world's going to hell."

Time to change the subject.

"Are you acquainted with a man named Eric Skipper?" I asked.

"No, ma'am."

"I find that odd, Mr. Tyne. Ms. King and I uncovered a police report stating that you and Skipper went at each other in a parking lot back in 2008."

Tyne's fingers froze. His lips moved as though trying out the name. "You talking about that prick who came to Yellowknife preaching e-cology?" Hitting hard on the long *e*.

"I am."

"That gasbag had a ton of education and not one ounce of common sense. His agenda? Write an article, get a name, score a university position. All off the back of a species that's about to go down."

"You disagreed philosophically?"

"Damn right we did."

"Wasn't Skipper's goal the same as yours? Saving the caribou?"

"The moron thought we should fight this new mine

the government's shoving down our throats. That's like trying to stop a train with your bare hands. I told him the only thing's going to help the caribou is a safe place to go."

"The guy made you mad?"

"Good thing he left town."

35

En route back to Yellowknife, King got a call. The spring melt had coughed up a lady in a lake.

"Need help?" I offered, truly not enthused.

"Nah. She and her boyfriend plunged their Ski-doo through a soft spot right before last fall's hard freeze. Up here, floaters overwinter well. The family will be able to order an open casket."

I also got a ring.

"Bergeron confirmed the Skipper ID," I said after disconnecting.

"Forward progress."

"What's your take on Tyne?"

"Sounds like he's got a temper. But the old duck's probably harmless."

"You don't see him as good for Skipper and Beck?"

"Because the two traded blows over ungulates?" She pooched air through her lips. "No."

"What do you think of Tyne fostering a mentally impaired seventeen-year-old girl?"

"You have to understand. Kinship is viewed differently up here."

Maybe.

I looked at my watch. One-fifteen. On cue, my stomach growled.

"Hungry?"

"Mm."

"There's probably a granola bar in the console."

"I'm good." I was starving. Regretted giving the muffin to Binny.

I settled into the seat and watched the same panoply of pines, tamaracks, poplars, and birches I'd watched when making this run with Ryan. I felt troubled, restless. Like something was hiding around a corner in my mind.

Chewing the ball of one thumb, I tried to pinpoint the source of my uneasiness. Had some clue stared me in the face and I'd missed it? What?

The feeling had started the day before. Had invaded my dreams. Had I seen or heard something on Saturday that triggered the pestering from my subconscious?

I reviewed the day in excruciating detail. The exhumation? Scar's murder? The Skipper ID?

No reaction from the old id.

King's voice snapped me back.

"Sorry to leave you, but I've got to view a body that's thawing fast."

"Drop me at the Explorer. I'll be fine."

She did.

I wasn't.

After grabbing a takeaway salmon burger and fries from the restaurant, I returned to my room. Minutes after downing the food, I was feeling more batshit-stir-crazy than ever.

I tramped out to the woods. Called for Tank.

Nothing. Of course not. The dog was dead. Why this obsession? Was I trying to save Ruben's dog because I'd failed to save her?

Annoyed with my pathetic psychobabble self-analysis, I returned to my room and opened the mining book. Too agitated to read, I glanced at pictures. A schematic of a kimberlite pipe. A shot of a panned sample. A close-up of diamond indicator minerals. An aerial view of the Diavik mine.

My subconscious nagged like an eyelash bent the wrong way.

What else happened yesterday?

Katy called.

Was that it? Was I merely worried about my daughter?

No. It was something here. Something I'd missed.

I'd also talked to Nellie Snook.

A cluster of cells sat up in my id.

Oh?

I closed my eyes and replayed the visit in my mind, bringing up every bit of minutiae I could recall.

The wildlife pictures, stickers, and calendars. Daryl Beck. Ronnie Scarborough. The photos of Ruben's dead babies. Murray the cat. The two mismatched goldfish.

Like the two mismatched sisters, I thought glumly.

I pictured the fish staring through the glass, colossal eyes bulging, redirected sun lighting their bellies.

I froze.

Adrenaline fired through me.

Heart thumping, I dug a file from my computer case, pulled out an envelope, and shook free the five-by-sevens I'd shot during my analysis of the window-seat baby.

With jittery fingers, I chose one photo and placed it beside a page in the mining book.

I pictured rainbow light reflecting off scales.

Jesus.

Diamond indicator minerals. DIMs. Each sister owned a small collection. Snook kept hers in an aquarium. Ruben kept hers in a black velvet sack.

My brain started jumping everywhere at once. A circuit of neurons landed on something Snook had said.

An idea began to take shape.

I checked a name on Google, an address.

I raced to the bathroom sink and rinsed my little ketchup container and replaced its lid. Then I repacked the file, grabbed my laptop, shoved the container into my purse, and bolted.

While Snook didn't slam the door, she didn't fling it wide in joyful welcome.

"May I come in?" I asked.

"I've got someone stopping by."

"I won't take long."

Sighing, Snook stepped back. I went directly to the kitchen.

The fish were still in their bowl. Murray was nowhere to be seen.

Either uncomfortable or genuinely hurried, Snook did not offer tea or a seat at the table.

OK. Plan B.

"Did Ms. King explain the results of the exhumation?"

"I shouldn't have done that with Daryl."

The change in attitude surprised me. "Why not?"

"It made people angry."

"What people?"

"It doesn't matter. They're right. It's un-Christian. The dead should rest in peace."

"But you were right, Nellie."

She twisted her lips to one side but said nothing.

"I'm so sorry about your brother."

"No one will do squat."

"I promise you. I will try my very best to find Daryl's killer."

Her eyes told me she didn't believe it.

I tilted an ear as though startled by a sound. "Oh, my. Is that Murray?"

"What?"

"Sounds like a cat in trouble."

Snook hurried to the laundry room. I heard the door open, then she called out. "Murray. Where are you, Murray? Here, kitty."

Wasting no time, I stepped to the fishbowl and, using the ketchup container, scooped a sample of the sparkly mixture lining the bottom. The fish skittered away from my hand, clearly displeased.

"Here, kitty."

Murray strolled in from the house's interior.

I moved to the laundry room.

"False alarm." I smiled. "He's here."

As though offering proof of his well-being, Murray joined us.

Snook picked up the cat.

I took my leave.

The Bellanca Building is Yellowknife's answer to the skyscraper. But Burj Khalifa it's not. Built in 1969, the eleven-story box has blue facade on its sides and LEGO-layered windows across its front.

I entered from Fiftieth Street and checked the directory. The Mineral Development Division of Indian and Northern Affairs Canada was on the sixth floor. The mining recorder's office was on the fifth.

I hurried to the elevator and pressed the button for five. When the doors opened, the MRO was straight ahead. Surprisingly, the office was unlocked.

No tax dollars had been wasted on interior design.

The reception area was Spartan, the walls decorated with framed pictures of rocks, underground shafts, large equipment, and aerial views of places probably not favored by tourists. Wooden chairs lined one wall. A desk sat at the rear. That was it. But would you really want frills at a mining recorder's office?

I called out.

No answer.

A corridor shot from a doorway to the right of the desk. Walking down it toward the back of the building, I wondered how I'd recognize the man I was seeking.

No problem. Each office had a name plaque. Jacob Rainwater's was at the end. His door was open.

Rainwater looked like the old professor from a Disney movie. Baggy sweater, bad haircut, wire-rimmed specs. The only thing that didn't fit was the snazzy new Mac where he was working.

The office was a claustrophobic's worst nightmare. An enormous desk and bulky file cabinets left only narrow passages for navigation about the small space. Every shelf and horizontal surface was covered with stacked papers and magazines, rolled maps, hunks of rock and petrified wood, and glass containers holding gravel and sand. If anything hung on a wall, it was hidden from view.

I cleared my throat.

Rainwater looked up. "Yes?"

"My name is Temperance Brennan. I have a few questions and was told you were very knowledgeable."

"What kind of questions?"

"About prospecting." Cautious.

"A prospector's license is two dollars for an individual, fifty for a company. The girl out front can help you with that on Monday."

Rainwater's eyes returned to the screen. His fingers resumed their hunt-and-peck ballet.

"If you need a prospecting permit, you're out of luck. Applications are accepted in December. Approved permits are issued effective February first of the following year. Permits are good for three years below the Sixty-eighth parallel, five years above. The cost is twenty-five dollars plus ten cents an acre." Rainwater's tone was robotic, suggesting he'd repeated the information thousands of times. "A prospecting permit gives you temporary but exclusive exploration and staking rights but not mineral rights."

"Sir, I—"

"You need a valid prospector's license to stake a claim but don't need a prospecting permit. A claim requires four tagged posts. Tags cost two dollars a set. The girl out front can sell you those on Monday."

"Mr. Rainwater—"

"It's mandatory to check with this office before staking a claim to make sure the area is available and not already staked, claimed, or leased by someone else. The girl out front can—"

"I also want to learn about diamond indicator minerals."

Rainwater's eyes rolled up. He studied me through the upper portion of old-fashioned bifocal lenses. "What about them?"

I pulled the ketchup container from my purse. "I have a sample." Lay it on. "I know this is irregular, and I know I'm being presumptuous, but your nephew says you're a genius with these things."

"You a friend of Joseph's?"

"Mm."

Rainwater hesitated, then waggled me in with up-turned fingers.

As I wormed my way forward, he cleared space on his blotter, unfolded a white cloth, and spread it flat with his palms. Then he exchanged the bifocals for glasses with a little microscope stuck to each lens.

I gave him the purloined sample. He poured the gravel onto the cloth, turned on and adjusted a lamp clamped to one side of his desk, and leaned in.

I waited.

Every now and then Rainwater poked at the sample, rearranging the mix with one gnarled finger.

Long minutes passed. The entire floor was absolutely still.

"Have you anything else?" No robot now. Rainwater sounded genuinely interested.

I lay the five-by-seven on his desk.

The old man's shoulders twitched, and I heard a sharp intake of air.

Rainwater switched back to the bifocals. Stared

some more at the photo. Finally, his eyes met mine.

"My nephew put you up to some kind of stunt?"

"No, sir."

"Sweet Lord in the rushes."

36

"Did you collect this?"

"No, sir."

"Who did you say you are?"

I repeated my name but offered nothing else.

"Got any idea what diamond indicator minerals are?"

"Crystals that form in the earth's upper mantle as companions to diamonds."

"Hm."

"The difference is, DIMs are millions of times more numerous, so they're worth next to nothing." Trying to impress.

Rainwater hit a keyboard combo to save his work. "Do you know how to look through a scope, young lady?"

"I do." Wishing Binny could have heard the appellation.

The old man swiveled and pulled the cover from a

microscope I hadn't noticed in the jumble behind his desk. The thing was primitive, probably from a student lab. "Prefer a scanning electron microscope, but this old gal will do."

Rainwater transferred my sample to the viewing plate. Then he flicked a switch, shoved his glasses onto his forehead, peered through the eyepieces, and adjusted focus.

"Look at this." Rolling his chair sideways.

I squeezed behind the desk and bent down.

And was amazed at the beauty of what I saw.

"That's magnified two hundred times."

"Wow," I said.

"Pretty, eh? When a prospector is out panning or bagging or however he does his sampling, he's mostly looking for hue."

I was mesmerized by the colors and shapes of the crystals.

"See the red and orange ones? Those are from the garnet group. The green to sort of lemony-yellow ones are from the pyroxene group. Olivine is one. The black guys are ilmenites."

"What causes the color differences?"

"Iron, manganese, and chromium content."

"So you're saying this sample contains diamond indicators."

"It's loaded. One of the richest I've ever seen. See those big green ones?"

"Yes."

"And this."

I straightened. Rainwater was holding the five-by-seven of the gravel in Ruben's velvet sack.

"Good call including a scale." He pointed at the green pebbles. "These are chunks of chrome diopside. Usually, they're microscopic. The biggest I can recall seeing was maybe one centimeter. These are almost two centimeters each. Hell, you could mount these babies and sell them in a jewelry store."

"Chrome diopside?" Calm.

"Crystals that form deep within the earth, then get carried to the surface in a rock called kimberlite, which is softer. Over the eons the kimberlite erodes away, leaving the crystals intact."

"So this came from a site near a kimberlite pipe?" Calm.

"I'd say there's a mighty good chance. I'd look for an infill lake or some similar formation." Rainwater steepled his fingers and eyed me over them. "You seem quite knowledgeable yourself."

"No, sir. Not really. But there's one other thing. I wonder if you can tell me how to research a claim."

"A mineral claim?"

I must have looked confused.

"A mineral claim must be recorded with this office within sixty days of the date it was staked. To do that, a staker files paperwork and a sketch of the claim and pays his fees."

"A mineral claim does what?"

"Gives the owner rights to the subsurface minerals for up to ten years if a specific amount of work is done on the claim each year."

I could hear Rainwater retreating into robot mode.

"If the required amount of work is done on the claim, a person or company can apply to *lease* the claim anytime before the thirtieth day after the tenth anniversary date of the claim. A mineral lease is good for twenty-one years and may be extended for another twenty-one years if the rental payments are up-to-date and the renewal fees are paid. If a person or company is going to begin production—meaning construction, mining, milling, etc.—then the claim must be taken to lease."

"Could we start with mineral claims?" I asked.

"You'd better pull up a chair."

As I did that, Rainwater tapped the keyboard. A new page appeared. The header said *Indian and Northern Affairs Canada* in French and English. A red sidebar offered a choice of links.

"I'm going into the SID viewer." Rainwater was entering a username and password. "SID contains a number of spatially integrated datasets."

A map filled the screen. I recognized the NWT and Nunavut. Hudson Bay. The places I'd viewed on the inside cover of the mining book. Rivers appeared in deep blue, lakes in turquoise, boundary lines and community names in black.

"Got to zoom to a scale of under a thousand. Otherwise, the mineral claims data won't appear on the table of contents. For now let's stick to NWT."

A red rectangle formed on the screen. Rainwater clicked an icon, and the area inside expanded.

A sidebar with choices ran vertically down the map's right edge. Rainwater chose to display two layers by placing dots in the selection boxes beside the categories. Active mineral claims. Prospecting permits.

He refreshed the map, and gray, green, and chartreuse boxes appeared superimposed on the topography. Each box had a number. Rainwater chose an icon from a panel on the left, and a query box appeared at the bottom of the screen. On a scroll bar under "field," he chose "C_Owners.owner_Nam1." Under "operator," he chose "=."

His fingers paused at the "value" field. "Name?"

"McLeod," I said.

He typed the letters, hit "add to query string," then "enter."

A pulsating silver bar said the system was searching.

Seconds later, a spreadsheet appeared below the map. It contained about twenty columns of data.

I skimmed the headers. Claim number. Claim status. Date claim was recorded. Acreage. Shape. Some abbreviations I lacked the expertise to interpret.

"McLeod was a busy boy." Rainwater was scrolling down through the rows. "Ninety-seven claims. Most recorded in the nineties. All withdrawn or lapsed, save three."

"Can you pull up information on the active claims?"

Rainwater hit some keys. "Looks like there are coowners on all three. Nellie M. Snook. Daryl G. Beck. Alice A. Ruben."

Pulse galloping, I forced myself calm. "McLeod died in 2008. How would that affect his claims?"

"Unless the deceased party left instructions otherwise, I assume the claims would belong wholly to the coregistrants as long as all fees were paid and use requirements met."

"Can you pull up one of the active claims?"

Rainwater tapped, and a block of green squares appeared on the map. They were dead north of Yellowknife, northwest of the Ekati mine, just below the border with Nunavut.

I stared at the cluster. Worlds were colliding. More accurately, separating.

Snook said it. I just didn't hear.

The only thing Farley McLeod gave his kids was a quick shot of sperm and a worthless piece of dirt in the middle of nowhere.

Farley McLeod had left his children mineral rights on land he'd staked. Ruben and Snook each possessed samples rich in diamond indicator minerals, probably given with the warning that they be safeguarded.

The samples probably came from the land McLeod had staked.

Sweet baby Jesus.

Beck and Ruben hadn't been killed in a battle over drugs. They owned mineral claims potentially worth millions. Someone wanted those claims.

But who?

A cluster of adjacent squares glowed the same bright green as those owned by Snook and her siblings. I pointed to them. "Are those active?"

"They are. Looks like someone snatched up the claims that McLeod let lapse." Rainwater clicked on a square. Then another. And another. "All owned by an entity called Fast Moving." He clucked his tongue. "The outfit's not moving all *that* fast. It's met the requirements for maintaining the claim but done nothing else."

"Is it some sort of corporation?"

Rainwater chuckled. "Sorry. Not my skill set."

The id cells had the band back together.

Fast Moving.

The name meant nothing to me.

While I was poking at my subconscious, my cortex conjured a terrible thought. Was Snook in danger?

"Thank you so much, Professor Rainwater." I rose. "This has been very educational."

Rainwater poured the sample back into the ketchup container. Handed it to me. "You are most welcome."

I maneuvered around the desk. I was at the door when Rainwater spoke again.

"Dr. Brennan."

I turned, surprised at the old man's use of the title.

"Your secret is safe with me."

"What?"

"Catch the bastards."

37

I was becoming a regular on Ragged Ass. Still, the atmosphere felt hostile.

As I pulled to my usual spot on the shoulder, I noticed a gray pickup in Snook's drive. It had a rusting tailpipe and a bumper sticker saying *Give Wildlife a Brake.* I'd seen it before, couldn't recall where. Rusty pickups were all the rage in Yellowknife.

I decided to hold tight.

Good call.

Ten minutes later, the side door opened, and a man stepped from the house to the carport. His face was in shadow, but his form looked familiar.

The man got into the truck and backed toward the street. While shifting gears, he glanced my way.

We registered mutual expressions of shock.

Horace Tyne.

Without a word, Tyne gunned it up Ragged Ass. Pebbles spit by his wheels ticked the side of the Camry.

What was Horace Tyne doing with Nellie Snook?

I got out, crossed to the house, and banged on the door.

Snook answered right away, holding a ball cap in one hand. "Don't worry. I've got it."

Realizing I wasn't Tyne, she frowned. "You're like a bad rash. You just keep coming back."

"Was that Horace Tyne?"

"What do you want?"

"You told me your father left land to you and your brother."

"Don't remember saying that, but so what?"

"Did the land also belong to Annaliese?"

"He did it to salve his conscience for ignoring us all our lives. That's my opinion, and I'll never change it."

"Think a minute. Do you own the land outright or the mineral claims?"

Snook's brows winged farther down. "What's the difference?"

"Where is the land?"

"All I know is it's not here in Yellowknife. A town lot might have value. This is a worthless hunk of nothing so far out on the tundra no one would buy it."

"Have you tried to sell?"

"Right." She snorted. "That'd happen. Now that the deeds belong to me outright, I'm going to offload the land to charity. I'm tired of shelling out for all three of us. Annaliese and Daryl never had a nickel to spare."

"You plan to donate the property to Horace Tyne?"

"Yes." Defensive. "I sign a few papers, I'm out from under the taxes, or the fees, or whatever it is I've been paying."

"For his preserve."

"When they open the new mine, the caribou won't have no place to go. Their migration routes will be shattered."

Something cold clammed into my gut. "Which new mine?"

"Gahcho Kué."

I grasped each of Snook's upper arms and locked my eyes onto hers. She stiffened but did not pull back.

"Nellie, promise you will do nothing until you speak to me again."

"I don't—"

"You own mineral claims, not land. The claims could be worth a great deal of money. Someone wants to get them from you. That person may have killed Daryl and Annaliese."

She looked at me like I needed a shot of Prozac.

"Who?" Barely voiced.

"I don't know. But I will find out."

I felt distrustful eyes on my back as I ran to the car.

Back in the Camry, I hit a key on my speed dial.

Come on. Come on.

"Hey, buttercup. You back in Charlotte?"

"Pete, listen to me."

Twenty years of marriage had sensitized my ex to

every nuance of mine. He caught the tension in my voice. "What is it?"

"You're a lawyer. You know how to research corporations, right?"

"I do."

"In Canada?"

"Mais oui." May we.

"Never speak French, Pete."

"Noted."

"How long would it take?"

"What do you need?"

"Just the names of the owners, or officers, or whatever they'd be."

"Probably not long."

"So you'll do it?"

"You'll owe me, sugar britches."

"I'll bake you a big batch of cookies."

"What's the name?"

"Fast Moving."

"Oh! là là. I like that."

"It's not what you think."

"Do you know if it's a partnership, a corporation, or just an assumed name used by an individual?"

"No."

"That makes it difficult. Do you know where it's registered?"

"No."

"That makes it even harder."

"Start with Alberta."

Ollie was coming out of G Division headquarters as I pulled in. The lot was small, and I almost ran him over.

Holding two palms high, he circled to my side of the Camry. I lowered the window. "Sorry."

"Slow it down, sister, or I'll have to write you up."

"You can't write me up. You're out of jurisdiction."

Ollie pointed a finger pistol in my direction.

"Haven't seen you since Friday," I said.

"Believe me." He tipped his head toward the building. "I'd rather be with you than those skanks."

"What's happening?"

"Unka's about to roll on Scarborough. Doesn't matter. It was endgame when his buddy nailed him to the wall."

"So Scar killed Castain, and Unka killed Scar."

"Cheap method of social cleanup, eh?"

"What about Ruben?"

"No one's owning that one."

"Ryan's still in there?"

"He and Rainwater will be at it awhile."

"He said you might be leaving."

"Flying out in two hours." Ollie grinned, but the tightness in his jaw belied unhappiness. "Thanks for coming west. Sorry we didn't get satisfaction on Ruben. But it'll all come out."

"I think her murder is unrelated to Castain and Scarborough."

"What do you mean?"

I laid out my theory.

"Who do you like for the doer?"

"I don't know. But Tyne has Snook convinced that her"—I hooked air quotes—"'land' is vital for his caribou preserve. That the opening of the Gahcho Kué mine threatens the herds. Here's the thing. Snook's mineral claims are way over by Ekati. They're nowhere near Gahcho Kué."

"What are you going to do?"

"I'm waiting for info on the owner of the claims adjacent to Snook's. In the meantime, I plan to dig in to Tyne's background."

"Good luck."

Our eyes held for a moment. Then Ollie reached in and stroked my cheek with one knuckle. "Do you still think I'm the most magnificent creature to ever cross your path?"

"I think you're a narcissistic pain in the ass." Smiling.

"I may start calling you again."

"Keep in mind they've tightened the laws on stalking."

Ollie laughed and stepped back.

Back at the Explorer, I booted my laptop and entered the name Horace Tyne.

Google sent me to an old photo of a Second Lieutenant Horace Algar, gazetted with the Tyne Electrical Branch of the Royal Engineers.

I tried a more detailed string. Horace Tyne. Caribou. Alberta. That bought me a link to Friends of the Tundra. Ryan was right. The site was primitive.

I decided to take a different approach. The Fifth Estate.

I started with the *Yellowknifer* but could find no link to its archives. I looped through a number of newspaper portals. The *Deh Cho Drum. Inuvik Drum. Nunavut News. Kivalliq News*. Each had interesting headlines and colorful photos. None offered access to archives.

Frustrated, I returned to the *Yellowknifer* and tried clicking through some of the drop-down menus. One presented a graphic of the newspaper's seventy-fifth anniversary collector's edition.

The cover displayed a black-and-white of a man in coveralls and a miner's hat. I clicked on it and downloaded the PDF file offered.

I was studying a shot of the Con mine circa 1937 when my mobile sounded.

"I'm thinking this is worth a lot more than cookies."

"What did you find, Pete?"

"Maybe buns?"

"Uh-huh."

While I listened, I scrolled to a story titled "The Golden Age of the 50s and 60s."

"Fast Moving is an LLP, a limited liability partnership. It's registered in Quebec. Because it's a partnership and not a corporation, this may take a bit longer."

"OK."

I moved on through a series of ads to a color shot of the Old Stope Hotel burning down in 1969. Prince Charles's visit in 1975. Strikers protesting in 1992.

I kept scrolling.

My eyes fell on a photo.

I stared in disbelief.

38

The world shrank in around me. Nothing existed but the image on my screen.

The article was titled "Ice Road Truckers." The black-and-white photo showed four men, all wearing parkas, fur-trimmed hats, and safety vests.

Three of the men were smiling and squinting as though facing into the sun. I recognized two of them.

The fourth man had his face turned from the camera. Though I couldn't see his features, something about him looked familiar.

"Are you there?"

"I'm here, Pete." Squeezing the phone between my shoulder and ear. "That's incredibly helpful."

"Are you OK?"

"I'm fine."

"You don't sound fine."

"Really. You're awesome."

"I know."

"I'm about to head out, so could you e-mail the partners' names when you find them?"

"Will do. How about Katy's news?"

"We'll talk about that later."

"Pretty ballsy move."

"I've got to go, Pete."

I clicked off, skimmed the article, then stared at the photo. The caption identified the three forward-facing subjects: Farley McLeod, Horace Tyne, and Zeb Chalker.

Facts zinged like popcorn in my head.

Charles Fipke had discovered diamonds in Canada, setting off a staking rush in the nineties. McLeod and Tyne had both worked for Fipke.

McLeod had staked claims during the rush. He had named his offspring—Nellie Snook, Daryl Beck, and Annaliese Ruben—as coowners.

Snook and Ruben possessed samples rich in diamond indicator minerals. DIMs point to kimberlite. A kimberlite pipe means diamonds. Diamonds can mean millions, even billions, of dollars.

Snook now held all of Farley McLeod's active claims.

Horace Tyne had confused Snook into thinking that she owned land. He'd persuaded her to donate the land for a caribou preserve. A preserve necessitated by the impending opening of the Gahcho Kué mine. But Snook's claims were nowhere near Gahcho Kué.

My ill-formed idea began to solidify.

I stared at the photo, heart pounding my ribs.

McLeod. Tyne. Chalker.

Zeb Chalker had bola'ed me at Snook's house. Blown me off when I'd reported Ruben's murder. Spread rumors about my drinking.

Had Chalker discredited me to divert suspicion from himself and his cronies?

McLeod. Tyne. Chalker.

McLeod died in a plane crash.

Tyne. Chalker.

One of these men wanted McLeod's claims. Maybe both.

Ruben and Beck were dead. Snook, the sole survivor, was easily manipulated.

Had that been the strategy? Kill Beck, disappear Ruben to Montreal, after seven years have her declared dead? Then get Snook to sign over the claims? Had Ruben's sudden reappearance spurred a change in plans?

Who had I seen in the woods the night Ruben was shot? Who had made off with her body?

Suddenly, I felt I was plunging.

I'd told Snook to do nothing. To sign no papers.

"No. Christ, no."

I'd gotten Ruben killed. Had I put Snook in danger?

I checked the time.

Seven-ten. Ollie was already at the airport.

I grabbed my mobile.

Voice mail.

Unka be damned. I had to talk to Ryan.

I pocket-jammed my iPhone, slammed the cover of my Mac, and headed out.

I was unlocking the Camry when I sensed a presence behind me. Before I could turn, a gun muzzle kissed my temple.

An arm snaked around my neck and pulled me upright.

I couldn't move or speak.

"Not a sound." Male. Had I heard the voice before? Tyne? Chalker?

I thought of dropping fast and rolling under the car. What was the point? My assailant had a gun. He'd squat and nail me.

The arm tightened and twisted my body to the right. "Move."

Probably wanting to avoid notice, the guy dropped the arm from my neck, stepped close, and lowered the gun to my back.

On rubber legs, I took a few very small steps.

"The truck."

I hesitated. Every cop I know says, *If taken, never enter a vehicle. Once inside, your chance of escape plummets.*

The muzzle gouged deeper into my spine. "Don't fuck with me."

I walked as slowly as I dared. Two feet out, I stopped.

I felt the guy's gun hand tense. I pictured the long dark tunnel, the bullet tearing through my bones, my heart, my lungs.

Instead, my assailant pushed me forward into the side of the pickup. With the gun back in place, he yanked my purse from my shoulder. "Get in."

I didn't move.

"I said get the fuck in."

Maybe fear. Maybe boldness. I believed he would shoot me but remained frozen.

I felt his body shift. Saw movement in the corner of my eye.

A shadow crossed my face.

I heard a sound like the snap of a piano wire.

The world broke into millions of white particles.

Went black.

I was at the bottom of a deep, dark pit, struggling to climb out and getting nowhere. A moth flailing in sap slowly turning to amber.

The pit shifted.

A pinpoint of light appeared overhead.

I strained to reach it.

Slowly swam upward.

To consciousness.

The place I was in sounded hollow.

I smelled moisture. Ancient rock and soil. An acrid scent unfamiliar to me.

The world lurched.

My body shifted.

I was curled fetal on a cold, gritty surface.

I listened.

Heard the crunch of rubber on gravel. A soft humming.

I was in a vehicle. But not a car. The engine was wrong.

A flash image. The parking lot. The SUV.

The gun!

I lifted my head.

Almost screamed.

I lay back until the pain and dizziness passed.

The pressure on my body changed. The vehicle was moving downhill.

I tried to roll to my back.

My arms wouldn't move. My legs wouldn't move.

Dear God! I'm paralyzed!

My heartbeat kicked into high.

The adrenaline helped.

Sensation crept back.

I felt tingling in my cheeks and fingertips. Drought in my mouth, my eyes.

I tried to swallow. Could barely muster sufficient saliva.

I attempted to open my lids. They were crusted shut. I blinked them apart.

Inky black.

The vehicle stopped. The motor cut off.

I held my breath.

Voices. Male. Close but all around. How many?

Trickling water. A faucet? A stream?

Boots on gravel. One pair to the left, one to the right. Moving away? Approaching?

Every noise echoed back onto itself. Nothing was clear.

The voices grew louder. Ricocheted wildly. Two? Three?

Banging.

More voices.

Footsteps.

I froze.

The footsteps clomped toward me.

Continued past.

Receded.

The pounding in my chest was supersonic.

I had to do something.

Ignoring the fiery arrows shooting through my brain, I twisted my neck and looked around.

I was in the back of a golf cart.

Moving gingerly, I finger-wrapped the safety bar on one side and slowly raised my head.

Ten feet ahead and to the left, a beam cut the darkness. Behind it, I could make out a form wearing some sort of helmet. Vapor swirled in the tight cylinder of light shooting from above its brim.

For a few feet to either side of the beam, the scene was visible through a milky-white haze. The contours of a tunnel. Snaking pipes. Yellow and orange numbers and letters hand-painted on rock. Beyond that, a black void.

My eyes traced the beam to a row of yellow barrels. Painted on each was a single red word: *Arsenic*.

My mind registered. Analyzed.

Subterranean shaft. Miner's helmet. Arsenic. Horace Tyne.

My blood chilled to ice.

I knew where I was.

The Giant gold mine.

Sweet Jesus. How far underground?

Tyne had brought me here to kill me. To hide my body.

As he'd done with Annaliese Ruben.

I had to get out. Or get help.

Please!

Moving with stealth, I fumbled for my pocket.

Yes!

I pulled out my iPhone and cupped the screen.

No signal. Too far underground.

Think!

An e-mail would go out automatically as soon as the device reconnected with a tower. It was the best I could do.

I opened mail. Dispatched my location to Ryan.

Noticed a text from Pete. Why not? Whichever medium worked first.

Pete's message was short: *Fast Moving general partner Philippe Fast.*

I sent a reply: *Giant Gold Mine. Call Ryan.*

Was I insane? Reading e-mail and texts? I had to get out.

Pulse gunning, I repocketed the phone, drew in one knee, and braced my foot on the floor of the cart.

Waited.
Breath frozen, I drew in the other foot.
Braced.
Waited.
A deep breath, then I flexed to spring.
One sneaker skidded.
Gravel ground between rubber and metal.
The sound was like a screech in the stillness.
The helmet beam whipped my way.
I caught a glimpse of the face below.
Disparate facts toggled.
A text message.
A photo.
Pieces. Players. Moves. Strategies.
Suddenly, I saw the whole board.

39

It clicked. The detail that didn't fit with the rest of the photo. The parkas, the vests, three truckers squinting into the sun.

A fourth trucker, face turned, white streaking the hair below a fur-lined hat.

Phil looks like a skunk.

A flyer showing Ralph Trees's brother-in-law behind the wheel of a truck.

Got it here? Want it there? We move fast!

Fast Moving.

Farley McLeod had allowed some of his mineral claims to lapse. An entity called Fast Moving had acquired those claims.

Philippe Fast was the general partner in that entity.

It wasn't Tyne bearing down on me with a gun in his hand.

It was Philippe Fast.

Who was his partner? Tyne? Chalker? Where had he gone? For how long?

No matter. These were the best odds I'd have.

I threw my legs over the safety bar and slithered to the ground. My knees buckled, but I kept my feet.

"Hold it right there!" The bellowed command bounced off rock and reverberated down the shaft.

All around me was blackness. I suspected we'd descended a ramp, but had no idea its location.

Fast drew closer, the light on his helmet pointed straight at the cart.

I was a sitting duck.

When Fast's beam was focused on the barrels, I'd noticed a spade propped to their rear.

I pitched into the darkness, rounded the row, dropped to a squat, and peered through a gap.

Fast's light swiveled left, as though he were searching for something. Then it swung my way. "Get out here. You're just delaying the inevitable."

Stall!

"Five syllables. Impressive." Blood leaping. Sounding much calmer than I felt. "Rocky said you were good with words."

Fast shifted his feet but held position.

"Fast Moving. Love the double entendre, Phil." My words leapfrogged one another, as though coming from everywhere at once.

"You're dead, bitch."

"Oh, dear. Now there you disappointed me."

I felt for the spade, talking to cover any sound I might make. "Did you kill Beck?" Wrapping my fingers around the spade handle. "Or did you have your buddy do it?" Taunting to draw Fast closer. "Or have I got that backward? Is he the brain and you're just the muscle?"

Fast took a few tentative steps, gun aimed in my direction. "Shut the fuck up."

"I get why you had to eliminate Beck." I eased the spade from the wall. "But why kill Eric Skipper?"

Fast again glanced left, then inched closer to the barrels. I sensed he was also stalling. Why? What had the other man gone to do? To get?

"Come on, Phil. Obviously, there's been a glitch. Since we're chatting here, waiting for your pal to get back so you two can murder me, why not lay out how it went down?"

Arms trembling, I lowered the spade. "OK. How about I give you my version. You just nod yes or no."

"How about you shut the fuck up."

Fast was now close enough for me to see his face. His skin looked autopsy-pale in the glow of the light from his helmet. A tangle of curls sparked white on his forehead.

"You learn that Farley McLeod has scored a rich kimberlite pipe. Maybe through Fipke, maybe on his own. You and McLeod and Tyne are all buddies. All ice road drivers together at one time. You know all about McLeod's mineral claims."

Fast's gun hand rose. I visualized his finger tensing on the trigger.

"You snatch up the claims that McLeod lets lapse. But he keeps active the three he says will deliver big. And he's registered these in the names of his kids. How am I doing so far?"

Moving ever so slowly, I laid the spade across my knees.

"McLeod buys it in his Cessna, so now it's just the three bambinos."

Fast was arcing the gun back and forth along the row of barrels, uncertain of my exact position.

"You and Tyne set up the Friends of the Tundra scam to get McLeod's children to sign over what they think is worthless land to help save the caribou. Tyne is the front man. He never mentions mineral rights. Eric Skipper discovers the caribou preserve is phony and confronts Tyne. I'm guessing he also tips Beck. Whatever. Beck won't play ball, so you cap him. Skipper also has to go. If he exposes the con, Nellie won't donate the land."

I kept goading.

"Very clever, your plan for Ruben. You know she's not competent to sign over anything, so you bury her in the Montreal sheet world under an alias, planning later to have her declared dead. The claims will belong to sweet, malleable Nellie Snook, who loves the caribou. This tracking right so far?"

Fast was now two feet from the barrels. I could

hear breath rasping in and out of his nostrils. See the Beretta trembling in his grip.

"When Tyne tells you Ruben is back in Yellowknife, you hightail it out here from Quebec. Time to up the ante on little Annaliese. We know how that story ends, don't we, Phil?"

With icy fingers, I groped the ground around me. Found what felt like an old rubber glove.

"You also snuff the babies? That how the big, bad ice road trucker rolls?"

A shot rang out and roared down the tunnel.

The rock beside me sparked.

I felt a jagged prickling on the side of my face.

Now!

Keeping low, I tossed the glove to the far end of the barrels.

Fast moved left. Another round exploded from the Beretta.

I sprang from my end of the row and, death-gripping the spade handle, sliced sideways with all my strength, aiming for the pale swath of flesh between Fast's collar and his helmet.

The blade connected with a sickening thunk.

Subsequent events exist in my mind as disjointed images and sounds. At the time, they seemed to go on for hours. In reality, the sequence lasted but minutes.

Fast windmilled forward, legs pumping. Finding no traction, he stumbled to his knees. The Beretta flew from his hand. His forward momentum sent him into the last of the barrels. His helmet popped off and landed upside down.

The barrel spun, careened off a wall, tipped over, rolled, and boomed against rock.

The lid popped free. Spotlighted in Fast's upside-down beam, a noxious mix of mud, stagnant water, and arsenic-laced sludge spilled from the barrel and spread across the ground. A form took shape in the muck.

Annaliese Ruben lay on her side, long dark hair pasted to her face, features blue and rubbery in the cast-off light. Her legs and arms were tightly flexed. Below her chin, a lifeless hand lay curled on her chest, translucent skin peeling from the fingertips.

My pain gave way to a wave of pity.

Annaliese resembled the poor dead baby she'd hidden under her bathroom sink.

The sound of frantic scrambling snapped me back.

With a guttural howl, Fast lurched to his feet, head canted at an unnatural angle.

I tightened my grip on the spade. My pulse thudded in my ears. Blood pumped in my throat.

Swing again? Go for the gun?

That second of hesitation gave my opponent the advantage he needed.

Moving surprisingly quickly, Fast kicked the shovel from my hands and several feet from me. He then dropped on all fours and began groping for the Beretta.

I heard the spade clatter in the darkness and lunged to retrieve it.

Too slow!

With an animal snarl, Fast grabbed my hair and brought the gun up to my head. "Now you fucking die!"

He spun me and drove the Beretta into the back of my skull.

Against my will, I cried out. For a moment all was silent except for the soft trickle of water.

Then. A swish.

Where? To the left? The right?

Or had I imagined it?

Fast dug the muzzle deeper. I smelled his sweat and hair cream. Would they be the last sensations my brain would register?

In my mind I saw Katy, Pete, Ryan, Birdie. Tears streamed from the corners of my eyes. I braced for the bullet.

Then. A scrape. Like a shoe being placed with stealth.

Fast tensed and pointed the gun in the direction of the sound.

The Beretta discharged with another thunderous crack.

A locomotive blasted my right side. My body went airborne, hit the ground hard. Almost instantly, I heard another shot.

Lungs in spasm and gasping for air, I strained to comprehend what was happening.

Blood and bone burst from Fast's shoulder and splattered the wall at his back. He gave a keening yelp, then toppled with a sound like meat hitting wood.

In the smoky haze lit by Fast's bottom-up helmet, I saw three figures. One squatted beside me. The other two crouched by the cart.

All three had weapons trained on my would-be executioner.

40

Two p.m. Tuesday. Out my window, the sun was a hard white ball in a perfect blue sky. The bay looked glassy and still.

Between the koi-pond plunge, my gritty cart ride, and ricocheting fragments from Fast's bullet, my face resembled postwar Dresden. And I ached in places I didn't know I had.

Nevertheless, my mood was upbeat. I was packing to go home.

Sunday night's abduction had left me with abrasions and a possible concussion. The latter had mandated twenty-four hours of hospitalization.

While under observation, hooked to IVs and very cranky, I'd gotten the story piecemeal. Mostly from Ryan.

One heroine in the tale was Nora, the conspiratorial desk clerk. Through the hotel's front entrance, Nora saw a man flatten me against a truck and yank my purse from my shoulder. Thinking she was witnessing a mugging, and still in Dick Tracy mode, she'd noted the license and phoned the cops.

When the plate came back registered to Horace Tyne, someone told Rainwater. Rainwater told Ryan.

During one of their long stretches together, Itchy and Scratchy had discussed my double-motivation theory, decided it had merit. Figured I could be in danger.

About the same time Nora was dropping her dime, Ollie contacted G Division. He'd also considered the possibility that I might be right. And therefore in danger.

I have to admit, these guys moved fast. Rainwater contacted Corporal Schultz out in Behchoko. He checked Tyne's house, reported no truck in the drive.

Ryan remembered Tyne's part-time job as a security guard at the Giant gold mine. Rainwater remembered the barrels of arsenic being stored underground. Both agreed that sounded bad. Told Ollie.

Ollie commandeered a rental car and sped from the airport. Ryan snagged a ride from Chalker and raced from headquarters.

The trio converged on Giant simultaneously. Just as Tyne was returning to the shaft with a crowbar and a Remington 700 bolt-action rifle.

The locomotive that ran me over was Chalker. He knocked me clear so Ollie could get off a shot at Fast. Turned out the guy was solid all along. Just doing his job as a cop and as a member of Snook's exceedingly extended family.

Two ambulances hit Stanton Territorial at the same time. Fast remained there. Tyne was in a cell at G Division.

And I was at the Explorer, throwing panties and socks into my roll-aboard. I'd called Constable Chalker to thank him for throwing himself into the line of fire to shove me out of the way. He'd said I was welcome.

I was collecting toiletries from the bathroom when I heard a knock. Thinking it was Ryan, I hurried to the door.

Ollie stood in the hallway, a Whitman's sampler in one hand. "Didn't think flowers would travel well." He proffered his gift. "Not Godiva, but selection here sucks."

"Chocolate is always good." I took the box.

"You doing OK?"

"I am."

"You look like someone pulled your life support."

"Thanks."

Ollie glanced past me into the room.

"Would you like to come in?" I stepped back.

Ollie entered and dropped into a chair.

"Did you find out how Scar got to Yellowknife so fast?" Not important. But the detail had been bugging me.

"Got a buddy's who's a bush pilot. The guy flew him up."

"What's happening with Unka?" I asked.

"Stick in the fork. He's done."

"Fast?"

"Lost a chunk of one shoulder, but he'll survive."

"Is he lucid yet?"

"Oh, yeah. He and Tyne are in a sprint to see who can give it up faster."

"They've turned on each other?"

"The boys are looking to deal. Got to hand it to you, Tempe. You were spot-on. Ruben had nothing to do with the drug hits."

"What are Fast and Tyne saying?"

"It seems originally, no killings were planned. They were just going to defraud McLeod's kids out of their mineral rights with the 'save the caribou' scam. Snook would donate willingly, and Beck could be induced to do it during one of his drug or alcohol blackouts. The bigger problem was Ruben. Since she wasn't mentally competent to sign over anything, she had to disappear long enough to be declared dead so her interest would pass to the other two.

"The plan ran off track when this Skipper dude showed up to whine to the review board. He discovered that one of the things Tyne was doing was collecting land claims. He confronted Tyne, and they came to blows. Skipper apparently learned that Beck was one of the people who'd been approached and went to see him. Someone followed, shot him and Beck, then torched the house. Bad crime scene work failed to reveal either a shooting or two vics."

"But things were back on track."

Ollie nodded. "Fast and Tyne simply had to wait out the remaining time to have Ruben declared dead, then get the mineral claims from Snook. When Ruben showed up in Yellowknife, they had to make her disappear again. And they were worried about what she could tell you."

Again the guilt that arises when my inquiries lead to someone being killed. I pushed it aside.

"I still don't get how they swept that scene so thoroughly."

"The rain and scavengers did it for them. According to Tyne, after carrying Ruben to his truck, they gathered up what evidence they could see, scattered armfuls of needles, then boogied to turn Ruben into arsenic soup."

"The morons thought arsenic would speed up decomp."

"Won't it?"

"From the Civil War until about 1910, arsenic was the main ingredient in embalming fluids used in North America. The stuff actually preserves tissue by killing the microorganisms that cause putrefaction. It fell out of favor because it's so toxic. And persistent. Elemental arsenic will never degrade into harmless by-products."

"Thus the gonzo cleanup at Giant."

"Exactly. That mine contains over two hundred

thousand tons of arsenic trioxide, a dust produced during the gold-roasting process."

"Bad news."

"Very. The dust is water-soluble and approximately sixty percent arsenic. The reclamation process involves permanently freezing it in storage chambers." I'd read that while under medical house arrest.

"What's that costing us poor taxpayers?"

"Somewhere north of four hundred million. Tyne and Fast planned to get their money's worth by stuffing Ruben and me into barrels and stashing us in one of the cooling chambers."

"That's cold."

"You're hilarious." I rolled my eyes. It did not feel good. "Do you know what the glitch was down in the mine?"

"You'll love this. The dolts forgot to get a key to open your barrel."

"Seriously?"

Ollie nodded.

"Here's something that bothers me," I said. "Snook's house was under surveillance. How did Ruben slip out that night without being seen?"

"Rainwater was bouncing the unit between Ragged Ass, Unka, and Castain."

I thought a moment. "Did Fast say why he came west now?"

"Remember the news article about Ruben's string of dead babies?"

White. The journalist who'd phoned the ME in Edmonton. Who'd gotten his tip from Aurora Devereaux.

I nodded.

"Fast read the story and phoned Tyne in an uproar just as Tyne was about to call him. When Tyne said Ruben was back in Yellowknife, Fast saw the plan going off track again."

"Whose brainchild was it in the first place?"

"Fast claims the con was Tyne's idea. Says he wouldn't have come aboard if he thought anyone would get hurt."

"Mr. Tyne gives a different version."

"On several points. Fast says Tyne killed Skipper and Beck, then torched the house. Tyne lays the shootings and fire on Fast."

"Honor among thieves."

"Here's a question." Ollie placed his elbows on his knees and leaned his weight on them. "How did McLeod score those claims in the first place?"

I'd thought about that. "Ever hear of Charles Fipke?"

"The guy who discovered diamonds in Canada."

"In the early days, Fipke was desperate for money, sometimes paid his employees in odd ways. In addition to trucking, McLeod piloted for Fipke. Maybe that was their deal. Or maybe McLeod recognized the value of the sites on his own. We may never know the answer."

"Think McLeod really found a kimberlite pipe?"

"Snook has experts working on that."

"She have good advisers now?"

"Rainwater and his uncle have hooked her up."

I didn't doubt the pipe's existence. Rainwater's uncle had gone gaga over Snook's fishbowl liner. I was sure the contents of Ruben's little sack would also ring his chimes. McLeod knew. And had told his daughters to safeguard the proof.

"OK, genius girl. Explain how you linked Fast to Tyne?"

"Remember Ralph 'Rocky' Trees?"

"The guy banging Ruben back in Saint-Hyacinthe."

I told him about the advert flyer for Fast Moving. The photo in the *Yellowknifer*. "Annaliese Ruben linked to Trees. Trees is Fast's brother-in-law. The photo tied Fast to McLeod and Tyne."

"Nice work."

I thought of another question. "Did you ask Fast if he's the john Ruben met on the night she left Edmonton?"

"The elusive Mr. Smith." Ollie snorted in disgust. "Fast admits driving Ruben to Montreal and setting her up in Saint-Hyacinthe. Says she wanted to go. God knows what the slimeball promised her."

"Who paid her bills?"

"Fast encouraged Ruben to do, shall we say, in-home entertaining. Sent tricks her way. If the income fell short, he and Tyne picked up the slack. Saw it as a business expense. Once Ruben's claim passed to Snook and Snook signed over the claims to Tyne's foundation, Ruben was out on her ass. Or worse."

"Those heartless bastards."

"Any word on paternity?" Ollie asked.

"Yes." I'd gotten the call during my discharge from the hospital that morning. "Rocky fathered the infant hidden under the bathroom sink. Because the others are mummified or skeletal, their DNA is degraded, so analysis will take longer. And may never be conclusive."

"You know what Fast told her?"

I gave a tight shake of my head.

"Apparently, the first kid was stillborn. He's fingering Tyne for that one, by the way. Not wanting to deal with the inconvenience of doctors or birth control, Fast told Ruben she had a genetic defect so all her babies would die. Said if she ever had another one, she should ignore it, then hide the body where it wouldn't be found."

A chaos of emotions short-circuited my tongue. Anger. Sorrow. Guilt. Others I couldn't label.

I swallowed.

"Ryan and I are going to grab some lunch. You want to join us?"

"Are you and Detective Douchebag—?" He shrugged. "You know."

"No," I said.

For a moment Ollie's eyes sought to reach inside

Kathy Reichs

my head. Then he palm-smacked his knees and stood. "I'll pass."

I walked him to the door. "Thanks for staying, Ollie. Really. It means a lot to me."

"Couldn't have Detective Douchebag blowing the takedown."

"You and Detective Douchebag make a damn fine team."

"Fill in the name. I hear that a lot."

I rose up on my toes and kissed Ollie's cheek. He tried for a bear hug, but I dodged.

"You know I'd give my left nut for an invite to Charlotte."

"Sergeant Hasty, I assure you, your nut is safe."

When Ollie had gone, I finished packing, rolled my suitcase downstairs and out to the Camry, then turned in my room key.

Ryan was at our usual table by the window.

I ordered a club sandwich. Ryan went with a cheeseburger.

We ate in silence. Good silence. Comfortable. Now and then I took one of Ryan's fries. He snagged my pickle.

I didn't ask about Lily. Ryan would set the agenda there, share when he wanted. I would listen.

During his visits to the hospital, Ryan and I had dissected every aspect of the past week's events. Neither of us felt the need to rehash that.

I gazed out the window. So much had happened.

406

Had it really been a week ago yesterday that we'd gathered in Saint-Hyacinthe?

I was dipping a pirated fry in ketchup when movement in the garden caught my attention.

A trash can toppled. Garbage winged out.

I watched idly, expecting an appearance by Rocky Raccoon.

Spindly legs backpedaled from the upended can, dragging a prize I couldn't see.

I felt a buzz that sent blood rushing to my face.

"Meet you at the Camry!"

Before Ryan could respond, I snatched the bacon from my sandwich and bolted.

The sole survivor of an odd family stood alone under the sun on a gently sloping hill. Insects boiled around her. Four cavities gaped black and raw at her feet.

Maureen King had told me where to look for Nellie Snook. And of Snook's plan to bury her kin.

Daryl Beck. Alice Ruben. Ronald Scarborough. I wondered what inscription would mark the common grave of the unnamed infants.

As Ryan and I crossed the cemetery, the smell of grass and turned earth triggered memories of my prior visit to Lakeview.

Snook turned at the sound of our approach. Watched in stoic silence as we drew near.

"How are you, Nellie?"

"OK."

"Detective Ryan and I want to tell you how truly sorry we are for your loss."

Snook regarded me, expression resigned. Once again life had not met her expectations. Or had.

"This is a very generous gesture." I tipped a hand at the graves.

"Blood takes care of blood."

"When will you be able to hold the funerals?"

"Ms. King will tell me."

"Please let me know if I can help in any way. You have my number."

"Thank you."

"I mean that."

She nodded. We both knew she would never punch those digits.

"Nellie," I said softly. "I have something for you."

I unzipped my windbreaker.

A head poked free, fur tufted and matted with grime.

Snook's eyes went wide. "Tank?"

The dog's snout whipped toward Snook. With a yip, he pushed from my chest, landed, and wagged the entire back half of his body.

"Here, boy." Snook spread her arms.

Tank scampered to her and sprang.

Snook caught the dog and buried her nose in his coat.

A soft pink tongue lapped Snook's face.

A long moment passed.

Snook looked at me, cheeks moist with saliva and tears. "Thank you."

"You are most welcome."

Snook smiled. It was the first time I'd seen her do it.

A heaviness wrapped my heart as we set out for the car.

I felt Ryan's arm drape my shoulders. My eyes met his.

"Ms. Snook is going to be a very wealthy woman," he said gently.

"Can any amount of money mend her perception of the world?"

"It can mend its reality."

I looked a question at him.

"She can spend it to save her beloved caribou."

I slipped a hand around Ryan's waist.

"To the caribou," I said.

Together we walked arm in arm, under that flawless blue sky, on that sunny spring day.

From the Forensic Files of Dr. Kathy Reichs

Hypotheses, plots, and vegetable soup

I am a scientist. I am a writer. I tease secrets from the dead. I tease stories from my mind. At first glance the two endeavors seem worlds apart. In many ways they are. Yet I approach a forensic case and a work of fiction in a similar fashion.

Whether analyzing bones at the lab or outlining a Temperance Brennan novel or a *Bones* TV script on my home computer, the process is like preparing vegetable soup. At the outset, I gather observations, ideas, and experiences—every legume for itself—and then they simmer together in my brain.

Eventually, disparate facts and details connect. A nicked phalange. A cranial fracture. A trip by train. An old woman observed on a beach. Out of brothy chaos, a complex potage is born. A story, with plot, setting, and characters.

Typically, I begin to contemplate Tempe's next adventure as I am wrapping up the current book. At the time I was finishing *Flash and Bones* and considering what would become *Bones Are Forever*, I was involved in three real-life child homicide cases. The victims died at various ages, in different cities, in unknown ways. One was a baby, wrapped in a blanket and left to mummify in an attic. One was a toddler, stuffed in a garbage bag and tossed in a wood. One was a preteen, buried on a riverbank below a bridge. All were girls.

One mother went to jail. One mother went free. To date, no suspect has been arrested in the third murder.

The death of innocents. This trio of disturbing cases gave rise to the dual themes of infanticide and the abuse of children (or the childlike) in *Bones Are Forever*.

I now had the main elements of my plot. Peas, carrots, and mushrooms swirling in the narrative broth. Next, a dip into the kettle for a setting. Where to send our heroine?

In June 2011, I had the great good fortune to be invited to the NorthWords Literary Festival in Yellowknife, NWT, Canada. In my two decades as forensic anthropologist at the Laboratoire de Sciences judiciaires et de médecine légale in Montreal, I'd often heard talk of the Far North. Until I made my own voyage there that spring, I'd sorely underestimated just how far that "far" really was.

While in Yellowknife, I met some of the most hardy and thermally tolerant souls on the planet.

Many were aboriginals. Some were writers, poets, or photographers. Warm and welcoming, all. But the highlight of the trip was the place itself.

Clinging to the shore of Great Slave Lake, on the edge of the Arctic, Yellowknife is the polar opposite of my native North Carolina. It is midnight sun and aurora borealis. Moose in the pines. Snow in June. Elk chops in the hotel restaurant.

And Yellowknife's past is as fascinating as her present. Once home to a prosperous gold-mining industry, the town's economic derrière now rests firmly and comfortably on diamond mining.

Diamonds on the Canadian tundra? Ridiculous, you say. My reaction, too. But the tale is true. Charles Fipke is the man most responsible for the diamond boom in Nunavut and the Northwest Territories. The founder of the country's first diamond mine, Fipke has dedicated the past four decades to pursuing the precious stones.

And the citizenry of Yellowknife is well versed on Fipke and his search for bling in the raw. Many know the man personally. Some helped in his pursuit of the sparkly little buggers.

The hotel at which I stayed, the Explorer, served as Fipke's base from time to time. His bush planes took off from a harbor visible through my window. Lying in bed, in wool socks and sweats, I'd wonder if Fipke once slept in the room I now occupied.

Equally soup-worthy were Yellowknife's abandoned gold mines with their dark, meandering tunnels and bright yellow barrels of arsenic. It took just one subterranean visit and I was mentally penning a scene for my embryonic book.

Tomatoes. Lentils. Beans. Yellowknife. Tundra. Diamond and gold mines. I had my setting.

Add characters. Stir.

In a fiction series or TV show the core ensemble carries through from book to book or episode to episode. On the cop front, each Temperance Brennan novel has Andrew Ryan, Luc Claudel, or Skinny Slidell. At the LSJML in Montreal or the ME Office in Charlotte, it's Pierre LaManche or Tim Larabee. In *Bones* there are Booth and the squints at the Jeffersonian. Since I interact with forensic scientists and members of law enforcement through my work, templates for these regulars are ever present in my cerebral stock.

But each story must introduce new personalities. Different good guys and bad guys to keep things lively. From whence these fresh ingredients?

Temperance Brennan is a professor in the Department of Anthropology at the University of North Carolina – Charlotte. So am I. When I need inspiration for a fictional professor, as in *Devil Bones,* fodder from my fellow academics is there floating in the pot.

Now and then Tempe works with an FBI agent. Case in point, *Flash and Bones.* For years I traveled to the FBI Academy in Quantico, Virginia, to teach a course on the recovery of human remains. Special agent needed? Memory bytes are ready for the taking.

In *Spider Bones*, Tempe goes to Hawaii to assist with the resolution of a case for the Joint POW-MIA Accounting Command's central identification laboratory. I once consulted for the organization and frequented that facility. Military personnel? JPAC scientist? Right there in the bisque.

Since 2004 I have served as a member of the National Police Services Advisory Council in Canada. The council provides strategic advice to the commissioner of the Royal Canadian Mounted Police on policing services such as the firearms program, the Canadian Police College, criminal intelligence, forensic and identification services, and technical operations.

Through the NPS council I have gotten to know many members of the force. I have learned about the role of the RCMP in Canadian law enforcement.

In *Bones Are Forever*, the action moves from Montreal to Edmonton to Yellowknife. The story involves murder. Clearly a Mountie was needed. No problemo. I ladled one out and seasoned him with a colorful past.

Okra. Onions. Oregano. A few corpses. A diamond-mining town way up on the tundra. An RCMP sergeant.

Mix thoroughly.

Simmer.

Bones Are Forever is served.

Kathy REICHS

ONLINE

Be the first to hear Kathy Reichs' news and find out all about her new book releases at

www.kathyreichs.com